FAMILIAR

MORWITCH SERIES
BOOK ONE

JENNIFER REDMILE

DEDICATION

This book is dedicated to those amazing people in my life who refused to let me give up and stop writing. Special thanks to my writing buddy and Editor, Alison Clifford, my long-suffering husband, Paul, and my children, Carly and Brendan. Without their never-ending tolerance and faith in my ability, Ellie and Jayce's story would never have been told.

CHAPTER ONE

Ellie

*O**kay. This was now officially the most bizarre day of her life!* Ellie stared at the woman who sat opposite her—the one claiming to be her previously assumed dead mother—and didn't know whether to laugh, cry, scream, or throw up. What the woman had just said was impossible. Both her parents had died seventeen years ago.

Closing her mouth and shaking her head, she tore her eyes away from the woman and turned to her aunts. "Serena...? Emelda...? What's she talking about?"

The look in their eyes confirmed the woman's story. Not that Ellie really needed them to answer. Her *heart* told her this woman was her mother. But her befuddled *brain* refused to accept the notion.

She shifted her eyes back to study the woman's face, the emerald-green eyes so like her own, the unruly red-gold hair threatening to burst out of the tight braid on her shoulder. Although she'd aged considerably, she was the spitting image of the smiling girl in the photo beside Ellie's bed, the one standing next to her father, holding a baby in her arms.

Ellie slid her shaking hands under her thighs, swallowing back the nausea rising into her throat. Lifting her chin, she continued to glare at the woman, seriously regretting getting out of bed that morning. How could her mother be alive all this time and not contact her?

An overwhelming sense of anger and betrayal rose to the surface. "Well, I guess you have a helluva lot of explaining to do then, *mother dear*... like about seventeen years' worth!"

"Please don't be angry, Ellie. Just give me a chance to explain everything before you judge me."

"Judge you? I've spent my whole life believing my mother died when I was a baby, and you waltz in here after all these years and think you can pick up where we left off? I don't think so! "

"So unless you're about to tell me you were recently raised from the dead or have been locked up in chains the entire time, I don't like your chances of convincing me to forgive you."

Ellie spoke more harshly than she'd intended, but this whole business had thrown her into a spin. *She was hurting, damnit.* The anger was a self-preservation mechanism developed over the years for when she felt out of her depth, and she was totally drowning here.

Emelda frowned at the woman. "Yvette... I—"

Yvette didn't take her eyes off Ellie's, ignoring whatever Emelda was about to say. "I don't expect you to forgive me; I just want you to know the truth. Not being a part of your life is something I would *never* have chosen. But the choice was taken away from me. I owe it to both of us to explain. Coming here today was one of the hardest things I've ever done. But you deserve to know what happened. Once you do, it is entirely up to you to decide what happens next."

Ellie looked into the woman's eyes and finally nodded. She didn't speak, knowing if she did, the anger and hurt raging through her body would taint what came out of her mouth. She owed this woman nothing, but she owed it to herself to find out what happened. Although she couldn't even *begin* to comprehend what could make a mother walk away from her only child and then wait seventeen years to return.

Yvette's face relaxed slightly, as if she'd feared Ellie would refuse her the opportunity to speak. With a sad smile, she fixed her eyes on Ellie's.

"A week ago, my grandmother died. On her deathbed, she confessed to having done something she came to realise over the years may have been a great injustice to me... and to you."

Yvette's face was a mask of pain and regret, her eyes radiating a terrible sadness; she faltered as if unsure what to say next. "It's probably best if I start at the beginning. You see, your father didn't know about me being a witch when we met—"

Ellie recoiled in horror at her words. "*Excuse me? Did you really just say you think you're a... witch?*"

The woman's eyes flew to the aunts in confusion. "She doesn't know? You never told her?"

Ellie slid from her perch on the arm of the chair onto the floor, suddenly needing the support of the lounge behind her back. She pulled her knees up and wrapped her arms around them, wishing herself anywhere but in this room.

Okay... so my mother is alive, and seriously believes she's a witch? Well, I guess that might explain where she's been for the last seventeen years... in an insane asylum! And knowing my luck, the insanity is probably hereditary.

Ellie's mind spun as she looked up at Serena and Emelda for their reaction, and a lump formed in her throat. The aunts had both turned deathly pale, wringing their hands and avoiding meeting her eyes.

This couldn't be happening. It had to be a nightmare, and she'd wake up any minute. And then the aunts' eyes finally met hers, their own filled with sorrow... and *guilt!*

Yvette sighed. "I should have known! Your father

and I drew up a will as soon as you were born. We stipulated that if anything happened to us, your great-aunts Serena and Emelda were to be your legal guardians. But we *also* requested they make you aware of your birthright."

Yvette turned her steely gaze back to the two old women cowering before her. "So you told her nothing? Stars save me! She turns eighteen in eight days. She has a choice to make, and she needs to fully understand her options. Or were you planning on completely denying her that too?"

Serena sat forward in her chair. "She doesn't need to make a choice at all! She can just continue to live the normal life she's been living here with us for the past seventeen years."

Yvette's eyes had taken on a burning intensity. "So you'd deny her the right—"

Ellie growled, anger rippling along every nerve. "Excuse me, but *she* happens to be right here in the room. And *she* would very much like to know what the hell you're all talking about!"

All three women's eyes flew to Ellie, their mouths gaping in the stunned silence following her outburst.

Yvette's mouth twitched, as if she were trying to hold back a smile. "Well, I see you inherited at least *some* of my traits. I'm sorry, dear, it won't happen again. We were talking about your powers, Ellie."

"Because you are half-mortal, you'll have exactly twenty-four hours from midnight on your eighteenth birthday to decide whether you want to embrace your heritage as a witch or choose to stay a mortal for the rest of your life. I know it's hard to believe, but I really am a witch... and so are you."

Ellie dropped her chin onto her knees and shuddered at the mention of the *witch* word again. Everyone knew that real witches didn't exist. Maybe Yvette was one of those weirdos who *thought* she was a witch. Like those women on the internet who claimed they could tell your future without even meeting you. Or the ones who offered 'spells' to fix anything. For the right price, of course.

Ellie sighed; her mind was way too overloaded to process the woman's delusional beliefs. She continued to stare at a spot on the wall. "Yeah, okay, whatever. How about you just get on with the story."

Yvette gave the aunts one more withering look before turning back to Ellie. "Yes. That's probably best. Your father moved into town halfway through our final year at school. I had already turned eighteen and completed my Coming-of-Age Ceremony as a witch. Witches have rules about not getting involved with mortals, but John wouldn't take no for an answer. And to be honest, the 'no' was a pretty half-hearted one anyway."

Yvette's face softened, a wistful smile lifting the corners of her mouth. "So we did what most irresponsible teenagers do. We fell in love, and I decided to deal with the consequences later." She sighed. "It was the happiest time of my entire life. We'd been together for just over a year when I fell pregnant. Your father was *so* excited and wanted to get married straight away."

Ellie couldn't help herself, she had to ask. "Let me guess... you still hadn't told him about the whole 'witch thing'?"

Yvette shook her head, tears welling in her eyes. "I'd been meaning to tell him for ages, but the time never seemed to be right. So when I finally *did* tell him, he blew up, slamming out the front door and driving away without another word."

"We were living here with Emelda and Serena at the time. The next day, the aunts asked where he went and when he was coming back, and I broke down and told them everything." Yvette smiled sadly at the aunts. "Funnily enough, they took the news much better than your father had and assured me he'd be back once he sorted his head out. It took him three days and nights, but in the end, he forgave me."

"So, what did *your* family say about all this?" Ellie asked, intrigued despite her resolve to remain aloof. Her mother's eyes turned hard, and she uttered a mirthless laugh.

"They reacted exactly as I expected. The Witch Council ordered me to give up the mortal man and dispose of the unborn child or face banishment from the Witch Realm forever. A mortal man and a 'mor-witch' or 'morlock', the child produced by such a union, would never have been welcome in that world." She shrugged. "I chose you and your father and walked away."

Until that moment, Ellie could have sworn the woman couldn't say anything more to shock her. *But seriously? A Witch Realm?* Her heart felt ready to jump out of her chest. "Whoa! Hang on a minute. What's with all the talk about mortals and morwitches and a Witch Realm? I mean, it's one thing to *think* you're a witch, but this is the real world, not some fantasy novel. You don't seriously expect me to believe all this... mumbo-jumbo hoodoo-guru stuff, do you?"

Yvette shrugged and held her empty hand out in front of her. Ellie's jaw dropped as a bottle of water appeared in the woman's hand.

"How did you...? Where did that...?"

"*That's* what I've been trying to tell you. I'm a *real* witch, just like in the fantasy novels." She opened the bottle and took a sip. "I 'fetched' the bottle of water using *real* magic."

CHAPTER TWO

Jayce

J ayce swore under his breath as he checked his watch. *Of course, Rhett was running late.* Even though Jayce hadn't been home in months, he felt torn between excitement and dread at the thought of going back to the Dragon Realm.

Maybe agreeing to fly home with Rhett for the night had been a mistake. He missed his home, but the price demanded of his soul to live there had become unbearable. He paced the floor, his hands clasped behind his neck, as he waited for the darkness of night to devour the light of day.

He smiled at the irony of his situation. He remembered this same sick feeling in his gut when he left the Dragon Realm almost two years ago. Dragon law dictated that all young dragons live in the mortal world for the final two years of their schooling. Something to do with helping them develop what the Council called their 'survival skills', far from the comforts and familiarity of home.

Fortunately, his best friend Rhett, whose birthday fell a couple of weeks after his, had come with him. Being sent to a strange world together definitely eased the transition. And saved his sanity.

Forced to survive in a world where releasing his dragon was only possible after dark, his life became a living nightmare. He shuddered at the memories of almost collapsing from the strain of maintaining his human form, his mind and body aching from the incessant need to change.

Back then, the small room in the boarding house in Darwin he called home felt like a prison cell. How many times had he paced like this, waiting for night to fall so he could escape the confines of his miserable existence?

But slowly, over the last few months, he'd come to see the room as his sanctuary, and life in the Dragon Realm as the prison sentence.

Although leaving home and coming to the mortal world to live had been difficult, the time away from his father quickly became like a dream come true. He loved the freedom and respect he was afforded in this world. It would be years before he attained a similar standing in the Dragon Realm.

Restless and bored with waiting for Rhett, he stepped outside onto his small balcony, resting his arms on the railing. In just over a week, on his eighteenth birthday, he would come of age, and the expectation to take up his birthright as a Raythawn dragon would become a reality. Lately, the prospect of entering the world of politics and constant warring, an integral part of life in the Dragon Realm, turned his stomach.

Then there was the mandatory five years' servitude to the Dragon Council, a requirement all dragons were obligated to fulfil once they'd completed their schooling. His father, Thomas Raythawn, was a highly respected member of the Council and expected Jayce to follow in his footsteps.

But Jayce was nothing like his arrogant and despotic father, and therein lay the main reason he didn't want to go home. The thought of living with the man again made his skin crawl.

Not that he had a lot of options. Either suck it up and go home, or face banishment as a rogue for the rest of his life. Just the thought of being declared a rogue made him nauseated—*almost* as sick as the idea of going back to live with his cruel, control freak of a father.

Sucking in a deep breath, Jayce looked up at the darkened sky. *What a mess.* The churning in his stomach had become a constant reminder of the indecision about his future. Rhett was right. A quick trip home, staying at his friend's house so he didn't have to deal with his father, might be just what Jayce needed to bring him to his senses.

"You all ready to go?" Rhett asked, stepping up beside him on the balcony. Jayce hadn't even heard his friend enter his room, too wrapped up in his own personal pity-party to register Rhett's arrival. *This was bloody ridiculous!* He needed to pull himself together and get back to reality.

Summoning a grin to cover his earlier quandary about his future, Jayce nudged Rhett's shoulder. "I've been ready for ages. Thought maybe you had a better offer and decided to stand me up."

Rhett chuckled. "Yeah well, it wouldn't be real hard to find a better offer than *your* company lately. Glad you've decided to at least pretend to be happy about going home."

Jayce scowled at Rhett, pulling a chair up close to the edge of the railing. The intoxicating thrill of releasing his dragon heated his blood as he balanced on the chair.

"You comin' or what? I'll race ya," he called back to Rhett, placing one foot on the railing and launching himself into the air. A heartbeat later, his dragon was free, his massive wings halting his body's rapid descent as they cut through the air, lifting his copper-scaled dragon's body into the night sky.

A quick glance over his shoulder revealed Rhett's silver-blue wings working double-time to close the gap between them.

Rhett's voice entered his mind, using the customary form of dragon speak to communicate. *You don't seriously think you can beat me? Even with a head start, I'll still whoop your copper ass.*

Never doubted it for a second, mate. Jayce chuckled, the exhilaration at being in the air displacing his earlier sombre mood. He continued to glide with minimum effort, not bothering to increase his speed. Rhett would work his guts out to catch and overtake him anyway, and Jayce was content to relax and enjoy the freedom of flying.

RHETT'S GRIN, and the impatient tapping of his foot as he waited in the courtyard, told Jayce he should expect a ribbing. Tucking his wings into his body, his talons touched the cobbled surface as he morphed back into human form.

"About time," Rhett crowed, slapping Jayce on the back. "You didn't even *try* to beat me, did you?"

"What do you think I am... stupid? I've seen how badly you sulk when you don't win."

"Yeah, right, I never sulk. You just knew you couldn't beat—"

Rhett's mother emerged from the front door of the castle. "Rhett... Jayce. What a pleasant surprise. I didn't think we'd see you, what with your Feast being next weekend."

Sonya Valdaran hugged her son and then turned to hug Jayce. "So Jayce, are you on your way home? I know your mother's been missing you terribly."

Jayce's heart ached, her words adding to the guilt he already carried. Before he could answer, Rhett hooked his arm through his mother's. "Don't start, Mother. We only came for a quick visit. Jayce's parents don't even need to know we were here, okay?"

Sonya looked at Rhett with raised eyebrows, turning back to Jayce. "Are you sure that's really what you want to do? Your mother will be devastated if she finds out you were here, and your father—"

"Mother... Enough." Rhett's voice held a warning tone.

Jayce sighed and ran his hands through his hair. He should have listened to his gut, instead of Rhett. What had made him think he could get away with visiting the Dragon Realm without his father finding out? Thomas had eyes and ears everywhere.

Jayce attempted to paste a smile onto his face, but from the looks on Sonya and Rhett's faces, he wasn't very convincing. "Nah, Rhett. Your mother's right. The last thing I want is to cause trouble for your family by asking you to keep my visit a secret. I'll head home now and catch up with you in the morning."

"No way, Jayce. We're not kids any more, remember? If you wanna stay here—"

"It's all good, mate; I'll catch ya later." Determined to avoid an argument with his friend, Jayce turned and launched himself back into the sky, his dragon revelling at another chance for freedom.

Jayce's stomach churned as he considered the flash of barely concealed fear he'd seen in Sonya's eyes. How could she have known how his father would react to the news that she'd kept Jayce's visit a secret?

Thomas had always been a bad-tempered bully at home, but it appeared his reputation had spread since Jayce left. He briefly considered turning around and heading back to the mortal realm, but what was the point? His father would find out he'd been here, and others would pay the price for his defiance.

Jayce landed in the castle courtyard of his own home, nostalgia washing over him. Memories flooded in; some good, some great, some horrendous.

His mother was out the front door and running across the courtyard within seconds of his arrival, her arms reaching out to him, tears of joy welling in her eyes. Two strides and Jayce had caught her up in his arms, lifting her petite body and swinging her in a circle.

"Hey, Mama, I've missed you so much," he said when he put her down, looking into her soulful blue eyes.

"Oh, Jayce, it's been ages. Why haven't you...?" She shook her head and linked her arm with his. "Never mind. You're here now. That's all that matters. How long can you stay?"

"I have to be back tomorrow night. Rhett's here too, so we were planning to hang out with a few friends. It'll be awesome to be able to morph and hit the skies in the daylight for a change."

Jayce stiffened as they stepped inside, the scrape of heavy boots crossing the tiled floor alerting him to his father's impending arrival.

"Jayce! I thought I heard your voice. We weren't expecting to see you, son, with your Feast being next weekend. How's school?"

Jayce clasped the wrist of the arm extended toward him, searching his father's almost black eyes for an indication of his mood. He breathed a sigh of relief at their flat, unemotional state. "Yeah, school's okay, I guess. I can't say I'll be sorry when this year's over, though. Homework sucks."

A hint of a smile lifted the corner of Thomas' lip, a calculating gleam in his eyes. "Excellent. Then you'll be pleased to know you won't be going back after your Feast. The other Council members have agreed to allow you to finish your trial in the mortal realm early."

Jayce stood as if frozen to the spot, desperately trying not to show any reaction to the words that felt like a death sentence. "But I thought we had the option of finishing the year out? Why would you do that?"

The fleeting smile was gone in a flash, replaced by Thomas' usual scowl. "I'm surprised you would even ask me that, *son*." His tone, more than his words, carried a veiled threat. *How dare he question his father's decision?*

"You have duties to attend to here. It is time to stop playing silly games with mortals. You will commence your training as a Council Guard the day after your Coming-of-Age Feast."

"What?" Jayce and his mother cried at the same time.

Thomas' cruel eyes flew to Jayce's mother. "Iridia, this has nothing to do with you. *I* will decide our son's future *without* your interference."

His mother dropped her eyes to the floor. "Yes, Thomas. I'm sorry. It won't happen again."

Jayce clenched his jaw, trying to quell the anger burning its way to the surface. He knew better than to try and defend his mother—she would pay the price. It was how Thomas always kept his son in line.

"Of course, Father. If you think this is for the best, then I will, as always, defer to your greater knowledge and experience. Now, if you'll excuse me, I think I'll retire for the night." He turned to his mother, the relief and gratitude in her eyes almost bringing him undone. "Rhett wants to get an early start in the morning."

"Please see me in the morning before you go running off with your friends. I may have some more important matters for you to deal with."

Jayce didn't miss the challenge in the older man's voice. Clamping his lips closed, he merely nodded, not trusting himself to speak lest he betray his bitter anger and hatred for the monster who called himself his father.

Jayce took the stairs leading to the second floor two at a time, then walked with long, determined strides toward his old room. Rhett was right about one thing: coming home for the night had definitely helped him decide his future. And it would be as far away from the Dragon Realm as was physically possible.

Without pausing, he opened the door to his bedroom, walked to the balcony and leapt into the air. He'd be dead before he would *ever* spend another night under the same roof as that man.

CHAPTER THREE

Ellie

Ellie's head ached, the ridiculous possibilities continuing to swirl around in her tired, overloaded brain. Okay, so even if witches really existed, and her mother just *happened* to be one, how could *Ellie* be one without knowing it? Surely, she would feel 'different' if she had special powers or something? The whole thing was utterly...

Wait. What if the weird feelings she got when something good or bad was about to happen were a by-product of being a witch? What did they call them... premonitions or something? She groaned, dropping her face onto her knees to hide the blush creeping up her neck.

Yvette's gasp drew her reluctant eyes to the other woman's face. "Ellie? Have some of your powers emerged? What is it? What can you do?"

Ellie's eyes widened at the woman's perceptive question. *Seriously? Did the witch read minds as well, or had that been a lucky guess?* Feeling her life slipping out of her control, and fueled by the stunned looks from the aunts, anger reared its ugly head again, and she directed toward her aunts.

"Don't you dare look at me like I've been hiding some huge secret? *You're* the ones who did that... remember?" Ellie bit her tongue, the hurt in her aunts' eyes making her regret her cruel words. She took a deep breath and reined in her ragged emotions. "I'm sorry. You didn't deserve that. I love you both so much, and I know you've always been there for me. I'm just struggling with all of this right now. Not to mention the blinding headache I'm getting from listening to all this ridiculous crap."

Emelda stood and rubbed Ellie's shoulder. "It's okay, sweetie, we understand. How about Serena and I make us all a nice cup of tea, and then Yvette can finish her story."

Emelda glared at Yvette from under furrowed brows, as if warning her not to do anything to upset Ellie while they were gone. Ellie almost giggled at her aunt's over-protective gesture, but the whole situation felt so surreal that giggling didn't seem appropriate.

A heavy silence hung in the air as the aunts left the

room. Ellie returned her face to her knees, determined not to say anything until the aunts were back in the room. She would *not* sit here and make small talk with Mrs Witchy-Woo-Child-Deserter.

"They did an excellent job of raising you. Seems your father and I did something right after all. Leaving you with them, I mean," Yvette spoke softly, almost as if speaking to herself.

Ellie raised her head and looked into eyes so similar to her own. "They've always been there for me. They're the only family I have... or should I say *had*."

Regret flashed in Yvette's eyes. Well, what had she expected? Ellie loved Emelda and Serena like the parents she never had. Then she remembered what Yvette had said about her own family disowning her, and her blood boiled.

What kind of family disowned their own child? "I can't believe your own family kicked you out? What kind of people do that?"

Yvette shrugged. "It was my own fault, really. I ignored the rules; my mother warned me often enough. Besides, my family didn't exactly have a choice; the Witch Council ruled me an outcast, and that was the end of it." Tears welled in her eyes as she smiled. "But I would *never* have agreed to abandon you. Magic can sometimes be used to cause great harm, even if the user believes it's for all the right reasons."

The return of the aunts, bustling back into the room with tea and cake, interrupted their conversation. Laying the impromptu afternoon tea on the coffee table, Serena frowned at Yvette. "I think it might be time you told us what happened *after* the accident. You mentioned earlier that your coming here had something to do with your grandmother's death?"

Yvette leaned forward and wrapped her hands around the hot teacup. Emelda and Serena settled back into their chairs, while Ellie stayed on the floor. All eyes focused on Yvette's face.

Tears began to trickle from Yvette's reddened eyes. "Oh, Stars… the accident. It all happened so fast. One minute, we were driving along talking about celebrating our beautiful baby girl's first birthday, and the next, a huge kangaroo came out of nowhere. John tried to swerve to miss it, and the car went into a spin. I wasn't wearing my seatbelt. Yeah, I know… stupid. But I was sick of it rubbing against my neck. Anyway, the last thing I remember is flying toward the windscreen, then everything went black."

Yvette paused for a second, swallowing back a sob and working to calm herself. After a few deep breaths, she resumed the tragic story. "I woke up covered in blood. I kept calling for John, but I couldn't find him. When it hit me that the blood was all mine, I quickly healed myself. I was about to start searching for John when the ground shook from an explosion at the bottom of the ravine. I teleported down there, but it was too late. A raging inferno consumed the car, with

John trapped inside. I c-couldn't get to him. There was nothing I could do..."

Yvette broke down and sobbed. A small chunk of the ice around Ellie's heart thawed at the pain in Yvette's voice. This woman—her mother—had endured nothing but rejection and hardship because of her love for Ellie's father and herself. And yet she'd ended up losing them both.

But Yvette had survived! Why didn't she come home to her daughter? Damnit, she didn't *have* to lose them both!

Tears flowed down Ellie's face as she tried to push the anger away, but the feelings of hurt and abandonment were deep-rooted. "But why didn't you come home?" she cried in a broken voice.

"Because my family wiped my memory. They removed every trace of you and your father from my mind!" A stunned silence followed Yvette's bitter words.

"What? But how did they find you? You were living here, in the mortal world."

"Apparently, I teleported home to the Witch Realm after the accident. I don't remember any of it, but my mother and grandmother found me sobbing hysterically in my old room, screaming about having lost everything. They assumed you were in the car when it burned, too."

"So, they wiped all memories of the years I lived in the mortal world. They thought it would help me to deal with my grief." She caught and held Ellie's eyes. "Until a week ago, I had no memory of ever being married, let alone giving birth to a child. That's why the memories are still so painful. I only just got them back."

Yvette wiped her face with a handkerchief that just appeared in her hand out of nowhere.

Obviously 'fetched' Ellie mused. Hysterical laughter bubbled up inside her. She must be seriously close to losing it if she could even consider the absurd notion of magic being real.

Ellie sucked in a calming breath, shocked by her lack of empathy for the broken woman sitting in front of her. Since when had she become such a heartless bitch?

Maybe she was in shock, too numb to feel anything. She felt somehow removed from the situation unfolding before her, like she was watching a movie or reading a book about someone else's life. Because there was no way in hell that any of *this* could be considered reality.

"I'm so sorry, Ellie. I tried to stay away and let you continue to believe I'd died. I know it was selfish of me to come here and disrupt your life like this. I'll understand if you want me to walk away and never come back, but at least I got to meet you. Thank you for giving me the chance to explain."

Ellie came back to earth with a thud. *Did she want*

the... her mother... to leave and never come back? Yvette had been just as much a victim of circumstances as Ellie. She didn't *desert* her child; her family *stole* the child from her. And suddenly, Ellie knew that she needed to find it in her heart to forgive this woman. She had no idea how, but she needed to try.

Ellie smiled for the first time since she'd walked in the front door and found her world tipped upside down. "Look, I don't know how to do this, or how long my brain will take to digest all this... stuff, but what if you... like... stay for a while, and we'll see how things go? Maybe we could try to be friends first? The whole mother/daughter thing might take a bit longer to get used to."

Ellie blushed as she turned to the aunts, realising she should have run her idea by them first. "Serena? Emelda? I'm sorry, is it okay if—"

"Welcome home, Yvette," Emelda said, and Yvette's eyes lit up like a kid at Christmas.

Jayce

JAYCE OPENED his eyes and groaned. The blinding rage from the previous night continued to burn through his veins. His only regret was that he had to leave his mother behind. *Damn, Rhett was going to be seriously pissed.* Jayce hadn't even thought to let his friend know he was leaving. Now Rhett would be stuck in the Dragon Realm all day, unable to fly back until after dark. Guess that put an end to their plans to party that night.

He spent the day in brooding silence, rehashing the details of his father's words. Every time he thought about the fear on his mother's face, Jayce wanted to punch something... preferably his father.

The familiar feelings of guilt and cowardice surfaced whenever he thought about his mother. As Jayce had grown older and more muscular, his father had learned that the threat of physical abuse would no longer keep his son in line. That's when the psychological abuse started. If Jayce stood up to him, or refused to do what his father wanted, Thomas would beat his mother instead.

Jayce remembered the first time his mother came down to breakfast with a black eye. At fourteen, Jayce was just shy of six feet tall and as strong as an ox. Excited by finally having a physical advantage over his father, he began to test the waters, rebelling against the man's bullying tactics. The previous night had been one of those occasions, and as his mother sat down to eat, the gleam of triumph in his father's evil eyes made him shiver.

"Mama, what happened to your eye?" the young Jayce had asked, the possibility of his father being responsible causing bile to rise into his throat.

Her eyes flew to his father and then dropped down to the table. "I... ummm... tripped and fell against the bedpost. It's nothing, honey. You just eat your breakfast."

After that, whenever Jayce thought about standing up to his father, his mother's eyes would fill with fear, begging him not to make trouble. So, as long as Jayce toed the line, and pretended to the world they were a happy and loving family, his mother was safe from Thomas' cruelty.

Which was why the fear he'd seen in Sonya Valdaran's eyes had shaken him so badly. Jayce knew exactly what Thomas was capable of, and it seemed his father's public facade had finally slipped, with people becoming aware of his true nature. And Thomas' position on the Dragon Council allowed him to get away with it.

But that was all in the past now. Since deciding to turn his back on the Dragon Realm and become a rogue, Jayce felt like a huge weight had fallen from his shoulders. He had a week to disappear and start a new life.

He planned to head to Sydney, somewhere busy

enough that the crowds would swallow up any trace of his existence. And when he was settled, he'd go back for his mother and take her away from the living hell that was her life. His father could go to hell.

CHAPTER FOUR

Ellie

The buzz from a text message woke Ellie the next morning. Reaching over to her bedside table, she read the words through sleep-blurred eyes.

Hey L, can u b ready by 7?

Ellie groaned at the message from her friend Sarah. *That stupid party was on tonight?* Damn, she'd completely forgotten about what everyone was calling the 'party of the year'.

The kids at school had been talking about nothing else for weeks, and Ellie had finally given in to Sarah's pressure to go a week ago. Ellie wasn't really into loud parties full of drunken idiots, but every time she thought about going, she got one of her 'good-feelings', so she figured she should go.

Ellie sighed, about to text Sarah back when memories of the previous day filtered into her brain. *Her mother was alive... and here in the house.* She dived out of bed and threw on jeans and a T-shirt, stuffing the phone into the back pocket of her jeans.

Sarah could wait until *after* she found out whether Yvette had plans for the evening. It was only a stupid party, and it wasn't every day a girl discovered her *dead* mother was actually alive.

Ellie had tossed and turned for hours after going to bed, replaying the events of what had become the weirdest day of her life. She needed to at least give this new mother/daughter relationship a go. And she had to admit to feeling the *tiniest* bit intrigued about the whole witch and magic thing. Sarah would just have to cope if Ellie changed her plans for the party.

Laughter greeted Ellie at the kitchen door, and she gasped at the change in Yvette's appearance. The woman looked so much younger than she had the previous day, her eyes sparkling, her face relaxed and creased with laughter lines.

"Good morning, Ellie. The aunts have been filling me in on some of the mischief you got up to as a child." Ellie didn't miss the underlying sadness and regret in her tone.

"Don't believe anything they say. It's all lies. Except for the good stuff, of course. That's all true." Ellie ducked to avoid the tea towel directed at her head and sat down at the table.

She grinned at Serena and poked out her tongue. "Missed me!" she teased.

"You'll keep. You're not too old to put over my—oh wait, yes, you are. As you were." She waved her hand and chuckled, turning back to finish off the pancakes.

"So, what's everyone up to today?" Ellie asked.

"Isn't that party on tonight, sweetie?" Emelda caught her eyes as she placed the stack of pancakes in front of them.

"Well... ummm... I could tell Sarah I can't go if... ummm... something else—"

Yvette put her hand up in front of her and smiled. "I wouldn't dream of letting you miss a party because of me. I have some business to attend to in the Witch Realm this afternoon, and I have no idea what time I'll be finished. I'll probably need to head off at about four, and I'll come back in the morning."

"Did you give any more thought to what we talked about last night? I mean, the part about your possible... magical ability?"

Had she *thought* about it? Her every waking moment had been *consumed* with thinking about it. The temptation to find out whether or not she had any 'abilities' was slowly eroding her initial resolve to decline the offer. *Surely, it wouldn't hurt to know one way or the other, right?* But she wasn't quite ready to share how she felt about it all just yet.

"To be honest, I'm still on the fence about the whole thing. My brain's struggling to wrap itself around the concept that magic is real, let alone the fact that I may be able to use it."

Yvette smiled. "Of course it is. So, it might be a good thing I'm leaving for the night? It'll give you a chance to absorb some of the information overload and think about what *you* want."

Ellie returned her smile and nodded. "You're right. Nothing like going to a party with music blasting where you're surrounded by drunken morons to bring what's important into perspective. I'll text Sarah after breakfast and tell her we're on."

Yvette's eyes were focused on cutting up the pancake on the plate in front of her. "So, anything else planned for the day? I mean... I'm not leaving until four... I thought, if you wanted, we could... talk or something?"

"That'd be awesome. You might be able to answer some of the gazillion questions buzzing around in my head."

"Sure, I'll do what I can to help. But first, you really should eat some of these pancakes. Trust me, *nobody* makes pancakes like the aunts."

Ellie ate a few mouthfuls of the warm, fluffy pancakes. "You know, I hadn't even considered how hard it must have been for you to come here yesterday." Ellie's cheeks burned as she met Yvette's eyes. "And I suppose I reacted exactly as you imagined in your worst-case scenario. I'm sorry I was such a rude cow."

Yvette chuckled. "Actually, *second* worst. In my worst scenario, you turned me into a toad or something equally gruesome."

They both laughed, and Ellie relaxed a little more, allowing the knowledge that her mother was alive and cared about her to melt a little more of the ice around her heart.

Jayce

THE PARTY WAS in full swing by the time Jayce and Rhett arrived, and within an hour, Jayce knew he'd made a huge mistake letting Rhett talk him into coming. He pushed his way through the crowd and headed for the balcony, the noise and constant press of drunken people making him want to scream.

He couldn't believe he'd been stupid enough to think the party atmosphere might distract him from his dark thoughts. *Yeah, right, like there'd ever been a chance of* that *happening.* But Rhett had already been pissed with him, and Jayce couldn't find the energy to argue.

Stepping out onto the balcony, Jayce sucked in the fresh air, the massive expanse of Star-studded night sky taunting his dragon to come out and play. But after eighteen months in the mortal realm, controlling his desire to morph had become as easy as flicking a switch. Still, the thought of escaping for a while was always incredibly tempting.

A shuffling sound from the shadows behind him took the decision out of his hands. *Someone else was out here.*

Annoyed at being denied the chance to carry out his plan, he turned and lashed out. "Hey, who's there? What are you doing hiding back there? Were you following me?"

A girl emerged from the shadows, the sparks flying from her startling emerald-green eyes piquing his interest.

"Seriously? What on earth would make you think anyone would be interested in following *you*?" She stared at him with hands on hips, her foot tapping the ground. "Besides, I came out here before you even arrived, so maybe I should be asking *you* that question?"

Jayce's bad mood evaporated, and he found himself grinning at the unexpectedly feisty response. "And what were you gonna do if I *was* following you? Push me over the balcony?" He chuckled at the thought of this whip of a girl trying to overpower him. "I'm Jayce, by the way."

The girl's eyes looked him up and down, dismissing him as unimportant. "I know *exactly* who you are. So where are all the usual *groupies, Jayce*?"

The way she said his name, as if it left a sour taste in her mouth, had him puzzled. What could he possibly have done to deserve her instant dislike? He was positive they'd never met.

Hell, he would *definitely* remember if he'd met this fireball before. The combination of emerald-green eyes, wild auburn curls, and spunky attitude made her almost irresistible. "I'm afraid you have me at a disadvantage then. I don't think we've met?"

"Well, that's probably because your nose is usually stuck so far up in the air it's impossible to notice us little people you consider beneath you!"

Jayce threw back his head and roared with laughter. No one had *ever* spoken to him like that before... and it was exhilarating. "Okay, now I *really* want to know your name. I need to remember one of the few people who ever had the guts to tell me exactly what they thought of me. I gotta tell you, it's a totally refreshing experience."

The wariness in her eyes changed to confusion, and then she burst out laughing too. "Okay, I admit that was *not* the response I'd expected. From your 'reputation' around town, you should've totally dismissed me, looked down your nose and flounced out of here."

Her expressive eyes sparkled with mischief, and Jayce was completely entranced. *This girl was amazing!* Her forthright honesty was like a breath of fresh air... so different from the girls he usually met!

She tilted her head to the side when he said nothing, then held out her hand and smiled. " Okay, so maybe you're not *quite* as bad as I've been told. Ellie Fiora... Oh, that was weird."

Jayce flinched at the zap of electricity running up his arm. From her puzzled expression, and the way she instantly snatched her hand away, she'd felt it too. *Weird was an understatement!*

Ellie backed away toward the open doorway, the wave of disappointment at her leaving catching him by surprise. Why would he care if a girl he'd just met, a *mortal* girl who obviously loathed him, left? Man, he was in a worse state than he'd thought.

"Well, I have to go. My friends will be looking for me. N-nice meeting you, Jayce," she stammered before turning and walking quickly away.

Jayce watched her leave, then shrugged and turned away. Staring up at the Stars, he couldn't shake the image of the sparks flying from a pair of dazzling emerald-green eyes.

He groaned when his friends found him a few minutes later, seriously not in the mood for their company. His friends, or *groupies* as Ellie called them, suddenly seemed insipid and boring, and he couldn't stop thinking about the electric shock when his hand had met Ellie's.

Faking a yawn, he smiled at the group around him. "Sorry guys, I'm beat. Think I'll call it a night."

Ignoring their disappointed faces, he brushed past them and re-entered the deafening chaos inside. Jayce vaguely registered the protests behind him but kept walking, heading for the front door and the haven of silence beyond it.

CHAPTER FIVE

Ellie

Fighting her way through the crowd, Ellie moved from room to room in search of Sarah. Why hadn't she done this earlier, instead of hiding out on the balcony? Because she was trying to kill time before telling her friend she wanted to go home. *What an idiot.* Well, Sarah would have to cope. She was going home!

The tingling sensation from Jayce's touch continued to surge through her body. Her heart pounded in her chest, the butterflies in her stomach playing havoc with her concentration. She needed to get out of there, as far away from the gorgeous guy she had just met as possible. Spotting Sarah's black tresses among a group dancing, she hurried over.

"Hey, Ellie! Isn't this party a blast?" Sarah leaned toward her ear and yelled over the noise.

"Sorry, Sar', but my head is pounding. I'm gonna head home."

Sarah smiled. "No worries; at least I got you here, even if you didn't last long. I'll call you tomorrow. Be careful walking home."

"Sarah, it's like two blocks. I'll be fine."

The cute guy Sarah was dancing with moved closer, trying to draw her friend's attention back to him. Ellie laughed and took the hint, squeezing Sarah's hand as she pushed her way towards the front door, and the sanity beyond.

Edging past a couple absorbed in a passionate kiss, Ellie stumbled in the doorway and tripped. Bracing herself for the impending collision with the wooden verandah, she wondered how the hell this all fit in with her earlier 'good-feeling' about the party. So much for relying on stupid *feelings!*

A pair of strong arms came out of nowhere, wrapping around her waist and pulling her back from the brink of disaster. She didn't even need to turn around to know who'd saved her. The electricity zinging along every nerve ending told her it was Jayce.

"Fancy meeting you here," a voice said in her ear as he held her against him for a few seconds longer than necessary before letting her go.

Ellie turned and pushed herself out of his arms. On

top of the painful zinging, just being near this guy made her pulse rate go ballistic. "Thanks for that. I thought I was a goner there for a second." Ellie tried to smile, her face burning with embarrassment.

"No worries. So, you heading home too?"

"Yeah... the crowd and the noise were starting to give me a headache."

"I can relate to that." He chuckled and ran his hand through his thick, dark hair, the movement accentuating the powerful muscles in his arms. Ellie gulped and tried not to stare.

"So, you right to get home?" he asked as if he were enquiring about the weather.

Ellie's legs almost gave out beneath her at his question. *No way did those words come out of his mouth.* Why would *he* care how she got home?

At school, Jayce hung out with the 'cool kids', which meant he and Ellie moved in completely different social circles. She often saw him around school, surrounded by his *groupies*, but he'd never seemed to even notice her before.

Maybe he was thinking of 'slumming' for the night? Well, he definitely picked the wrong girl for *that*.

Ellie put her hands on her hips and lifted her chin. "Look, thanks for saving me from looking like a complete idiot, but right now, I just wanna be home. I only live two blocks from here. So thanks, but I'm fine."

Jayce shrugged and stuffed his hands in his pockets.

"Sure... just checking. Well, I'm heading for the lake to clear my head. Thought it might be on your way, and I could walk along with you. Night, Ellie." He turned and headed down the front steps.

Ellie's mind whirled with indecision. He was going that way. Walking home with someone *would* be nice; she hated walking alone after dark. Not to mention that he was gorgeous, and she felt drawn to him.

Maybe after they'd chatted, he'd prove himself a total jerk, and she could forget all about him. *Oh, what the hell... nothing ventured and all that stuff?*

"Hey, Jayce." He stopped and turned as she ran down the steps toward him. "I'm going that way too. My house is right across the road from the lake. I suppose it wouldn't hurt if we walked together."

Jayce

JAYCE'S HEART hammered in his chest as Ellie came closer. What was it about this girl that threw his usual controlled indifference into a spin? The electricity running through him since he'd caught her made his hair practically stand on end. But it had been totally worth it to have her in his arms for those few seconds.

What really freaked him out was the gut-wrenching longing to hold her again that continued to surge through him. To say he was happy she'd agreed to walk with him would be an understatement.

"So... do you live near the lake too?" Ellie's question snapped him out of his thoughts.

"Nah, I just like to go there when I need to think."

"Yeah, me too. Sitting and watching the water is my regular 'destressifier'. Lately, I seem to be spending more and more time there."

"Really? Same here. Must be something in the air. You doing year twelve, too?" When she nodded, he smiled. "Let me guess. The old 'what-am-I-gonna-do-with-the-rest-of-my-life' question is driving you nuts?"

She shrugged and smiled, but he'd caught a flash of fear in her eyes. *Okay, something about her future had her seriously freaked out.*

"Something like that. Last year of school, turning eighteen in a week, and I still haven't decided what I wanna do."

She chewed on her lip, and he had to suppress a burning desire to kiss her. *Whoa, where did that thought come from?*

"So do you mean your birthday's in exactly a week? It must be close to mine, then. I turn eighteen next Saturday. And yeah, I've been hanging out at the lake thinking about the same stuff." *Well, that and the fact that I'm not sure I want to be a dragon anymore.*

"No way. We have the same birthday. The twenty-first. Weird, eh?"

Jayce stuffed his hands in his pockets and tilted his head to the side, trying to work out why being around Ellie made his heart race and his palms sweat. He'd never been this into a girl before. "Well, seeing we share the same birthday, we should celebrate at least some of the day together. Got much planned for Saturday?"

"Ummm... I'm not sure yet. Probably just some family stuff."

"Yeah, my family will want me to hang around too, I guess. So what about Friday night? If we stay out long enough, it'll turn into our birthday anyway. How about dinner and a movie?" Jayce felt like a five-year-old asking for a treat, fighting the urge to cross his fingers.

Ellie blushed and smiled, her sparkling eyes giving him his answer before the words left her mouth. "Sure, sounds great. What time?"

Jayce quelled the desire to pick her up and hug her. The poor girl would probably freak out and never speak to him again if he did. Not that he'd blame her. He was acting like a complete tool. He reined in his over-enthusiastic emotions and tried to appear calm.

"Ummm... how about I come by around five o'clock? Any preferences on the restaurant?"

"Nope. I'll leave it up to you. I eat pretty much

anything. Well, this is my house. Thanks for walking me home, Jayce."

Jayce nodded, disappointment flooding through him as she turned and opened the gate. His eyes followed her until she went inside, exchanging waves as she closed the front door. His brain was still scrambling to work out what was going on.

This was crazy. He'd known her for what?... two hours, and it was as if the sun rose and set according to his proximity to her. The worst part was that right then, it felt like the sun had set, and the world was a dull and boring place.

A week ago, feeling this way about someone like Ellie would have sent him running for cover. Everyone knew that relationships between mortals and dragons never ended well. But now that he planned to stay in the mortal world...

Bugger! What happened to leaving for Sydney on Friday? Stuff it. That would just have to be put off until first thing Saturday morning. The Coming-of-Age-Feast didn't start until the afternoon, and he would be long gone before anyone realised he was missing.

Wait, so he was putting his whole life on hold for a date with a mortal girl? *Seriously?* Jayce groaned, shutting the annoying little voice of reason in his head down. Now, his only problem was how to survive without seeing her again until Friday.

Ellie

ELLIE CLOSED the door behind her, a goofy grin spreading across her face. *Wow!* She was pretty sure she knew what the 'good-feeling' about the party meant now—six-foot-two-inches of golden-eyed, dark-haired, male-model material, Jayce Raythawn. And he'd asked her out on a date!

Not wanting to disturb the aunts, Ellie slipped quietly up to her room. She undressed and climbed into bed in a euphoric haze, so happy she thought she might burst. Her life had changed so much in the last twenty-four hours, and meeting Jayce tonight had been like the icing on the cake.

Wait 'til Sarah heard about the infamous Jayce Raythawn asking her out. Ellie knew at least twenty girls who would be green with envy. Even though he had a reputation as an arrogant snob, which she had yet to see any evidence of, she'd never argued with the general consensus that the guy was seriously hot!

The zapping thing when they touched was a bit

weird, and from the shock on his face, he'd felt it, too. Maybe it had something to do with her powers? She giggled at the idiotic thought. *Yeah right.* That would be the powers she didn't even know whether she had yet. It was funny how, since meeting Yvette, she'd started to believe that *anything* was possible.

Ellie had spent most of that day talking to Yvette and trying to decide whether she wanted to have magical powers or not. Not having them would make life a lot simpler and save her from having to make a choice on her birthday. On the other hand, she couldn't help but wonder what it would be like to have the use of magic. *I mean, seriously? Who wouldn't?*

She smiled as she recalled the excitement on Yvette's face when Ellie had told her mother about her 'feelings', describing them as good, bad and totally weird.

Yvette had said they sounded like premonitions, which often indicated some form of magical ability. Ellie had laughed, sharing the disastrous stories of the two occasions she ignored her 'bad-feelings', both of which had ended up in trips to the hospital.

Rather than laughing with her about the near catastrophes, Yvette's eyes took on a haunted look. "I'm so sorry, Ellie. If I'd been around, those things would never have happened."

"Hey, kids have accidents all the time. It's part of growing up. Besides, you're here *now*. Better late than never, right?" She'd chuckled, rubbing Yvette's shoulder, and been rewarded by the return of the woman's smile.

Yvette had explained that, because of Ellie's mixed-blood, her powers might range anywhere from none to phenomenal. Until they performed a ritual to open her 'third eye', it was anyone's guess what would happen. They'd agreed to wait until the next day for Ellie to decide what she wanted to do.

She wasn't sure exactly when it happened, but when she woke up the next day, she'd decided to go through with the ritual. She'd been waiting all her life for *something* to happen, and this could be it. Hey, everything in her life was so out of control anyway; why not stay on the rollercoaster to the end of the ride?

So what about Jayce? She had no idea how he fit into the big picture, but somehow, she knew he did. Just thinking about his warm, honey-gold eyes, his hands running through his thick dark hair, and his well-toned physique made her pulse skitter.

Ellie had never met anyone who affected her this way. She knew she should be terrified by the intensity of her feelings about an almost stranger, but his easy charm had broken through her usual sturdy defenses the first time he'd opened his mouth.

The memory of his arms wrapped around her, holding her close for an instant longer than necessary, turned her legs to jelly and sent chills racing up and down her spine.

Jayce had managed to crawl under her skin in an

incredibly short time, and she couldn't wait to see him again. She buried her face in the pillow and groaned. Friday seemed *so* far away. She knew it was pathetic, but she actually missed him already.

CHAPTER SIX

Ellie

Ellie was pleased to find Yvette had returned when she entered the kitchen that morning. She was looking forward to telling Yvette about her decision, and starting the whole third-eye-ritual thingy.

"Did you enjoy the party?" Yvette smiled as she looked up from buttering a piece of toast.

"Yes, thanks," Ellie said, unable to hide the blush creeping up her neck as she dropped into the chair beside her mother. She braced herself for the inevitable ribbing from the three women in the room, but to her surprise, they all just continued with what they were doing. *O-kay. More weird stuff.* Why was she even surprised?

"Great. So have you decided yet? About the ritual, I mean."

Ellie stared down at her empty plate as three pairs of eyes bore into her. Whatever she answered, someone would be disappointed. "Well, I've given this a lot of thought... and I've decided I'd like to know either way."

A whimpering sound from the other side of the room made her heart ache. Serena stood with her hand over her mouth.

"I'm sorry, Serena, but I have to do this. I don't want to spend my whole life wondering *what-if*." The woman nodded, turning back to the sink with a sigh.

"Serena will be fine, sweetheart," Emelda said with a sad smile. "She's just worried about you; we both are. But you have to do what your heart feels is right. We'll always be here for you, no matter what happens. Actually, we've decided to go away for a few days and catch up with some old friends. You and Yvette can have the place to yourselves and use the time to get to know each other."

Ellie knew her aunts were hurting, that they had hoped she'd turn her back on her heritage and continue on the way they'd always been. But everything had changed so much since her mother's arrival. Going back to the way things were was no longer an option, and probably not something she'd choose if it were.

She jumped up and embraced the aunts in a huge hug. "Thank you for understanding. I can't explain it, but I know this is what I'm supposed to do. Hey, the whole thing could turn out to be a big fat fizzer yet. But enjoy your trip, and I'll see you when you get back."

Ellie glanced over at Yvette, barely able to contain the excitement racing through her.

Yvette smiled and raised an eyebrow. "So, when would you like to start?"

Ellie shrugged and grinned. "I'm ready whenever you are."

ELLIE'S KNEES TWITCHED, her heart thumping in her chest and her palms sweating, as she sat on the floor in her room surrounded by candles. Her mother stood outside the circle, chanting witchy mumbo-jumbo in some foreign language while making weird signs in the air with her hands.

Ellie stiffened as a tingling sensation started in her fingers and slowly spread throughout her entire body. Whatever her mother was doing was obviously work-ing. Ellie couldn't decide whether to be disappointed or excited. Closing her eyes, she tried to slow her breathing and calm her erratic heartbeat.

Just when she thought she had it under control, a

burning sensation flooded her body, her eyelids refusing to reopen.

The tingling grew into a warm, pulsating buzz, her brain turning to mush. Unable to fight the lethargy seeping into her bones any longer, she curled up into a ball and embraced the darkness.

THE VOICE SEEMED to be coming from a long way off. Ellie tried to concentrate on the words, but she didn't seem to have the energy. Besides, she liked this place. She felt warm, and safe, and—

"Ellie, you need to listen to my voice so you can find your way back. Try to focus on it, and then move towards the sound... this is really important, honey... we need you here..."

Someone needed her. She had to leave now. She couldn't let them down. She forced her mind to focus on the sound, fighting the desire to continue floating in the void of nothingness.

Reaching out her hand, she slowly moved toward what she hoped was the source of the voice. The flow of words continued, getting louder as she got closer. A bright light flashed in front of her, and when it faded, she was back on the floor in her bedroom.

Ellie pushed herself up, feeling like a total idiot for

falling asleep. *So, was it over?* Damnit, she didn't *feel* any different. She bit her lip, trying to hide the disappointment. Her mother's worried eyes stared into hers, as if waiting for her to say something. What could she say? *Yeah sorry, but your daughter's a witch reject?*

"So... what happened?" Ellie finally asked, surprised by the dry, croaky voice she hardly recognised.

Yvette's shoulders slumped as she released a long, slow breath. "I'm not sure, honey. I kind of hoped *you* could tell *me* that?"

Ellie frowned and shrugged. "No idea, sorry. I think I fell asleep for a while... didn't I?"

Yvette chuckled. "Yes, you did. But slightly longer than 'a while'. I've been trying to wake you up for the past twelve hours. I thought you might be able to tell me something about where your mind's been?"

Ellie's jaw dropped as she took in the dark shadows in her room, broken only by the candles Yvette must have replaced at some stage. *Twelve hours? Where the hell did she go?* Memories of being cocooned in a warm, safe place floated through her mind. The peace and contentment, and not wanting to leave. Then she'd heard the voice.

Yvette watched her intently as Ellie sighed and told her what she remembered. The worry faded from Yvette's eyes, her smile softening her tired features.

"Stars Ellie... it sounds like you experienced some kind of rebirth. Do you feel any different?"

Ellie shrugged. "I don't really *feel* different... but

now that I think about it, things *look* a bit different. There's like, a fuzzy kind of glow around you. What's with that?"

"That means your 'third eye' is open, and you can detect auras. Everyone has one, although some are more revealing than others. And any supernatural will glow a little more than those who don't." She waved her hand in dismissal.

"Auras are a huge topic you can read up on later. But the fact that you can *see* them means you have at least *some* magic. Seems you've got a *lot* more in common with my side of the family than your father's, after all."

Realising her mouth hung open, she snapped it shut, the reality of the situation hitting her. *She was a real witch! She had magic!* Not that she had any idea what that meant. But it was a helluva lot better than nothing!

"SO, DO I NEED A WAND, or a book of spells or something?"

Ellie sat at the kitchen table devouring a stack of toasted sandwiches, her stomach growling as if she hadn't eaten in a week. Well, she *did* lose an entire day. Of course, she was starving.

Excitement bubbled up inside her. She had a thousand questions she wanted to ask. But she couldn't talk and eat at the same time, and right now, food took priority.

Yvette smiled at her eagerness. "To be honest, I'm not sure how this is going to work, honey. It depends on what abilities you have and how strong they are. Usually, you'd have 'grown into them', so to speak, so I guess it's going to be a lot of trial and error for a while. Can you skip school tomorrow so we can start working on your magic?"

Ellie laughed at the irony of the situation. Here she was, having breakfast with a woman she'd thought dead, and her *mother* was asking her to skip school for the day. Life was just *full* of surprises.

"What's so funny?" Yvette asked, watching her spluttering and choking on her food.

"Well... it's just that *you're* the parent, and normally it would be *me* asking *you* about skipping school. The whole situation is a bit weird, that's all. Anyway, I'm sure I can miss a day. I'll text Sarah and ask her to take notes about anything important."

Her mother smiled and nodded absently. Ellie suddenly realised the poor woman looked ready to collapse. Spending the last twelve hours trying to bring Ellie back from *wherever* must have been exhausting. "Ummm... I think you might need to go to bed for a while. Sorry, but you look terrible."

Yvette rubbed her hand across her face and sighed.

"I don't remember the last time I slept, actually. A few days ago, maybe?"

Ellie chuckled. "Here we go with this whole 'role reversal' thing again. I really think you need some sleep. My questions can wait."

Yvette closed her eyes and pointed at the table in front of her. A pile of well-worn books appeared out of nowhere.

Ellie grinned, her excitement growing. "Wow... where did they come from?"

"I used a simple fetching spell and brought them from home. In case you wanted to do some reading before you go to bed." Yvette yawned and stretched, her eyes sagging from weariness.

"I'm looking forward to sleeping in our old room again. The aunts haven't changed a thing since John and I..." She pushed her chair back from the table and stood, tears welling in her eyes.

They shared a smile that warmed Ellie's heart before Yvette headed off to her old bedroom.

Ellie grinned at the pile of books waiting to reveal their secrets. She grabbed the top one and pulled it toward her, running her hands across the aged leather-bound cover. *Auras Explained* she read, sighing happily as she opened the book. Maybe this whole being a witch thing wouldn't be so bad after all.

Jayce

JAYCE SPENT most of Sunday hanging around at the lake, trying to convince himself he was there for the calming effect the waters had on his mind. *Yeah, right.* If he *happened* to see Ellie, that would just be an *unexpected bonus.*

He'd originally planned to spend the day scouring the internet for accommodation and jobs in Sydney. He figured he had enough money saved from his monthly allowance to survive for about a month before he'd need to find work.

But Ellie's image invaded his every waking moment, not to mention dreaming about her when he slept. She was like an addiction, and it scared the crap out of him.

He'd spent the last eighteen months simply going through the motions of living in the mortal world while he completed his education. A relationship, especially with a mortal, was the last thing he wanted or needed.

He groaned and cursed under his breath. Something about this girl had seriously messed with his head. And dammit, the after-effects of holding her wouldn't go away. Ever since his arms released her, he'd been like a junkie needing his next fix.

It wasn't just that he *wanted* to hold her again—it felt more like a burning *need*—and it freaked the hell out of him. He'd never considered himself the emotional or sentimental type. Sure, there'd been a few flings with mortal girls in the past, but he'd never even entertained the thought of getting serious with one.

But then, that had been before he decided to turn his back on his dragon heritage. Maybe now the decision was made, he'd subconsciously let down his defenses, and Ellie had just been there to slip between the cracks.

His eyes shifted toward her house for probably the hundredth time. There'd been no sign of movement in the two hours he'd spent sitting and pining for a glimpse of her. He stood and brushed the grass off his jeans, angry with himself for acting like a lovesick idiot.

Time to start the research. This is ridiculous and getting me nowhere. He strode toward the boarding house where he lived, determined to put all thoughts of the green-eyed redhead from his mind. He needed to focus on his future.

He would get on the bus to Sydney on Saturday morning and then vanish into anonymity. His heart was heavy but filled with determination. No matter how much he wished things could be different, this was how it had to be.

But if he needed a break later, he *would* be going back to the lake.

CHAPTER SEVEN

Ellie

Ellie's excitement about learning to use her newly awakened magic almost managed to push thoughts of Jayce from her head. *Almost!* But when she least expected, images of his honey-coloured eyes and bone-melting smile would invade her mind.

Which, of course, made focusing on her magic lessons almost impossible. *It was so frustrating!* She had already wasted most of Sunday floating in some void. Why did everything always have to happen at once?

Mastering the art of fetching turned out to be relatively simple. She only needed to picture where the thing she wanted was, and it appeared in her hand within seconds. Her mother had burst out laughing at the shock on Ellie's face the first time it worked. Ellie had just stared at the pillow she called for as if an alien had landed in front of her.

"Well done, honey. See, I told you it was easy."

Ellie's shock had turned to excitement, and she added her favourite pink jacket and her laptop to the pile of fetched goods.

"Okay, looks like you have that one under control. How about you try to put them back where they came from?"

"What if I'm not sure of exactly where something came from? I mean, I knew this jacket was in my room somewhere, so I just pictured the general area. Will it go back to the same place if I'm not specific?"

"The problem with that is, it might end up where you'll never find it again. It's best that you think of sending it somewhere you can picture in your mind. Oh, and having seen your room, I'm thinking hanging the jacket up in the cupboard would be a refreshing change." Yvette winked.

"Yeah, yeah. Didn't take long for the nagging mother thing to start, huh?"

They both grinned, and Ellie formed a mental picture of her jacket hanging in the cupboard. As soon as she was done, she sent her pillow back to what she hoped was her bed. Deciding she might need the laptop, she left it where it was on the table.

"Aren't you going to run and check if it worked?" Yvette asked, raising an eyebrow.

Ellie shrugged. "Nah, I'll check later. Can we start on something else?"

Yvette sighed and nodded. "Ah yes, the impatience of youth. I remember being just like you once upon a time."

Ellie reached for one of the books she'd been reading the previous night. Bored with *Auras Explained,* she'd picked up the next book in the pile, *Witches and their Familiars.* Intrigued by the weird-sounding topic, she'd read the first couple of chapters before giving in to exhaustion and going to bed.

"So what's the go with familiars? Do you have one?"

Yvette smiled and reached into the pocket of her skirt. When her hand came back out, she held a cute little white mouse. "Ellie, meet Squeak. He's been with me since I was twelve."

Ellie grinned as Squeak ran up Yvette's arm and perched on her shoulder, rubbing his tiny head against her neck.

"Wow... pleased to meet you, Squeak," Ellie said softly. "I hope I find my familiar soon. I reckon it would be kinda cool to have a 'forever friend'."

"You will. There's still almost a week to go until you turn eighteen. I'm sure something will happen before then. So, do you really want to get into this topic right now? I thought you were busting to learn some more magic."

Ellie closed the book and pushed it aside. "You're

right. I'll deal with that one when it happens. So what's next?"

"How about we try teleporting?"

Ellie's eyes lit up. "That'd be awesome. But do you really think I'll be able to do it?"

"Only one way to find out." Yvette smiled at Ellie's enthusiasm. "How about I do it first and take you with me? That way, you'll be used to the sensations before you try to teleport alone. We could go to your room and see how you went returning the things you fetched earlier."

"Sounds good to me... let's go."

Yvette grabbed Ellie's hand and pulled her close. "You need to be touching the person who's doing the teleporting to travel with them. Oh, and you might want to close your eyes. The first few times can be a little nauseating. Ready?"

Ellie nodded and closed her eyes. Her stomach dropped to her knees as the floor fell away from under them, followed by a jolt as her feet touched the ground again, making her stomach bounce back up into her throat. Not the most comfortable way to travel, but definitely the quickest.

"We're here," Yvette's voice announced beside her. Ellie opened her eyes and clutched at Yvette's arm, her head spinning. As her stomach settled and her eyes came back into focus, she felt a rush of pride at the sight of her pillow on the bed. She glanced towards the cupboard and laughed at her pink jacket in among her shoes.

"Oops... guess I forgot about the coat-hanger part."

"Sometimes it's hard to remember all the details. So, how was the trip? Not too bumpy?"

Ellie shrugged and grinned. "I'm sure I'll get used to it. Can I try it now? On my own?"

"Why not? If you think you're ready. It'll either work or it won't. Just make sure you focus on *exactly* where you want to go."

Ellie closed her eyes and focused on the kitchen. Immediately, her stomach dropped again and then leapt into her throat as she landed. She opened her eyes and burst out laughing. She was standing on top of the table! A heartbeat later, Yvette appeared at the kitchen door, grinning from ear to ear.

"I said *exactly* where you wanted to go. What did you think about?"

Ellie climbed down off the table, still laughing. "I'm sure I thought *at* the kitchen table, not *on* the kitchen table."

"But you only pictured the table and the kitchen? Lucky you didn't try to go to the lake."

They both cracked up laughing, sitting back down at the table and relaxing in each other's company.

"To tell you the truth, I'm still amazed that you managed to teleport so easily—regardless of the less-than-perfect landing. You're a natural." Yvette beamed with pride, and a warm glow of contentment wrapped around Ellie's heart.

"We might try doing it a couple more times, only as far as the front gate and back. The one thing you need to remember is that using certain types of magic drains your energy. If you try to do too much in too short a period of time, you could collapse. Restoring your energy requires food, water and rest."

"O-kay. Will I get a warning or something before I collapse?"

"With me, the first sign is that I'm starving. You'll be able to do more once you start practising regularly. Building up your strength and resilience is a bit like weight training. The more you do it, the stronger you'll become. Before long, your energy levels won't drain as quickly, and you'll take less time to recover."

"Right, I get it. So what about spells? Do we do them too? Do we need wands or something?"

"Spells are a whole different kettle of fish. They require specific words to do their job. As you can imagine, there are literally thousands of word combinations for different spells. But obviously, they'll only work if you use them in the right order."

Yvette chuckled. "And no, you don't need a wand. Using your hand works just as well. But you *do* need to direct the spell where you want it to go. You don't want to target the wrong place. Trust me, that's never pretty."

Jayce

BY THE END of lunchtime on Monday, Jayce had decided that if he didn't see Ellie again soon, the men in white coats would be carting him away in a straitjacket.

Spending most of Sunday distracted by thoughts of where she could be and what she was doing had been bad enough. Damnit, the need to touch her again had become a mindless obsession.

Jayce declined his friends' invitation to go for coffee after school, not in the mood for company, and desperate to at least catch a glimpse of the girl who'd taken over his mind. His friends gave him puzzled frowns, uncertain how to act around this sombre stranger. Not that he blamed them. He was just as confused by his uncharacteristic behaviour as they were. Maybe he could try walking it off.

What the hell is wrong with me? I'm acting like some kind of lovesick jerk. Ellie had somehow managed to crawl under his skin, and he had no idea what to do about it.

Unsure how long he'd been walking along in a daze, he stopped and took in his surroundings. Relief flooded him as he caught sight of the sparkling waters of the lake. Of course, his feet had automatically carried him here. Where else would he go?

He glanced hopefully towards Ellie's house and froze. There she was... sitting on the front verandah, reading. She looked up as if she felt someone watching her, and their eyes met.

Unbridled anger surged through his body. *Ellie was glowing... she was a supernatural. That explained everything!*

The damn girl had to be a witch, and she must have put a hex on him. But how had she hidden her aura from him when they first met? Only one way to find out. Seething, he crossed the road and opened the front gate. He would make sure this *witch* regretted ever setting eyes on him.

Ellie

AFTER THEIR BUSY morning spent practising magic, Yvette suggested they take a break for a while. Ellie had managed to devour a huge amount of food, a good indication of her depleted energy levels. Yvette decided to use the break to take care of a few things in the Witch Realm, promising to be back in a couple of hours.

Ellie made herself a coffee, carrying that and the book on familiars out onto the verandah. Dropping down on the oversized outdoor swing, she breathed in the fresh spring air and started to read. The whole idea of having a familiar for life sounded awesome. How long 'til they found each other? She didn't even know where to start looking or what to look for. *Hmmm. A cat might be nice...*

She'd been reading for over an hour when the sensation of someone watching her made her look up. Excitement bubbled up inside her at the sight of Jayce. But the welcoming smile on her face froze at the rage burning in his darkened eyes.

Whoa! Was that anger directed at her? Why? What the hell could she possibly have done? And then her vision expanded to take in the glow surrounding his body, and everything fell into place. He was a supernatural, and from the scowl on his face, he realised she was too.

Before she could even begin to make sense of what was going on, Jayce stood on the verandah in front of her. "Who the hell do you think you are? How dare you put a hex on me! I don't know how you hid your aura the other night, but your secret's out. I'm sure you've been having a good old laugh at my expense."

Jayce literally growled the words through clenched teeth. Ellie's mouth fell open as she stared at the feral beast standing in front of her. He bore a startling resemblance to the gorgeous guy she'd met at a party two nights ago, but she was having trouble reconciling this rabid lunatic with the Jayce from her dreams.

"S-sorry? I must have missed—"

"Oh, you'll be sorry, alright, if you don't lift this damned curse right now. I should've known something was wrong. As if I'd ever be attracted to someone like you. Did you seriously think I wouldn't work it out eventually?"

Ellie recoiled as if he'd slapped her in the face. She fought against the tears welling in her eyes, biting her lip, determined not to cry in front of this delusional jerk.

Jayce's anger seemed to escalate at the sight of her tear-filled eyes. "Don't even think about turning on the waterworks. I know—"

"You know *what,* young man?" Yvette appeared next to Ellie on the verandah, her hand protectively resting on her daughter's shoulder. "I have no idea who you are or why you're here abusing my daughter, but trust me when I say you will live to regret the next nasty word that comes out of your mouth." Yvette spoke quietly, but the threatening tone in her voice was hard to miss.

Jayce turned his fiery gaze on her mother, and Yvette drew in a short, sharp breath. "Stars... this can't be happening. How... why... where did you come from? What do you want with my daughter?"

Ellie's eyes slid from Jayce's to her mother's and back again. *What the hell was going on?* These two were seeing something she wasn't, and now it was her turn to be angry.

"Hey... remember me...? The one caught in the middle of all this? I have no idea what either of you are talking about, but I want some answers... *now!*"

Yvette and Jayce both turned to stare at Ellie, effectively silenced by her outburst. Jayce's eyes narrowed, some of the anger fading as he turned back to her mother.

"Your daughter put a curse on me on Saturday night, and I want it removed right now."

Yvette frowned for a second, and then burst out laughing. Seeing the rage building in Jayce's eyes again, Ellie gave her mother a filthy look. As if realising her mistake, Yvette stifled her laughter and went back to glaring at Jayce.

"What on earth makes you think Ellie put a curse on you? And did you say this happened on Saturday? That's utterly ridiculous. She didn't even know she had any powers until I woke them yesterday."

Now, it was Jayce's turn to stare with his mouth open. His eyes flicked from mother to daughter, and they both nodded. He groaned, punching the wooden post beside him. "Then what the hell is going on? Why can't I get her out of my head? And why do I feel like I'm being electrocuted every time we touch each other?"

Ellie screamed in frustration and jumped to her feet. "What is it with people talking about me like I'm not here? I am sick to death of it!"

The fire in Jayce's eyes flared into an inferno. "Hey, welcome to my world. *I'm* sick to death of being manipulated. If you didn't—"

Yvette raised her hand. "Enough!" she said in a loud calm voice. "I think I may know what's going on here. I sincerely hope I'm wrong, and it's not something I'm prepared to discuss out here in public. So... how about we go into the kitchen and have a rational conversation? I'm hoping you two will be able to refrain from clawing each other's eyes out long enough for us to solve this puzzle."

Yvette glanced down at the chair where Ellie had been sitting, raising her eyebrows at the book her daughter had been reading. "You might want to bring that with you."

CHAPTER EIGHT

Jayce

ayce hesitated, sizing up the possible threat from the mother/daughter witches. He didn't trust either of them but decided he could handle anything they might throw at him. Besides, not knowing what was going on was driving him nuts. Taking a deep breath, he shrugged and stepped inside the house.

The house appeared old but spotlessly clean, and the furniture was obviously chosen for comfort rather than aesthetics. Jayce followed the two witches through the lounge room and into the kitchen, sitting down at the table opposite Ellie. She avoided looking at him, which was both irritating and a relief at the same time. Yvette placed a jug of iced tea and three glasses on the table and pulled her chair close to Ellie's.

"Right. Much better." Yvette sighed and poured them each a drink. "Now, what we're about to discuss must not leave this room. Just talking about it probably breaks half the laws ever written. So, we know how Jayce feels about you, Ellie, but I'm afraid you need to tell us honestly if you've had a similar reaction to him."

Ellie's face turned fire-engine red.

Jayce looked at the two women, even more confused than ever. *Why would Ellie be feeling the same as me? I was the one who'd been hexed... wasn't I?*

With her eyes still glued to the table, Ellie sucked in a deep breath and let it out slowly. "About the same as Jayce, I suppose." She lifted her glowering green eyes and met his, the jumble of raw emotions flickering in their depths seeming to bore into his soul. "Up until just now, of course."

Yvette cleared her throat and reached for the book Ellie had been reading earlier. "I was afraid you might say that. It appears we have a big problem." She turned to Jayce. "But first, let me explain about Ellie's powers."

She related the shortened version of what Ellie had been through since Yvette came back into her life on Friday afternoon. By the time she'd finished her story, he felt like a total jerk.

Yvette turned to her daughter and smiled. "Now, unless I'm completely mistaken, Jayce here is an underage dragon... and therein lies the root of all our problems."

Jayce almost fell off his chair when Yvette said the word 'dragon'. *How did this woman know that?* Ellie's eyes were like saucers when they looked into his. He cringed, wishing he could take back the cruel things he'd said to her earlier.

Yvette ignored both of their responses and continued to talk. "About five hundred years ago, the dragon and witch Councils passed a law forbidding any contact between the two races prior to their eighteenth birthdays. I don't know the details of how or why this came about, but after listening to what you two have been going through, it's not too hard to work out."

A sour taste grew in Jayce's mouth as an inkling of what Yvette was suggesting crept into his brain. She took a deep breath and continued. "A witch and her familiar will usually seek each other out when they are both quite young. For obvious reasons, great care is taken when a young witch or dragon's parents place them in a mortal school."

"If a witch is already attending the school, the dragon's parents will take their offspring elsewhere, and vice-versa. This prevents accidental meetings. *Unless*, of course, the witch is unaware she's a witch and her powers are still bound. Do either of you see where I'm going with this?"

When neither of them responded, she shrugged.

"You are both going through the exact symptoms a witch and her familiar experience when they first find each other. I'm sorry, but it sounds like the bond has already been invoked. And the bad news is... the bond is irreversible. It can only be broken by the death of one or the other."

Totally dumbfounded by what the woman was telling them, Jayce risked a glance at Ellie's face. Still staring at the table, her pale face and dazed expression told him she was just as horrified as him. Only the loud ticking of the clock on the wall broke the stunned silence.

Then the anger came flooding back, overwhelming him as it pushed its way to the surface. Unable to control the warring emotions surging through his body, he rose abruptly to his feet, his chair flying backwards as he turned and stormed from the house.

Slamming his way out the front door, Jayce headed for the park across the road. His dragon screamed to be released, the rage almost overpowering the rigid control he'd spent years developing. *I seriously need to wake up from this damn nightmare... now!*

It was one thing to *choose* not to follow his destiny, opting to rebel and reject his pre-ordained life. But from what Yvette had told them, the decision about his future had been taken out of his hands *again*. Meeting Ellie had caused his entire existence to be ripped out from under him.

His head throbbed, his stomach threatening to

empty its contents right there and then. He reached the edge of the lake and flopped down on the ground, resting his aching head in his hands.

"Unbelievable!" he shouted to no one in particular.

Ellie

ELLIE SAT in a state of numbed shock as Jayce's chair flew across the room, her eyes following him until the front door slammed. *This couldn't be happening... I'll wake up any minute and discover it's all been a horrible nightmare.* But the devastated look on her mother's face told her it was all very real.

"So, what do we do now?" Ellie whispered into the silence.

"I have no idea, honey; this is all way out of my area of expertise."

"Well, do you at least know someone who can help us? There's got to be a way to reverse what's happened... this will ruin Jayce's life."

Yvette raised her eyebrows and smiled at her.

"Interesting that you're more worried about how this will affect Jayce than yourself?"

Ellie's face grew hot, and she threw her hands in the air. "I didn't even know dragons existed until five minutes ago, but I gather he can't choose *not* to be a dragon like I can choose *not* to be a witch?" A glimmer of hope surfaced as an idea popped into her head. "That's it! What if I just choose not to—?"

Her eyes full of regret, Yvette shook her head. "I'm afraid it doesn't work like that, Ellie. Even if you choose to deny your birthright and stay a mortal, Jayce will still be bound to you for life. Either way, as a witch's familiar, he'll be banished from the Dragon Realm forever and branded a rogue. As you will be from the Witch Realm."

"So, we'll be outcasts no matter where we go or what we do? A morwitch and her rogue dragon familiar. If this wasn't all so real, it might be hysterically funny."

Yeah, real funny. If only we could turn back time. I'd have left the party early... hell, I'd never have even gone!

"My life couldn't possibly get any worse," she moaned, dropping her head into her hands.

"Sorry, honey, but you may be wrong about that. I'm not sure how the law is written in the Dragon Realm, but in the Witch Realm, this union, whether an accident or a deliberate act, is punishable by death."

Ellie hadn't heard Jayce come back into the house or noticed him hovering in the doorway, but at Yvette's words, she looked up, and their eyes met. The horror washing over her was reflected in those golden depths.

Before she could even begin to grasp the repercussions of what Yvette had just revealed, her head had started to spin. Suddenly, the world tilted crazily as the floor seemed to rise up to meet her, and the enveloping darkness offered a soothing escape from a world gone mad.

CHAPTER NINE

Jayce

J ayce scooped Ellie's unconscious body up off the floor, the electricity surging through him setting his entire body on fire. He carried her into the lounge room, wanting to kick himself for being such a selfish jerk. He'd been too wrapped up in his own self-pity and anger to consider how all this might affect her. Ellie was as much a victim of circumstances as he was in this nightmare.

Placing her gently onto the lounge, he stepped back so her mother could check her vitals. His heart ached at the sight of her pale face, and he had to shove his hands into his pockets to stop himself from gathering her back into his arms. It would be worth the pain just to hold her.

"She'll be fine, thank the Stars," Yvette said as she

tucked a blanket around Ellie's body. "I think the traumas of the last few days finally caught up to her."

Jayce sighed, looking down at the floor as shame flooded his entire being. "I'm so sorry for acting like an inconsiderate jerk through all this. It took me a while, but I get it now. None of this is any more Ellie's fault than it is mine. I guess I kinda lost the plot."

Yvette dropped into an armchair, letting her breath out in a long, slow stream. "Your reaction was perfectly normal; I don't think anyone who found themselves in a situation like this would react much differently." She looked into Jayce's eyes. "Except Ellie. After you stormed out, she was more concerned about how all this would affect *your* life than her own. It appears my daughter has inherited one of her father's most irresistible traits—a selfless and caring nature."

Jayce groaned as he dropped into the other armchair. "Of course she did, and I just lashed out at her like the self-centred idiot I am. I wish I could take back everything I said to her on the verandah. I totally hate myself right now."

Yvette smiled. "Don't worry; I'm sure she knows you weren't yourself. Besides, I think there are a few slightly more important issues to deal with at the moment... like how to keep you both alive."

"Yeah, I see your point. So, do you have any ideas about how we might do that? Stay alive, I mean."

Yvette frowned, chewing her lip in concentration.

"Well, we've got until Ellie's birthday on Saturday to come up with a solution. When do you turn eighteen?"

Jayce almost smiled. "Would you believe Saturday?"

Yvette's eyes widened, and then she shook her head, chuckling. "Of course you do. Why would I be surprised? Makes perfect sense, really."

This time, Jayce did smile. "How do you figure that?"

"The week leading up to a dragon's Coming-of-Age is always a vulnerable time. All of a sudden, the life you were so eager to dive into becomes a reality, and questions and doubts start to rise to the surface. You wouldn't be the first dragon to turn rogue rather than endure the prospect of years of servitude."

Jayce tilted his head to the side and studied the woman sitting opposite him. "How is it you know so much about dragons? I didn't realise our customs and laws were such public knowledge."

Yvette shrugged. "You would be surprised how much witches and dragons know about each other. I've met a few rogues over the years, and their stories all sounded similar."

Jayce sighed and leaned back in his chair. "So I guess it's a good thing I was already considering going rogue. But I *was* hoping to have a little more say in what happened *after that*."

He jumped as Yvette slapped the arms of her chair with her hands in excitement. "That's it! I can't believe I didn't think of it before. I have an old friend who may be able to help us, or at least give us some answers."

"But I'll need to go now, and I don't want to leave Ellie here alone. Her aunts are out of town for a couple of days. Can you stay until I get back?"

"He doesn't need to stay. I don't need or want a babysitter." Ellie's voice drifted over from the lounge, her eyes still closed.

"How long have you been awake?" her mother asked, jumping up to check on her daughter.

"Long enough..." Ellie replied, opening her eyes and casting a confused glance in Jayce's direction. "You go do what you need to. I'll be fine here on my own. " She tried to plaster a smile on her face and failed miserably.

Yvette paused, looking anxiously from Ellie to Jayce and back again. "I would rather Jayce stayed here with you. I don't need the added stress of worrying about you while I'm trying to—"

"Okay, okay... he can stay. Now, would you please just go? We don't exactly have much time to spare. Saturday isn't that far away."

Yvette bent and kissed her daughter on the forehead, cast a quick glance at Jayce, and vanished. An uncomfortable silence hung in the air for a couple of minutes, and then they both started talking at once.

"Jayce, I'm so sorry—"

"Ellie, can you ever forgive me—"

They both stopped talking to let the other continue

and then burst out laughing at the absurdity of their situation.

"Man, that feels good," Jayce said, grinning. "I was starting to think I'd never laugh again."

Ellie sat up and smiled back at him. "Tell me about it. What a mess!"

Jayce stiffened, fighting the urge to join her on the lounge. Unsure of his reception after the way he'd been acting, he opted to stay put. The space between them felt more like light-years than a couple of paces.

He sighed and cleared his throat. "So I'm thinking we might need to take a rain-check on Friday night's plans? Somehow I can't see us factoring dinner and a movie into the new arrangements."

Ellie shuffled over and patted the spot beside her. "It's okay, you know; I promise I won't bite."

Jayce's jaw dropped. "What makes you think I want to come join you?"

Ellie grinned. "Are you serious? It's written all over your face. For a minute there, I thought you might be calculating the dimensions of the lounge and whether the two of us would fit without being too cramped."

Jayce opened his mouth to argue, and instead chuckled as he stood and moved to the lounge. "You are way too intuitive for your own good, girl. Fine, I'll join you, but only because you insisted."

Ellie sighed and snuggled into her corner. "So... a dragon, huh? Unlike my mother, I know absolutely

nothing about dragons. Guess you should start enlightening me."

Ellie

ELLIE KEPT her eyes glued to Jayce's expressive face as he told her stories of growing up as a dragon. He explained about the expectations of both his family and the Council, and how he was questioning what *he* wanted before he'd even met her.

"I seriously didn't mean what I said earlier. I was attracted to you from the minute I set eyes on you, way before the bond even came into play. The way you came out of the shadows with all guns blazing was the most amazing thing I'd ever seen. You were spectacular."

Ellie blushed and giggled. "It was all bluff. I knew who you were, and your reputation, but something about the way you were standing there on that balcony all alone told me there was more to you. So I guess I just wanted to find out for myself."

Jayce threw his head back and laughed. When he could talk again, he wore a sheepish grin, like a naughty boy caught with his hand in the cookie jar. "Well, you certainly made a great first impression. I was only angry 'cos you stopped me morphing into my dragon form and taking off."

Ellie's eyes widened. "You mean I nearly saw you change? Damn. Cheated out of the experience of a lifetime by an ant bite. Which is the only reason you heard me shuffling, by the way."

Jayce's happiness faded, replaced by a frown. "Maybe we'd both be better off if I *had* morphed. You'd have run away and avoided me like the plague, and I would be totally unaware of your existence. I'm pretty sure the bonding didn't happen until I shook your hand."

Ellie smiled, shivering at the memory. "Now *that* was just plain weird. And it was even worse when you caught me at the party. Like when there's heaps of static in the air, and you bump into someone and get zapped, except about a million times stronger."

Some of the sadness left his eyes as they met hers. "Tell me about it. When I carried you in here from the kitchen, it felt like my entire body was on fire."

"Sorry about that." Ellie blushed, wishing she'd been conscious when he picked her up and held her in his arms. The pain from the zapping would have been so worth it.

She dragged her mind away from the images his words conjured and cleared her throat. "What I don't understand is why it keeps happening. If we are what my mother seems to think we are, surely having physical contact shouldn't be painful." A thought popped into her head, and Ellie jumped to her feet. "Hang on a sec'. I'll be right back."

She ran into the kitchen and grabbed the book about familiars, slapping her forehead and chuckling as she flopped back down on the lounge. "I keep forgetting I don't need to physically move to get what I want any more. Yvette taught me how to fetch things. Totally awesome. Remind me to show you later."

Ellie opened the book up to the page she'd been reading earlier. "So, I was reading this before your... less-than-spectacular arrival. Maybe something in here can explain why the zapping thing is still happening."

She flipped through the next couple of pages and then pointed to a section she hadn't read before. "Here it is, listen to this:

A WITCH and her familiar can be drawn to each other without necessarily being aware of it. In order for them to recognise their connection, each will give off an electric charge when there is physical contact between them.

So, if you keep getting zapped by the cat at your feet, or a bird brushing you with its wings has the same effect, you can guarantee you have found your familiar. Once the bond is recognised and acknowledged, this effect will cease imme-diately.

ELLIE TURNED her head to look at Jayce, only to find him a lot closer than she'd thought, their faces almost touching. "Ummm... I th-think it means we have to... ummm... say we ack- acknowledge each other. So, ummm..."

Jayce was so close she could hardly breathe. Butter-flies were doing back-flips in her stomach, and she couldn't for the life of her make herself move away. From the look in his eyes, Jayce had no intention of moving either.

"Okay. I'm game if you are. I acknowledge that I am this witch's familiar," he whispered into her ear.

Ellie gulped. "A-and I acknowledge that I am a witch, and this is my familiar," she said, never taking her eyes from his.

"Well, I guess we should see if it worked..." Jayce's lips touched hers gently, almost hesitantly, ready to pull away at the first sign of pain. When there wasn't any, he moaned softly against her mouth, his arms wrapping around her and pulling her in closer.

Ellie's heart screamed at her to melt against him, but she lifted her hands to his chest and reluctantly pushed him away. "I'm sorry, Jayce. I don't think I'm ready for this yet. So much has happened in the last few days, and my head is still spinning. We don't even know how much of what we're feeling is real and how much is due to the bond."

Jayce looked into her eyes, disappointment and confusion on his handsome face. He sighed and nodded, running his hands through his hair. "Yeah, I know. Sorry, I didn't mean to... Yep, you're right. We need to take a step back and give it some time, right? Friends?"

He smiled and reached for her hand. Ellie sighed with relief, entwining her fingers in his. She understood the need for physical contact, and this seemed a safe enough alternative while they sorted out their feelings.

"So, at least we've solved the zapping problem. Now, if the rest of this mess could be that simple, everything would be fine." The husky tone in his voice sent shivers up and down her spine.

Ellie couldn't decide whether to be relieved or disappointed that Jayce had agreed with her. She wanted him to kiss her so severely she ached, but she needed to be sure his feelings were for *her*—just plain Ellie. Not Ellie the witch he was bonded to. And although he'd apologised, his cruel words from earlier still stung.

Ellie had seen the beautiful girls who usually hung off Jayce's arm, and she was nothing like them. But if his need to be with her were anything like what she was going through, it would be almost impossible for both of them to keep their distance.

No, she refused to give her heart to someone who only wanted her because of a random magical anomaly. *Besides, it wouldn't hurt either of us to wait... would it?*

CHAPTER TEN

Jayce

Jayce looked down at Ellie's hand in his and sighed, fighting the urge to pull her back into his arms and kiss all her arguments away. Hell, he was almost certain it's what *she* really wanted him to do.

But she was right about one thing. The emotions raging through his body were way out of control. No way this overwhelming compulsion to be with her could be called normal.

What if this *was* all just a side effect of the bond? They might never be able to sort out what was real and what was caused by the bond. They needed to learn to trust and rely on each other's support first. Somewhere safe where they could explore their feelings.

Their immediate concern was dealing with the

slightly more urgent problem of finding a place to hide for a while. Preferably *before* the Councils found out about their bond, and until all the outrage and excitement had died down. Surely, if they disappeared, they would be yesterday's news in no time?

Well, they could live in hope anyway. He was surprised by the fierce protectiveness surging through him. It was just another totally new experience to add to the list. Apparently, Ellie's safety had become his first priority. He squeezed her hand and got to his feet. Maybe coffee would help.

"Excuse me? Where do you think *you're* going?" Ellie said, tugging on the hand she still held.

He knew she was only playing, but he stiffened and shook off her hand, annoyed by the inferred reference to a familiar's servitude. With an angry scowl, he turned and looked down at her puzzled face. "No, excuse *me!* I am not your servant, and I don't need your, or anyone else's, permission to do *what* I want *when* I want."

Furious, he marched into the kitchen, his hands shaking as he filled the kettle and tried to make sense of his jumbled emotions. *Where the hell had that come from?* There was no excuse for snapping Ellie's head off like that.

Okay, it's time to pull yourself together and stop acting like a Neanderthal.

Taking a deep breath, he acknowledged the real reason for his anger. Everything he knew about witches and their familiars screamed the word servitude. So, basically, he'd just traded one life of servitude for another. Jayce fought the urge to throw the damn kettle against the damn wall and scream with rage. He would not be anyone's slave... ever!

The sound of Ellie clearing her throat behind him made his hackles rise. He turned and growled at her. "What?"

Her emerald-green eyes shot sparks at him across the room, challenging him to argue with her. She pointed down at the open book on the table in front of her. "I would say sit and read, but you might misinterpret that as an order. So, would you please sit down and read the page I have open? I think you may find it enlightening."

Jayce moved to the table and stood looking down at the book. Fine, he would read it, But he'd be damned if he'd sit to do it. She couldn't have it *all* her way.

A FAMILIAR DOES NOT REQUIRE training—they are born with the innate skills and qualities needed for an effective partnership and are, therefore, an equal to their witch, just as a witch must be born with a talent for magic.

An independent spirit is prized in a familiar. They are never servile, and no decent witch would ever treat their familiar as anything but a friend and an equal. These companions also serve as a moral compass for their witch. A familiar will leave a witch who turns to the Dark.

. . .

JAYCE'S FACE burned as he read the passage. *Bloody hell, I did it again. Jumped to conclusions and made a complete ass of myself.* He turned his head to where she stood beside him, hands on hips and a long-suffering look on her face.

"Well...?"

Jayce grinned. "Ummm... oops?"

Ellie burst out laughing and punched his arm. He shrugged, mumbling about being sorry as he went back to making the coffee. Knowing Ellie was still standing there, he lifted his head and gave her a sheepish grin, holding up a cup with a cute puppy dog on the front. "So... coffee?"

Ellie

ELLIE AND JAYCE SPENT the next few hours learning a little more about each other. They enjoyed sharing stories about their childhoods, laughing and consoling one another, each gaining a better under-standing of who the other one was.

Ellie showed off her newly acquired skills, fetching a few items and sending them back to where they came from. Teleporting from the kitchen to the lounge room and back, arriving exactly where she'd intended both times, was her crowning achievement. Jayce had cracked up laughing at her story of finding herself standing on top of the kitchen table.

Finally, she told Jayce about what would happen on her birthday and how she had to choose whether to take up her birthright as a witch or stay a mortal. Since Jayce's future would be affected by whatever decision she made, she thought it only fair to consider his input.

"Wow, so which way are you swinging at the moment?"

Ellie chewed on her lip. "I have no idea. Although, since all this latest crap started, I'm thinking it'd be crazy not to take up the option of having the use of magic. I mean, it would sure come in handy if we're going to be hunted criminals—Damn, that sounds ridiculous. I feel like I'm living inside a B-grade movie or something."

Jayce smiled and put his arm around her shoulders, the contact making her heart hammer painfully in her chest. *Get a grip, girl. He's being a friend and offering comfort. Nothing more.*

"I'm sorry, Ellie. This must all be so weird for you. I

don't suppose the existence of witches and dragons is something you considered before this all started."

"Ya think? Honestly, when Yvette started rabbiting on about witches and stuff, I was ready to call the men in white coats." Ellie chuckled and gazed into his gorgeous golden eyes. "And to be honest, no matter how long I listen to you talk about being a dragon, it still just seems... impossible. Think about it. How the hell could this guy beside me be what I always believed was a mythological creature? Sorry, but I can't even begin to go there."

"Well, time we rectified that, I'm thinking. We've been cooped up in this house for hours, and I don't know about you, but I'm suffering from the onset of cabin fever. Whadya say we grab some fresh air and clear away the cobwebs? We'll leave a note for Yvette and tell her we won't be long."

Ellie jumped up off the lounge, a thrill of excitement rushing through her. "You mean go to the park so I can watch you fly?"

Jayce grinned. "That's what I had in mind."

Ellie raced to the kitchen, grabbed a pen and paper, and scribbled a note for Yvette. Jayce was at the front door waiting for her when she came back out, holding the jacket and scarf she always kept hanging in the hallway.

"Here, put this on. It might be cold down by the lake at this hour." He helped her to shrug into the jacket, wrapping the scarf around her neck, lifting her hair and pulling the scarf snugly. He was so considerate and so close that she wanted to throw her arms around his neck and kiss him for hours. And from the flash of frustration in his eyes, he wanted the same thing.

She pulled herself together with a sigh of regret and took a step back. Frustrated and kicking herself for not acting on her desires, she wrapped her hands around the arm he extended politely towards her, and they headed for the park.

Never having been to the lake at night, Ellie was amazed by how different everything appeared. The trees that looked so lush and shady during the day took on a ghostly appearance, the gentle breeze making their shadows play eerily over the ground around them as they walked. Ellie shivered, and Jayce instantly pulled a torch out of his pocket and flicked it on, lighting a path to the lake.

"Are you always this organised? I never even thought to bring a light."

Jayce chuckled. "It was on the hall stand where I found your jacket. I thought it might come in handy. Besides, I figure *one* of us needs to be organised."

"Hey... I can be organised when I need to be," Ellie quipped, punching his arm at the skeptical raised eyebrows. He pretended to wince in pain, rubbing the spot where she'd punched him.

She was about to apologise for hurting him when he dropped the charade and pulled her close, chuckling softly in her ear. "Gotcha!"

"You *will* pay. You know that, right?" Lifting her head, she was again caught in the spell of his gorgeous honey-coloured eyes. She sighed, amazed at how comfortable she was around him after such a short time. Almost as if they'd known each other forever.

"I never doubted it for a minute," Jayce said, his arms still holding her close. Why did being in his arms have to feel so awesome? "Ellie... I..." he groaned and let his arms fall to his sides.

And as if she'd been hit by a bolt of lightning from the heavens, everything became clear. They could both be dead this time next week, and she was worried about why she felt this way about the amazing guy standing in front of her?

Seriously? This entire situation was insane!

So stop being a lunatic and just kiss the guy!

Ellie pulled his arms back around her and couldn't help smiling at Jayce's confusion. "Jayce, I don't know if what we're feeling is real or not. But then, I don't understand much of anything that's happened in the last few days. The one thing I'm sure of is that all my life, I've had these feelings when something good or bad was about to happen. And when I'm with you, the only feeling I get is a good one. So maybe—"

Jayce gave a huge sigh and bent his head to kiss her. His lips were soft and gentle, tentative almost, as he gauged her reaction. Fireworks exploded inside her head as new and exciting sensations raged through her body.

Ellie opened her lips, and he moaned, deepening the kiss and pulling her hard against him. The world ceased to exist as she floated on a cloud of contentment, refusing to let the doubts and fears about their uncertain future ruin this perfect moment.

Jayce lifted his head and grinned. "I have wanted to do that since the first moment I set eyes on you. And I'm *sure* that was before the bond thing kicked in. I know everything's pretty weird right now. But I agree that the *us* part of all this craziness just feels right. Now stop distracting me and get moving. At this rate, we're never gonna make it to the lake, let alone have time for a quick flight."

Ellie stepped back out of his arms and crossed hers in front of her. "Well, it's your fault we got distracted. Here I was, walking along, minding my own business, and then *BAM*, some gorgeous hunk of a guy started kissing me. I mean... what's a girl to do?"

"Gorgeous hunk, huh? I like the sound of that. Well, if you've changed your mind and don't want to see my dragon, I'm happy to continue—"

With a wicked grin, she stepped backwards as he reached for her. "No way I'm missing out on this sight. Besides, aren't your wings getting itchy or something? C'mon, let's go... I'll race you."

Ellie turned and sprinted towards the edge of the lake, laughing at the sound of Jayce's footsteps pounding behind her. Then the footsteps changed to a flapping sound, and a huge creature flew over the top of her head and out over the lake.

Ellie stood at the water's edge, transfixed by the beauty of Jayce's dragon. His copper-coloured wings sparkled as the soft moonlight bounced off their surface. Jayce the dragon was every bit as breathtaking as Jayce the man.

Did I mention that dragons communicate telepathically? And I think you're breathtaking, too.

Ellie almost jumped out of her skin when she heard Jayce's voice—*inside her head.* A slightly more gravelly version, but his, nevertheless.

Oops, I guess I better stop admiring the view, then. I wouldn't want you to get a swelled head. Jayce's husky voice, chuckling in her mind, told her he'd heard her reply.

She tried not to think about his spectacular demonstration as Jayce swooped and dived across the sky above her. She couldn't even begin to imagine what it must be like to be able to fly.

Within seconds, Jayce had landed beside her, the sight of his dragon up close totally mesmerizing. His head was almost as big as her entire body, yet she felt no fear. The eyes of this fearsome-looking creature belonged to Jayce, and fear was the last emotion she'd use to describe her feelings for *him.*

Okay, so if you really want to know what flying's like, hop on. Jayce's voice rumbled inside her head.

What...? I... how...?

Jayce chuckled. *I have no idea; this is a first for me, too. I never met anyone I wanted to invite until now. There must be somewhere back there where you can sit. Just make sure you hold on!*

But how do I... ummm... get on?

Oh yeah. Good question. Ummm... can you step back for a second?

Ellie moved backwards, and Jayce swung his huge tail around and laid it on the ground in front of her. *Your carriage awaits, princess.*

Climbing up onto the scaly tail, she straddled it as if sitting on a horse. She shivered as his tail lifted her into the air, until she hovered next to the massive expanse of his scaly dragon body. Carefully throwing her leg over, she slid onto his back. It was already the most amazing experience of her life.

Jayce's body rose and fell as he breathed, making it a definite challenge to cross his broad back. Every time he exhaled, her feet almost went out from under her.

Are you right up there? Have you found somewhere safe to sit yet?

Hang on, Mr Impatient. I only just got here. Give me a minute, will ya?

The massive body shook as Jayce chuckled, and Ellie, still trying to find the best place to sit, toppled over and landed on her butt.

Enough with the laughing already. Balance was never my strong point.

Now she tells me, Jayce muttered.

Ellie chuckled as she moved towards his neck, looking for somewhere secure. She reached the narrowest point, ripped off her scarf and managed to wrap it around his neck. At least that would give her something to hold onto. With her legs straddling his scaly neck, she laid down and wrapped the ends of the scarf around her hands.

She took a deep breath and exhaled slowly.

Okay, ready as I'll ever be. But are you sure this is a good—

Before she could finish the thought, Jayce's ginormous wings stretched out either side, and with one smooth downbeat, they were in the air.

CHAPTER ELEVEN

Jayce

Jayce tried not to laugh as Ellie's squeals of delight filled his mind. This was rapidly turning into the most mind-blowing experience of his life. He loved flying and never ceased to feel a thrill every time he launched himself into the sky. But knowing Ellie was here with him increased the thrill to nothing short of ecstasy.

How ya doing back there? You've gone awfully quiet.

That's because there are no words to describe how incredible this is. Thank you so much for sharing this with me, Jayce.

A surge of contentment ran through his body. It was so weird. Everything felt so right when they were together, their connection so strong he couldn't imagine his life without her already.

I couldn't have explained it better myself. Ellie's voice floated into his head.

If you two lovebirds could put this on hold for a while, I have some important information to share with you. I need you back at the house... NOW.

Jayce groaned as Yvette's voice boomed inside his head. Of *course,* Ellie's mother could hear their thoughts as well.

Damnit, who knew having your mother back in your life could be so annoying? I suppose we should get back before we're grounded or something. And suddenly, that punishment has a whole new meaning...

Ellie sounded like she was trying not to laugh. He smiled as he banked and headed back to the park.

Seeing no signs of life anywhere, Jayce landed closer to where the park met the road. He lifted his tail and swung it around to where he had previously, waited for Ellie to message him she was ready, and gently lowered her to the ground.

As soon as she was on her feet, he morphed back into his human form. Only to be almost knocked off his feet as Ellie threw her arms around him, pulled his head down to hers, and kissed him.

Jayce was so surprised that he almost forgot to breathe. Their first kiss had been almost tentative, exploratory. This one made his knees shake and his stomach churn. And the fact that she'd initiated it made him almost deliriously happy.

As Ellie's lips left his, he grinned down at her starry-eyed face. "Your mother is going to kill us if we don't hurry. She sounded amused, but there was worry as well."

Ellie stepped back out of his arms and sighed. "Yeah, yeah, you don't need to say it. Duty calls." They turned and walked towards the house in silence. Their brief respite from the real world was over. Jayce sucked in a deep breath and released it slowly. From the tone of Yvette's voice, he had a feeling she didn't have good news.

Ellie

ELLIE WAS HORRIFIED by her mother's dishevelled appearance when they entered the lounge room. She looked haggard, her hair a chaotic mess, and her eyes sunken and black-rimmed.

"Hey, are you okay," she asked. "You look terrible. What happened?"

"Gee, thanks, just what every woman wants to hear," Yvette groaned. She waved her hand over her head and muttered a few words. Her appearance improved immediately, except for the still faint dark circles under her eyes.

"Sorry, I meant to fix that before you got here. So, how did you like your first flight? You certainly *sounded* like you were both enjoying yourselves. I gather you decided to put your differences behind you and move on. Wise choice, under the circumstances."

Ellie's face burned, and a quick glance at Jayce told her he was in the same state.

Could anything be more embarrassing than your mother overhearing a conversation between you and your boyfriend? Ewww.

"Anyway, I hate to be the bearer of bad tidings, but we have a huge problem. Maybe you should both sit down before I tell you what's happened."

Ellie and Jayce moved to the lounge and sat down. Instinctively, Ellie moved closer to Jayce, and his arm went around her. She met Yvette's eyes, and fear began to gnaw away at her insides. Something was terribly wrong.

Yvette took a deep breath and sat forward in her chair. "They know," she said, tears welling in her eyes. "I don't know how, but apparently, the Councils from both realms know about the bond and are up in arms."

"I'm afraid we can't wait until Saturday for you to leave. The only reason they haven't come for you already is that both Councils are still too busy debating what to do about you and how to best enforce the law."

Jayce's arm had tightened around Ellie after Yvette's first two words. Ellie was too stunned to speak, her mind numbed by the reality of someone wanting them dead. *How the hell had my life become so crazy so fast? This couldn't really be happening... right?*

"Did you manage to find somewhere we can hide?" Jayce asked through gritted teeth. "It'll be daylight in three or four hours, and we need to be gone before then."

The worried frown on Yvette's face eased a little at Jayce's words. "Yes, *that* I managed to achieve. It took some convincing, but an old friend in a small rogue dragon community has agreed to take you in. Although he was concerned that it would be the first place the dragons would come looking for you."

Jayce sighed. "Your friend is right, you know. A community of rogue dragons is the first place *I'd* go looking."

Yvette nodded. "So, I promised to work on a charm to disguise you so that you won't draw attention. Lots of the rogues have mortal partners, so if I place a glamour spell on you both, you should blend in fine."

Ellie finally found her voice. "Will you be able to come with us? I only just found you, and I d- don't..." the words stuck in her throat, and the tears she'd been fighting against burst the walls of the dam and spilled down her face. "I c-can't believe this is h-happening to us..." she stammered between sobs.

Jayce scooped her up off the lounge, holding her tenderly against his chest until the sobs began to subside. Then he put his finger under her chin and tilted her face up. "Hey, we'll be okay. I have no intention of letting *anyone* hurt you—*ever*. But you need to trust me. Can you do that?"

Ellie saw the fire burning in his eyes and nodded, a watery smile lifting the corners of her mouth. "Thank you."

Yvette cleared her throat, probably thinking they'd forgotten she was there, and smiled. "You two remind me so much of your father and me. We were prepared to take on anyone who tried to ruin what we had. You are both strong and intelligent, and I don't think the Councils have any idea what they're up against."

"As for me going with you, honey, I'm afraid I can't. They'll be watching me closely, hoping I'll slip up and lead them to you. It won't be easy maintaining the pretense that I knew nothing about your bonding or disappearance.

The Witch Council knew I was coming here to meet you, but I'll tell them you refused to forgive me, and I gave up and walked away. I'll need to act as shocked and appalled by the news as everyone else."

"I know you're right. But I was just getting used to having you around."

"Hey, when this is all over, we'll have plenty of time

to do all the things we'd planned. Make sure you practice what I taught you to increase your energy levels, but no teleporting until you reach your destination. Teleporting leaves a magic trail for a few minutes, a bit like footprints. It can be seen and followed by anyone who's nearby and looking."

"But what about my choosing ceremony? I don't even know what I'm supposed to do."

Yvette moved to kneel in front of where Ellie sat in Jayce's arms. "I'll make sure someone is there to help you on Saturday. I would prefer it was me, but that may not be possible. I'll see what I can do. I promise I'll do everything I can to keep you both safe. Just seeing you two together, I think the odds for success are definitely in your favour."

ELLIE SKIMMED through the small spell book her mother had given her, excited at the thought of trying some of them out. But she couldn't help wishing her mother could be with her the first time she tried them. Being around Yvette made her feel like a little girl again, and Ellie loved the glow of pride in her mother's eyes when she succeeded at something new.

Yvette had already placed a glamour on Ellie, that of an old scrubber woman, an image she was relieved to learn she would only see if she looked in a mirror. It was still weird knowing *that* was the image she'd be projecting to the world. It was definitely going to take some getting used to.

Yvette had almost finished Jayce's glamour as well. "Now remember, this will only work on you when you're in your human form. I can't even begin to imagine what it would take to put a glamour on a dragon.

Under no circumstances should you morph during daylight hours. Your unique dragon colouring would be like waving a red flag."

Jayce nodded and walked over to the mirror hanging in the hall. He roared with laughter at the sight of his reflection. "I thought Ellie's disguise was good, but this one takes the cake. I look like a wasted old bum with a bottle-a-day habit. Elle, you *gotta* come see this..."

Ellie moved toward him, a shiver running down her spine at the way he used the shortened version of her name. She didn't usually like it, but somehow, Jayce made it sound... intimate.

Her 'old scrubber' matched the 'bum' perfectly. "Mmmm... what a gorgeous couple we make. No wonder women find you *hot*. That scraggly beard is totally irresistible," Ellie said, winking at him in the mirror.

Jayce grinned at her reflection. "Hey, you're *so* not in a position to judge. The grey bun goes well with—"

Yvette cleared her throat, again. "Just be grateful you can still see each other as you really are. I did think about making you put up with looking at each other's glamours, but I weakened." She chuckled and then quickly sobered.

"Okay, it's past time you weren't here. There's probably less than two hours left until daylight, and you need to be a long way from here before then. Here are your new driver's licenses and credit cards in the name of Mr and Mrs Jones."

"Okay, so where exactly is this community we're going to?" Jayce couldn't believe he hadn't asked where they were going before this.

"Tasmania." Yvette grinned at the astonished looks on their faces. She snapped her fingers, and a map appeared in her hand. "This should help you find the way, and Jasper said he would keep an eye out for you."

"The community is in a small valley surrounded by mountains, so it's very secluded. The local mortals believe they're some kind of religious commune and usually steer clear of the place."

Jayce chuckled. "Brilliant. Sounds like the perfect place to hide. How long do you think it will take us to get there? Darwin to Tasmania is a little more than a hop, skip and a jump."

Yvette frowned. "At least eight to ten hours flying time. So you'll need to make sure you're settled somewhere to sleep during the day, and you need to be out of your dragon form well before daybreak."

Ellie had turned white. "Are you saying I'll be on Jayce's back for like hours and hours? How am I supposed to stay on for that long? And what am I going to hold on *to*?"

Jayce shared a look with Yvette. "Do you wanna tell her, or will I?"

Instantly, sparks flew from Ellie's eyes. "What did I say the last time I was referred to as *her*? *Stop. Doing. It.*" she yelled, and to everyone's surprise, Jayce flew backwards until he was pinned against the wall.

Ellie's eyes widened, and her hand flew to her mouth. "O-kay, what the hell was that?" She turned to her mother for help. Yvette waved her hand and released Jayce from the wall, and they all burst out laughing.

Yvette was the first to recover enough to speak. "Oh dear, it seems your powers aren't going to stay dormant much longer. What you just did is called a 'power-thrust'. I'm amazed you were able to do it without any practice. It might be a good idea to keep a tight rein on your temper until you learn a bit more control, especially if you're pointing at someone. I'll leave some instruction books in your room for you to fetch if you need them."

Jayce was still on the floor, groaning. "Yep, that'd be much appreciated, Yvette. Not sure how long my back will hold up if this is what I can expect every time I do or say something wrong."

Ellie sat beside him, holding her stomach. "I am *so*

sorry, Jayce. I seriously didn't mean to..." she spluttered, then went back to rolling around hysterically.

Yvette stood watching them, shaking her head. "I hate to remind you both, but people want to *kill* you, and they could be on their way here as we speak.

Oh, and Ellie, what Jayce and I were talking about before you so lovingly pinned him against the wall was that we've devised a harness of sorts to help you when you're flying. Now, can we please get moving? I keep expecting a knock at the door any minute."

Ellie smiled sheepishly as Jayce helped her to her feet. "So... I promise I'll *try* not to lose my temper. At least not at you."

"My back would be most grateful." He grinned as they linked arms and headed outside.

CHAPTER TWELVE

Ellie

Ellie sat on Jayce's dragon's back as she finished strapping herself into the homemade harness. She looked down at her mother, her heart aching over their time together being cut short. "Please come and see us the minute you think it's safe."

Yvette just nodded, her eyes filled with tears. "Just remember I love you... always have and always will. Take care of my baby, Jayce. NOW GO!"

Don't worry, Yvette. I'll keep her safe. And thank you... for everything. Jayce's gravelly dragon voice had a determined ring, and Ellie suddenly felt sorry for anyone who tried to harm them.

Jayce's massive wings spread out beside them,

almost taking out the back fence as they lifted into the air. Ellie watched her mother standing alone in the backyard until she was a tiny speck in the distance.

Ellie? You okay?

Jayce's voice acted like a soothing balm to her tattered emotions. She wiped the last of the tears away and sat up a little straighter.

Yeah, I'll be fine. I can't believe how totally insane my life has become over the last few days. It's like I'm watching this all happen to someone else. And I would've liked to spend a bit more time with my long-lost mother, ya'know? Anyway, have you thought about where we should stop for the day?

No idea, this is all new territory to me, too. But I'm sure we'll find a decent-sized town before dawn.

Cool. The sooner, the better. It feels like ages since I last slept, and you must be exhausted, too.

Jayce chuckled. *Okay, I can take a hint. I guess as long as we're well away from the house, we can pretty much stop anywhere. We're only recognisable when I'm in dragon form. I'll start looking for somewhere soon.*

Almost an hour later, as Ellie's blinks were getting longer and longer, Jayce's voice popped into her head again. *How about the town up ahead? We could land in the scrub and then walk to a motel?*

Sounds good to me, Ellie said, not even opening her eyes. Her stomach did a backflip as Jayce started the descent toward the town. Her eyes flew open, hands scrabbling for the handholds attached to the harness.

Struggling to find the left one, she glanced down

and thought she saw a movement below and slightly behind them. Once her hand was safely secured, she checked again, but there was nothing. She shrugged and held on tight, eager to be on solid ground again.

AS SOON AS JAYCE LANDED, Ellie removed the harness and waited for Jayce's tail so she could climb on and be lowered to the ground. The streetlights of the town gleamed not too far off, and her mind wandered to delicious thoughts of climbing into a soft bed and sleeping the day away.

The emotional upheavals of the last few days had finally caught up with her, and she felt like she'd been hit by a bus. She bent over, attempting to stuff the harness into the overfull backpack, when she found herself wrapped in a pair of warm arms.

"Jayce, I need to—"

"Ahuh..." he murmured as his lips found hers. Ellie forgot all about the backpack, and her arms stole up around his neck of their own accord.

Crushed against his chest, she decided that flying might be awesome, but nothing compared to *this*. Jayce's arms made her feel warm and safe, the kiss soft and comforting.

Jayce lifted his head and grinned. "Sorry to interrupt, but I missed you."

Ellie chuckled. "Ummm... I didn't go anywhere. I've been with you the whole time."

"Yeah, but that was with *dragon* Jayce. *This* Jayce missed being able to kiss you—"

"You're a nut! You know that, right?"

"Only since I met you. I used to be relatively sane."

"Oh no, you're not pinning this on me—"

They froze at the sound of rustling in the bushes behind them. Jayce put his finger to his lips, grabbed her hand, scooped up the backpack, and then they were running toward the streetlights of the town. They crashed through the bush, making so much noise that it was impossible to tell if anyone followed them.

They reached the street a few minutes later, breathing hard and looking wildly behind them for any sign of pursuit. The soft dawn light picked up a movement among the trees, and Jayce pulled her behind him.

A tall, scruffy-looking man stepped out of the shadows, a nasty smile on his face and a gun in his hand. His aura told Ellie he was a supernatural, and her stomach clenched with fear. He was probably what she'd spotted before they landed. Which meant he was a dragon, and he'd been following them.

"Mornin' folks. Nice day for a run through the bush, eh?"

Jayce growled softly. "Who are you, and what do you want?"

The stranger broke into a wheezing chuckle. "Well, cain't say as I want anythin' from *you*. It's the witch behin' ya that I'm lookin' for. I gotta tell ya, though, I never woulda

picked you pair as the ones I'm lookin' for. If'n it weren't for the fact that I seen ya change outta them sparkly lookin' copper wings a'yours, I'da walked right past y'se in the street and been none the wiser."

Jayce squeezed Ellie's hand a little tighter, the muscles in his back tensing under her other hand. "And why would you be looking for us?"

The stranger wheezed again and slapped his thigh. "What planet you been livin' on? Y're witch girlfriend's got a truckload 'a gold bounty on her head, and I aim ta be the one ta claim it! So if ya jest step outta me way, ol' man, me and the 'old lady' 'll be on our way back to the Dragon Realm."

Jayce

Jᴀʏᴄᴇ ꜰᴇʟᴛ Ellie stiffen and then groan behind him. The man's words didn't make any sense. *Why would the Dragon Council put a bounty on Ellie's head and not mine?*

Jayce snapped his mind out of its numb state and tried to think of a solution. Damnit, he should have landed earlier. It was all his fault this slimy bounty hunter had found them.

But whining about *'if only'* wouldn't help them now. He calculated the distance between them and the bounty hunter, cursing as he realised he wouldn't be able to reach the man before he had a bullet in his chest.

Think! His mind screamed in frustration. *There must be something...*

An idea came to him, and he prayed Ellie would get the message.

"Are you sure you want to mess with my girlfriend, mate?" Jayce sneered at the man in front of them. "Take it from someone who knows from experience. She has an *incredibly* bad temper. I don't think you want to see what she does when she *gets angry*." He squeezed Ellie's hand as he spoke the last words.

Ellie returned the squeeze, and he heard her take a deep breath. *Yes!* She knew what he wanted her to do. He just hoped the last time she'd done this hadn't been a fluke. Stepping up beside Jayce, she pointed toward the sniggering worm with a frown.

"You heard my boyfriend. So *Back. Off. Now*," Ellie yelled. Before the man could react, he was flying backwards through the air, slamming into a nearby tree and crumpling to the ground. Jayce ran toward him, bent and picked up his gun, and then stood staring down at the unconscious man, shaking his head.

Ellie joined him within seconds, her shaking body sagging against him. He slipped his free arm around her waist and kissed the top of her head. "You are amazing. I didn't even know if it would work or whether you'd get what I was saying, but I figured it was worth a try."

"Yeah, I got what you meant, but I still can't believe it worked. So what do we do now? He knows what we look like and that we're headed south," Ellie said, a quaver in her voice.

Jayce shook his head. "Yeah, I was thinking the same thing. So what the hell are we supposed to do with him now?" His stomach recoiled in distaste at the thought of having to kill someone.

Ellie stiffened beside him and sighed. "Hang on a sec. I have an idea." She held out her hand, and her spell book appeared. Rubbing her eyes, she flicked through the pages. He figured she'd found what she was looking for when she released a long, slow breath, the mask of exhaustion and fear she'd worn only minutes ago melting away.

"Yes! I thought I saw this when I was skimming through earlier. Yvette said this little book was full of easy spells, so I'm assuming I can manage one. There's a spell here for erasing memories."

"Seriously? That is awesome." Jayce sagged with relief, grateful he wouldn't be forced to kill the man. And then he frowned. "Are you sure you're up to it? You look about ready to collapse. And how will we even know if the spell worked?"

Ellie shrugged and dropped her eyes back down to the book. "Well, it's not like we have a choice. This *has* to work. Apparently, I just need to form a mental picture of what we look like, and all memories of us will be erased." She moved closer to the man still slumped unconscious at the base of the tree.

Pointing her hand towards his face, she recited the words of the spell:

Dedisco Occursus.

The man's face instantly went slack, a gurgling snoring sound emanating from his open mouth.

Jayce shook his head in wonder and grinned at Ellie. "I guess *that's* how we'll know it worked."

Ellie smiled, practically swaying on her feet as he slipped his arm around her waist. "Okay, enough witchy stuff for today. Let's go find somewhere to sleep."

He picked up the backpack they'd discarded earlier, removed the bullets from the bounty hunter's gun, and stuffed it all into the bottom. It might come in handy the way things were going, and he could dispose of it when they reached their destination.

He looked down at Ellie stumbling along beside him and knew she wouldn't make it much further.

Reaching down behind her knees, he swung her up into his arms, loving the feel of her arms sliding up around his neck.

"Mmm... I think I could get used to this," she said, her eyes fluttering closed.

"That makes two of us, beautiful girl," he whispered against her hair, pulling her close and striding toward the brightly lit motel sign up ahead. Yvette had explained to him how the magic would drain her. She needed sleep, food and water to restore her energy levels.

He pushed aside the exhaustion creeping into his own body. His needs could wait until he'd ensured his precious cargo was safe. Somewhere over the last twelve hours or so, Ellie had become the most important thing in his life, and he had no intention of letting some bounty-hunting jerk, or anyone else for that matter, take her away from him.

CHAPTER THIRTEEN

Ellie

_E_llie opened her eyes and tried to make sense of her unfamiliar surroundings. *Unbelievable! No idea where you are or how you got here. Way to go, Ellie.*

She tried to recall the last thing she remembered, but the sensation of someone using a cattle prod on her head told her that *thinking* might not be such a good plan just yet.

Moaning, she rolled onto her side, relieved to find a pair of turn-a-girls-legs-to-jelly eyes gazing into hers. At least that answered one of her questions. She smiled as Jayce leaned over and kissed the tip of her nose.

"Afternoon, sleeping beauty." Jayce's soft, gravelly voice sent shivers down her spine.

"Did you say afternoon?" She winced as the cattle prod zapped her again.

"Well, it *was* daylight before we even got here." He frowned when she put her hand to her head. "Hey... are you okay?"

"Just a headache," she whispered so the sound wouldn't hurt her head so much.

Jayce rolled over towards the bedside table behind him and pulled open a drawer. Popping two tablets out of silver foil, he handed them to her with a bottle of water. "I sorta guessed you might need them."

He moved closer to help her sit up and swallow the tablets, and then she snuggled back down into his waiting arms, her aching head resting on his chest.

"So, how much do you remember?"

She smiled. How did he always seem to know what she was thinking? "Casting the memory spell," she whispered, and his chest moved under her cheek as he chuckled.

"No surprise there. You were pretty out of it after that, so I ended up carrying you here to the motel. I had to explain to the frowning man at the reception desk how you took a sleeping pill *before* our car broke down. Although, he still looked a bit suspicious when he gave me the key. I reckon he thought I was just some dirty old man who slipped you a roofie.

Ellie giggled at the image Jayce's words painted in

her head. She kept forgetting that the world saw them as an old couple.

Damn! She suddenly realised she'd stuffed up, *big-time.* Ignoring her sore head, she sat up and stared at Jayce in horror.

"Jayce, I can't believe I was so stupid. When I wiped the bounty hunter's memory, I was so tired that I pictured the *real* us. What if he remembers what our glamours look like?"

Jayce frowned, and then his face broke into a smile. "Hey, calm down. I don't know much about magic and spells or how they work. But surely, if he can't remember ever meeting us, he won't be able to recall our glamours either. When you think about it, the people we're glamoured to look like don't exist without us. Besides, if he *did* retain a memory of the old couple, he wouldn't know who the hell they were. So stop stressing and relax."

She sighed and slid back down into his arms. He tucked a stray curl behind her ear, kissing the top of her head.

"Now, where was I? Oh yeah, so when we got to the room, you started mumbling about being starving. I said I'd grab a quick shower and then go out to find us something to eat."

"When I came out of the bathroom, you were fast asleep, so I went and got the supplies anyway, figuring we'd still need them eventually. I didn't have the heart to wake you when I got back. You looked so peaceful."

The pain in her head began to ease as she listened to Jayce's soothing voice, the soft rhythm of his steady heartbeat comforting beneath her. Jayce wouldn't let her go back to sleep until she'd eaten one of the sandwiches from the previous night, and drank at least half the bottle of water. She smiled at his bossy fussing, secretly loving his concern.

Feeling slightly better with the food and water in her stomach, she nestled back into the comfort of Jayce's protective arms. *Damn,* she loved having him to watch over her. A comfortable silence settled over the room, and before long, the change in Jayce's breathing told her he was asleep. She sighed, her eyes heavy from the painkillers, and drifted off to sleep again.

Jayce

JAYCE WOKE WITH A START, reaching for Ellie and finding her gone. Cursing himself for falling asleep, he dived off the bed and scrambled for his clothes. If anything had happened to her, he'd never forgive himself. Then, the sound of the shower running in the bathroom penetrated his panicked brain, and he slumped back down on the bed in relief.

Damnit, would he ever get used to the surge of protectiveness that flooded his body every time he thought about her? He shook his head and went to put the kettle on. Life had certainly changed over the last few days.

A smiling Ellie emerged from the bathroom, still towelling her hair dry, as he finished making two cups of coffee.

"That coffee smells awesome. I was debating which was more tempting... staying in the shower for another ten minutes or the coffee." She shrugged. "The coffee won."

"Ah, I see... so I didn't even come into the equation? Spending more time with me should have at least been *one* of the options," Jayce tried to paste an offended expression onto his face, but the corner of his mouth kept twitching into a smile.

Ellie sauntered over and sat down on his lap. "Oops! Did I forget to mention that spending time with you *and* the coffee was a package deal I couldn't resist?" She winked and threw her arms around his neck, kissing him to prove her point. The scent of strawberries invaded his senses, her body soft and warm from the shower as she snuggled against him. *Damn, she was gorgeous.*

She lifted her head, a cheeky sparkle dancing in her eyes. He chuckled, scooped her up, and dumped her on the chair next to him. "Drink your coffee, you wicked witch. Otherwise, I won't be responsible for my actions, and the coffee will get cold."

Ellie blushed and giggled, picking up her coffee and sighing as she took her first sip. She grinned, and his heart skipped a beat. Who knew that meeting her would be the best thing to ever happen to him? Even if it did mean being banished and hunted by his own kind.

He frowned at the thought of telling Ellie about the internal debate he'd conducted while she slept. His heart ached at the possibility that she might agree with him, but he had to at least address the question playing over and over in his mind.

"Uh-oh, what's with the frown and the serious face? What's going on?" She moved her chair closer and put her hand on his leg. Already, just the thought of having to live without her touch almost convinced him to change his mind.

"Jayce? What is it?"

Jayce focused his eyes on his hands, wrapped tightly around his coffee cup, and shrugged. "I had a lot of time to think today while I watched you sleep. Something the bounty hunter said, how he only found us because of my dragon colouring, started me thinking. Being with me almost got you killed." He lifted his head and met her eyes. "Maybe you'd be better off going into hiding without—"

Ellie flinched and held her hand up in front of his

face. The anger in her eyes told him he was in deep trouble.

"Hey, if you don't want to risk being around me anymore, Jayce, that's fine. We both know it's me they want and not you. So, I understand how hard it was for you to lose everything because of me, but please don't try to justify your decision to leave by saying you're doing what's best for *me*. If you want to leave without me, then just go, okay?"

Jayce stared at her in stunned silence. How the hell had she managed to twist his words around enough to reach the conclusion that he *wanted* to go? If the entire situation hadn't been so sad, it would have been funny.

"How on earth did you interpret what I just said as being *me wanting* to leave you behind?"

"Well, that's how it sounded to me! How else was I supposed to *interpret* it?"

"Damnit, Ellie. The thought of not being near you makes me want to throw up! What I was trying to say is that I think *you* would be safer if you didn't have a dragon hanging around that may as well be wearing a neon sign blazing the words *here we are* for all the worlds to see. I was praying you wouldn't agree to send me away, but I need to put your safety before what I want."

The anger melted from her eyes, tears welling as she moved back into his lap and laid her head on his shoulder. "I'm so sorry, Jayce. I just thought... well, I feel so guilty for ruining your life and putting you in danger, so I wouldn't *blame* you if you wanted to walk away. But if you're asking me if *I want you* to leave, the answer is a definite no. I know it sounds ridiculous to admit this when we only met like, three days ago, but I don't *ever* want to be without you again.

Jayce shuddered and wrapped his arms around her. "I was terrified you'd agree with me and say we'd both be safer on our own. I don't give a toss about the life I walked away from. This one is a thousand times better already because *you're* in it."

Ellie sniffed and lifted her head, making his pulse race at the fire in her emerald-green eyes. "Excellent. Because if you ever mention us being better off apart again, I swear I'll put a spell on you that won't let you sit down for a week!"

Jayce threw his head back and laughed. "Don't worry... I promise I will *never* make *that* mistake again," he spluttered.

Brushing a stray curl back off her beautiful face, he leaned down toward her waiting lips.

Ellie

ELLIE PULLED the curtain aside and peered out at the darkening sky. The moon was little more than a thin crescent, perfect for concealing them as they travelled.

"About another half hour, and we should be good to go," she called over her shoulder, and then jumped when she felt Jayce beside her. "I thought you were in the bathroom?"

"I thought you were having a sleep?" he countered, and they both grinned.

Ellie turned around and pushed against his chest. "I just thought I'd pull the harness out and check it before we leave. My mother won't be here to help like last time, so I wanted to make sure I had all the clasps sorted in my head before I tried doing it in the pitch dark on my own."

"Hey, you won't be on your own. I'll be there."

"Uh-huh... as a bloody great impatient dragon grumbling about what's taking so long."

Jayce chuckled. "Yeah, well, I'm working on that, okay. Dragons aren't exactly known for their patience."

Ellie shook her head and stretched the harness out on the bed. Yvette and Jayce had done a brilliant job of creating it. The straps were made from strips of torn bedsheets in a variety of colours. It may not have been colour-coordinated, but it was undoubtedly effective.

The harness consisted of two parts. A wide strap with handholds and foot-loops attached, similar to stirrups, which wrapped around Jayce's neck at its narrowest part, and clipped together in front of where Ellie sat.

The harness itself wrapped around her shoulders and waist and clipped together at the front. The two clips snapped together and locked into place, allowing her to either sit upright or flatten herself against Jayce's neck.

"Right, I think I've got it all sorted now. You want another coffee before we go?"

Jayce nodded and sat down at the small table. "So, I was thinking—"

Ellie turned and raised her eyebrows. "Oh no, not again. Didn't we already do this?"

"Yeah, yeah, you're so funny. Seriously though, remember when we were flying over the park, and your mother heard our entire conversation? I don't understand how she did it. Dragon speak is called broadcasting, but I always assumed you only broad-casted to the person you wanted to hear you."

Ellie carried the coffee cups to the table and sat down. "Yeah, I meant to ask her about that, but with all the excitement, I forgot about it. Maybe she used magic to locate me, and it somehow allowed her to join the conversation?"

Jayce picked up his coffee, about to take a sip, when his eyes widened. "*Or...* what if learning how *not* to broadcast is something I would have learned after I turned eighteen?"

"That would definitely explain a lot of the trouble I

got into when I was a kid. I used to wonder how my parents always knew what I was up to. And I often got the impression they were communicating, and I couldn't hear it." He banged his hand on the table.

"Damnit! That's probably how the bounty hunter first found us. I have no idea how far we're broadcasting when we use the mind speak. Which means… we won't be able to communicate while I'm in my dragon form."

Ellie reached for his hand. "Hey, don't stress over it. There's sure to be someone at the rogue community who can teach you how to not broadcast."

"But we'll be flying for hours. I don't want to go that long without your voice in my head. There has to be a way around it."

Ellie waved her hand at the table, and the *Witches and their Familiars* book appeared. She chuckled. "Did I mention I really like this fetching thing? It gives a whole new meaning to having 'everything at your fingertips'." She flipped through the pages until she found the section she'd been looking for, turning the book so Jayce could read it. "You never did finish reading this, did you?

Telepathic Abilities

WITCHES WHO POSSESS strong telepathic powers may be able to use this to open the channels of communication with their familiar. The ability to read each other's thoughts can only be achieved when the bond is strong, and trust unconditional, and is a rare and powerful addition to their partnership.

However, if the familiar is unwilling to share their every thought with their witch, the witch's telepathic powers, no matter how strong, will be unable to open the necessary channels.

BY THE TIME he'd finished reading, Jayce's eyes sparkled with excitement. "So, do you think we can do this?"

"Don't ask me. I have no idea what I can and can't do, remember? But I suppose we can give it a shot if you want. According to this, it's up to you anyway."

Jayce grinned. "I don't think whoever wrote this had a *dragon* familiar in mind. We already do this when I'm in my dragon form... remember? If it works, the only difference will be that the rest of the world won't be able to hear us. It'll be like having our own private channel. This is exactly what we need."

Ellie stood and threw her hands in the air. "But the stupid book doesn't even mention *how* to do it. I hate this, not knowing how to do anything or what I'm capable of doing or not doing. Seriously, what's the point of having magic if I don't know how to use it?" She paced back and forth in the small space between the bed and the table. "Aargghh, where do I even start?"

Jayce jumped up and grabbed her shoulders, effectively stopping the pacing. "Okay, calm down. You're not gonna be able to do anything in this state. Close your eyes, take a deep breath, and let it out slowly." Ellie did as he suggested, her racing heartbeat slowly returning to normal.

"Better?" he asked, and she nodded. "Good. Now keep your eyes closed, and think about what you do to reply to me in dragon speak. Can you do that?" Ellie nodded again, calm now. "Okay, now try to reach my mind and send a message to me."

Ellie tried to reach out to Jayce's mind, but she had no idea where it was or how to find it.

Convinced the whole thing was a complete waste of time, she allowed the thought that had been playing in the back of her mind all afternoon to come to the surface.

Okay, this is totally crazy, but I think I might be falling in love with you, Jayce Raythawn. She didn't really send a message, so much as form the thought in her head.

When he didn't reply, she shrugged and opened her eyes. "See, I knew it wouldn't work..." But the fire in his eyes sent her heartbeat into overdrive. "Wait. You didn't...?"

I feel the same way, beautiful. The words entered her mind as he gathered her into his arms and kissed her. The kiss was hungry, conveying the way he felt better than any words. She clung to him, wishing they could stay right here like this forever. Stuff the realms and their stupid laws. Nothing this perfect should *ever* be outlawed.

I know, babe. But for now, we just need to keep going. Hopefully, once we get to the rogue community, we can take up where we left off.

She grinned as his words caressed her mind. *Damn, how cool was it to be able to talk and kiss at the same time? Now, that's what I'd call progress.*

CHAPTER FOURTEEN

Jayce

*L*ess than an hour later, Jayce held Ellie's hand tightly in his as they walked hand in hand down the street. He smiled as Ellie blew out a long, slow breath when the bounty hunter they'd encountered earlier that day. was nowhere in sight.

"Well, *that's* a huge relief. I had visions of that dirtbag bounty hunter still sitting here waiting for us. Not that he would even remember who we were, but try convincing my over-active imagination of that. I keep thinking another bounty hunter will jump out from behind a tree and..." She shuddered and held his hand tighter. "Oh, that reminds me. What happened to his gun?"

Jayce squeezed her hand. "I unloaded it and stuffed it into the bottom of the backpack, just in case. We can get rid of it later. Hey, stop stressing. I reckon we should be safe for now. Anyone who saw me as a dragon last night or this morning had all day to make their move. I'm just dreading morphing and exposing us again."

"Hey, as long as we land way before daylight this time, we'll be fine," Ellie reassured him. "Plus, we won't be broadcasting to anyone who happens to be in range again, either. So everything is looking good."

Twenty minutes later, they were up and flying again. The moon was a faint sliver, the night air crisp and exhilarating. The tension of the last twenty-four hours eased as Jayce moved his powerful wings with confidence. As a dragon, and being in the sky, his self-doubt about keeping Ellie safe melted away. He would get them to their destination in one piece if it killed him.

JAYCE HAD STUDIED the map Yvette gave them for almost an hour before they left the motel and figured they should be getting close to their destination. He assumed from Ellie's silence that she was asleep. For a while there, he'd thought the night would never end, but finally seeing land below them instead of an endless ocean meant the nightmare was almost over.

He banked to the left to take a closer look at the terrain below and felt a thump against his side.

What the...?

Jayce, help! Ellie's voice screamed in his mind. When he spotted her below him, her arms flailing as she plummeted toward the ground, his veins filled with ice.

I'm coming! Jayce turned and nose-dived in her direction, her screams echoing inside his head. His heart clenched in fear. He hadn't been that high up, dropping down to look for landmarks. Which meant he didn't have much time to get between Ellie and the ground.

She was almost within reach when he realised he didn't know how to stop her fall. He thought about flying underneath her, but at the speed she was falling, she might bounce off his back, and they didn't have time to test it out.

The only other way would be to use his teeth or his talons, either of which would hurt her. Still, a few scratches were definitely better than being dead.

Jayce pulled out of his nosedive and hovered above Ellie's rapidly descending body. *I'm sorry, babe, but I'm gonna have to grab you with my talons. This may hurt—*

I don't care... just don't let me hit the ground! The terror in Ellie's voice spurred him into action. Stretching out his talons, he clamped them onto her falling body, her body jerking as her fall came to an abrupt halt, barely above tree height.

He felt Ellie sag, both physically and mentally, and he assumed she'd passed out. Heading for a clearing large enough to accommodate his dragon body, he lowered her gently to the ground, released her slumped body and moved to land beside her.

He morphed the second his feet touched the ground, cursing as he wasted time untangling himself from the oversized harness still hanging from his body. He ran to Ellie and pulled her into his lap, wincing at the sight of the ripped flesh running down her left side. The pain must have been excruciating, but she hadn't made a sound.

"Elle... can you hear me, baby? I'm so sorry I hurt you, sweetheart. I couldn't think of any other way to stop your fall."

Ellie opened her eyes and smiled up at him. "I'm alive... and you saved me. The rest doesn't matter. But *damn*, my side hurts. Remind me to trim your nails."

Jayce leaned down and kissed her on the forehead. "We'll get you fixed up in no time. I think the harness has done its job now. I can use some of the strips of sheeting to wrap you up and stop the bleeding."

"It was my fault, Jayce. I forgot to lock the clips between my harness and the one attached to you, so when I fell asleep... I'm sorry. But don't wreck the harness. You can use this," Ellie said, wincing as she pointed at the ground beside her, where a first-aid kit appeared.

Jayce shook his head and smiled. "Clever girl. Just what the doctor ordered," he chuckled as he opened the box, looking for whatever he'd need to patch her up. "And stop beating yourself up about making a mistake. It was dark, and you did the best you could. Besides, I already did a good enough job of beating you up while trying to rescue you."

Ellie

ELLIE FOCUSED her pain-filled mind and managed to fetch an old tent she remembered seeing in the storeroom back at the aunts' house in Darwin. Jayce pitched it at record speed, and she fetched pillows and blankets, before crawling wearily inside. Her side ached terribly, but Jayce had cleaned and dressed the wounds and given her painkillers, so sleep was the next thing high on her agenda.

Apparently, they were in a dense section of forest not far inland from the Tasmanian coastline. Jayce said he remembered flying over lights not too far north of them and planned to walk into town and rent a car after they got some sleep. Ellie silently thanked Yvette for the fake driver's license and credit card.

Jayce climbed in beside her and gathered her into his arms. Her mind felt like marshmallow, the painkillers finally kicking in and blocking out everything else. Feeling safe wrapped in Jayce's arms, she sighed and floated off to sleep.

Jayce

JAYCE WOKE IN A SWEAT, the last traces of his nightmare clinging to his mind as he shuddered, grateful to be awake. He sat up, sucking air into his lungs and wiping the sweat from his face, taking slow, deep breaths until his heartbeat returned to normal. Relief flooded through him at the sound of Ellie's soft breathing beside him.

In his nightmare, she'd been lying on the ground crushed and broken, because he'd been too slow to save her. He could still feel the agony that had ripped through his heart as she hit the ground.

Ellie stirred and opened her eyes, cloudy and unfocused from the painkillers. "What's up? You okay?"

Jayce checked the time, surprised to find they'd been asleep for a good six hours. He smiled and slid back down under the blankets, Ellie instantly snuggling in beside him as her eyes closed, and she drifted back off to sleep.

"I am now, beautiful girl," he murmured, brushing her hair back from her face. He gasped and laid his hand on her forehead. Damnit, she was burning up.

Infection must have set in for her fever to be so high. Why hadn't he thought to ask her if there was a healing spell in her little book she could use on herself? He scrambled for the backpack, rifling through it in search of Ellie's little book of spells.

Jayce finally located the book and pulled it out, flipping through the pages in search of a spell that would help. He'd need Ellie to heal herself before delirium set in. Relief washed over him as he found the spell he'd been looking for.

Jayce crawled back up beside her, shocked by the heat radiating from her body. "Hey, gorgeous. I found a healing spell. I need you to focus on me and listen carefully." Ellie's eyes opened, and she nodded.

Jayce glanced down at the book in his hand. "You'll need to point to the wounded area, and the words for the spell are *Lenimentum Vulnus.*"

Ellie looked at him and smiled. "Lebinmeminum Valus...got it."

"Elle, this is really important. If you pass out before you cast the spell, I can't help you. I want you to try pointing to the spot, thinking about the wounds, and repeating *exactly* what I say. Can you do that, baby? For me?"

Ellie seemed to rally herself at his words. She nodded her head as he moved closer, lifting her hand so she could point to where the bandages were. He just hoped she had her thoughts focused as well.

"Lenimentum," Jayce said in a loud, clear voice.

"Lenimentum," Ellie repeated, not as loud but just as clearly as Jayce.

"Vulnus." Jayce held his breath as he waited for Ellie to repeat the word.

"Vulnus." As soon as the word left her mouth, Ellie gasped and slumped over onto her back.

Jayce touched her forehead, relieved to find she didn't feel quite so hot. He didn't know what else to do. She needed to be in hospital, and he had no idea where to find one. Besides, they had no way of getting anywhere.

Wait, if the spell had helped with her fever, it might have at least slowed the infection.

As gently as he could, he rolled Ellie on her side to check her wounds. Tenderly unwrapping the blood-soaked bandage closest to him, he reeled in shock. The wound was completely healed.

The torn flesh had knitted itself back together, and the scar looked like the injury was weeks old. He quickly unwrapped the other bandage to find the second wound in the same condition. The spell hadn't just worked. It had all but performed a miracle!

Sitting back on his heels, he sent a prayer of thanks to whatever deity had helped them. The possibility of Ellie dying from injuries inflicted by *him* had terrified him. Living without her would have been bad enough, but living with *himself*, knowing she'd died because of something he did, would have killed him.

Removing the rest of the bandages, he cleaned away all traces of the dried blood and slipped back under the covers, sliding his arm underneath her and gathering her close.

Ellie sighed in her sleep, and Jayce's heart contracted. Almost losing her twice in one day, three times if you count the dream, had ripped his emotions to shreds. He rested his head on hers and let the tears fall in silence.

CHAPTER FIFTEEN

Ellie

Ellie woke to find herself alone, the heat in the tent suffocating. Scrambling to unzip the door, she crawled out into the fresh air.

It appeared to be late afternoon, and she couldn't see Jayce anywhere. She held out her hand and fetched a bottle of water from the pantry back home. She was about to take a swig when a twinge in her side brought memories of her wounds flooding back. She frowned, trying to establish a timeline between then and now.

The pain of Jayce's talons digging cruelly into her side had been excruciating. She remembered thinking it might have been less painful to just hit the ground and die. Seeing Jayce's anguished face at the sight of her wounds had made her heart ache, and she'd tried her best to hide the pain.

So how was she so much better? Lifting her shirt, she stared in confusion at the neatly healed scars. Woah, someone had obviously used magic to heal her.

Who could Jayce have found to cast a healing spell out here in the middle of nowhere?

Wait... where was Jayce anyway? Panic began to set in as her mind imagined scenarios where he'd been captured or killed.

Why would he leave me here alone? And where the hell would he go?

Hey gorgeous girl, glad to hear you're finally awake. The panic subsided, replaced by bone-melting relief as his voice popped into her mind.

Jayce... where are you? Are you okay? Why'd you leave?

Hey, calm down. I'm fine. I went to town to hire a car. I'm on my way back. How are you feeling?

Well, I'm a bit confused. Who healed my wounds?

Jayce chuckled. *I'll explain everything as soon as I get back. I'm about ten minutes away. And I've got coffee and muffins.*

Ellie's stomach rumbled, her mouth watering at his words. *Did you have to mention the food before you got here. Hurry up, I'm starving.*

Yes ma'am. Be there soon.

She reached into the tent and pulled out a blanket, spreading it out on the ground so she could sit in the fresh air and think. Or even better, *lie* in the fresh air.

Stretching out on her back, she sighed, pulling the pillow under her head. Closing her eyes, she soaked up the late afternoon sun, the gentle breeze lulling her back to sleep.

FOOTSTEPS CRUNCHING through the bush roused Ellie from her nap. Hadn't she just closed her eyes? No way it had been ten minutes since she'd talked to Jayce... right?

She sat up, excited at Jayce's return and the thought of food. But instead of Jayce, a dirty, old, weather-worn face loomed in front of her.

The man jumped back, looking as shocked as she felt. "Crikey. And here I thought you was dead. What're ya doin' out here alone, woman? Don't you know it ain't safe? There've been women raped and murdered in this here forest before now."

Ellie's throat closed from fear, ice running through her veins. Was he really warning her, or was he the one responsible for those crimes? He leered at her through bloodshot eyes, probably trying to gauge her reaction.

Ellie swallowed down the fear and tried to smile. The memory that he wouldn't see an eighteen-year-old girl, but an old grey-haired scrubber, eased her mind slightly. Surely he wouldn't be interested in *this!*

"Oh, I'm waiting for my husband. He should be back any minute; he just ducked into town to get coffee."

The old man's lecherous eyes scanned the deserted area before returning to hers, his face breaking into an evil grin. "Nice try, sweetheart. Ain't no one else around here but you and me. Guess that means we might be havin' some fun, eh?"

The man pulled a wicked-looking knife from the back of his belt, moving toward her slowly.

Ellie's brain kicked back in at the sight of the weapon. Then she realised he didn't have a magical aura. *Phew.* He wasn't a bounty hunter, just some low-life predator who'd probably been preying on women for years. *I guess it might be time I did a service for the local community.*

"Listen here, you lecherous old goat. I have had the day from hell, and yours is about to get a whole lot worse, too."

She held her hand out in front of her, and the gun they'd taken from the bounty hunter appeared in it. Ellie knew it wasn't loaded, and she had no idea how to use it, even if it was. But *he* didn't need to know that. The man took a step back, his astonishment turning to fear.

"So, tell me... are *you* the one who committed those crimes you mentioned earlier?"

"No, ma'am," the man spluttered, his eyes darting around, looking for his best escape route. "I just thought I might cash in on the rumours and fear and have a bit of fun."

"Well, you picked the wrong woman to mess with, because I don't believe a single word that's come out of your mouth. So… what I'm saying is… *No. More. Lies!*" she yelled, pointing at the disgusting creep's chest. Ellie smiled at the shock on his face just before he slammed into the tree behind him. "Not bad for an old scrubber, eh?"

Ellie started laughing so hard she was crying. *Yep, hysterical much?*

Less than a minute later, Jayce came crashing through the bush. The confusion on his face when he saw her sitting on the blanket, laughing and crying, *with* a gun in her lap, sent her into further fits of laughter. The rush from having the power to defend herself was exhilarating. This whole magic thing could be seriously addictive.

Jayce

JAYCE HAD HEARD ELLIE'S raised voice as soon as he opened the car door. He'd sprinted the two-hundred-odd meters from where he parked to where he'd left her, his heart hammering with fear.

If she was in trouble, why hadn't she messaged him? And who the hell was she yelling at?

He'd arrived back at the tent to find Ellie sitting on the ground with a gun in her lap, laughing hysterically. The fear turned to anger when she laughed harder at the sight of him. "What the hell is going on? Elle? Who were you yelling at? And why is the bounty hunter's gun in your lap?"

Ellie reacted as if he'd slapped her, the laughter gone in an instant. "Don't you dare yell at me! Where were you when some lecherous old goat with a knife threatened to rape me? Huh? You're the one who left me here in the middle of nowhere on my own!"

Jayce growled, running his hands through his hair and linking them behind his head. "Sheesh, Elle, I went to town for a car! For us. And then I hear you yelling, and run like a maniac thinking you're in danger, only to find you sitting here laughing with a gun in your lap. Heck yeah, I'm angry. Because I was worried about you! I nearly lost you twice today already. How else did you expect me to react?"

Ellie's anger evaporated at the pain and exhaustion etched into his face. Jayce had been to hell and back, trying to protect her. He didn't deserve her anger.

"Jayce, I'm so sorry. I know you only went to get us

a car. I think the hysterical laughter might have been a reaction from dealing with Mr Lecher."

Jayce's eyes went wide, and he dropped down beside her. "You mean there really *was* some guy here threatening you? Why didn't you message me?"

Ellie shrugged. "It all happened so fast. At first, I thought he was another bounty hunter. But by the time I'd worked out he was just some human scumbag wielding a knife, I already had the gun in my hand. And then I decided he needed to pay for his crimes, so I did that power thrust thing and... Well, see for yourself." She nodded toward the unconscious man slumped against a tree and sighed with relief as Jayce's lips twitched into a smile.

"Man, I would've loved to see the look on the guy's face when that gun appeared in your hand. Not to mention when he was suddenly flying through the air. I'm sorry I yelled at you, sweetheart. I totally over-reacted. Can we please put it down to the stress of the last couple of days?"

"I'm sorry, too. We both snapped and overreacted. But I have so gotta ask... where are the coffee and muffins?"

Jayce laughed and pulled her into his arms, loving how quickly her anger cooled. They could both be hotheads when under pressure. It was something they needed to work through.

"In the car. So what do you plan on doing with Mr Lecher?"

Ellie giggled. "Well, I thought we could tie him up and somehow contact the police with an anonymous tip. I don't suppose you remember seeing a public phone in your travels?"

"Even better," he said, pulling a mobile phone from his pocket. "I picked this up in town."

"Good thinking! Oh, and I *happen* to remember the words for the truth spell. Might help the police when they question this jerk."

Jayce threw back his head and roared with laughter. "You really are a wicked witch. How about you send all this bedding and stuff back where it came from and fetch me some rope so I can tie him up? Then you can cast this truth spell, and we can get outta here."

Ellie

ELLIE ENDED the call to 000 Emergency and returned the phone to the backpack. She continued to sip happily on her coffee, having devoured two muffins in quick succession, and leaned back against the car seat.

"Okay, now that we've done our good deed for society, do you think you can fill in a few of the gaps for me? Like who healed my wounds?"

"Only if you promise *never* to put me through another day like today. You scared the crap outta me, witchgirl." He grinned, casting sidelong glances to where she sat.

"Well, if I could remember what happened, I *might* consider your request to never do it again. But not having all the facts, I'm not promising anything." She gave him a cheeky grin. "Actually, before you tell me, can you pull over at the next tree? I need to go to the little girls' room, or bush, or tree, or whatever."

Jayce chuckled as he pulled over to the side of the road. "Do you need any help?"

She rolled her eyes, blushing at his wicked grin as she opened the car door and slid out. "You stay right here and keep your eyes on the road, thank you very much. I'll be back in a minute." He chuckled as she headed off towards a tree with a massive trunk.

He climbed out of the car and couldn't resist calling over his shoulder. "Just remember to yell if you need me. I'll be there in a flash." He laughed out loud at the thoughts going through her mind, none of them complimentary.

Jayce pulled out the map and placed it on the bonnet of the car. According to his calculations, the secluded valley should be just beyond the mountains in front of them. They'd been so close this morning before Ellie fell... He shuddered, trying to shut out the images from his nightmare.

Ellie came up behind him and slipped her arms around his waist. "Okay, seriously, you need to tell me what happened. How come my wounds don't hurt anymore? Who did the brilliant healing job on me?"

Jayce turned and enveloped her in a bear hug, kissing the top of her head. "What's the last thing you remember?"

"Ummm... fetching the tent and bedding from home. After that, the next thing I knew I woke up in the tent, alone."

"That's about when the painkillers would have kicked in. I woke up about eleven o'clock, and you were burning up. I figured an infection had set in. By the time I found the healing spell, you were close to being unconscious."

Ellie lifted her head and looked at him. "*Healing spell?* How did you get a spell to work?"

" I didn't. *You* got the spell to work. I only helped you focus so you could do it." Jayce looked up at the sound of a car approaching. He hustled Ellie into the passenger seat, folded the map and headed around to lean against the driver's door.

The car slowed and pulled over next to Jayce. "Hey, you guys alright? Car trouble, or lost?" the young man yelled through the window.

Jayce smiled and waved his hand. "Yeah, we're fine,

thanks, son. Just stopped for a wee break and to check the map."

"Where ya headed?" the man asked.

Jayce hesitated before shrugging his shoulders and answering. If the man wanted to know where they were going, he could easily follow them. "Apparently, there's a religious community near here somewhere. Our son moved down here a year ago, and we told him we'd come visit once he was settled."

The young man nodded and smiled. "Sure is. Turn-off's about fifteen minutes drive in the direction you're headed. It can be easy to miss, so you're lucky I stopped. Once you've turned off, follow that road until you come to the first house. Old Jasper'll be happy to point you in the right direction. Well, you folks, enjoy your day. Tell Jasper that Bill says hello. He's a good bloke." He tipped his hat to both Jayce and Ellie, then drove off, tooting his horn in farewell.

Jayce dropped into the driver's seat, grabbing the steering wheel with both hands and resting his head on it. "Damn, I hate it when people ask questions. And how paranoid is it that we think everyone we meet is after us?"

Ellie rubbed his back, her hand moving in soothing circles, relieving some of the tension. "Ummm... maybe because most of them *are*. Hey, we're almost there. The light at the end of the tunnel is getting brighter."

Jayce chuckled. "Yeah, right. The way our luck is

running, the light's probably from a train heading straight for us.

CHAPTER SIXTEEN

Ellie

Ellie growled as her head smacked against the side window for the gazillionth time. She was seriously wishing she was wearing a helmet. The 'road' leading into the rogue community turned out to be more like a track, consisting of compacted dirt and gravel.

Carved through the mountain itself, the road ran between smoothly hewn rocks rising sharply toward the sky on either side. Jayce edged the car along slowly, swerving from one side of the narrow road to the other in an attempt to avoid the deepest potholes. Not that he was having a lot of success. At this point, Ellie was thinking that walking might be a safer option.

She was sure Jayce's lips twitched at that last thought. If not for the fact that both her hands were occupied trying to anchor herself in her seat, she would happily have punched him.

"Lucky for me then, eh?" Jayce burst out laughing just as they hit a pothole the size of a crater. Caught off guard, his head bounced off the steering wheel, and they came to an abrupt halt.

"Not so funny now, huh?" Ellie crowed, and they both dissolved into fits of laughter. *Damn, it felt good to laugh.* The stress of the last few days had almost turned them both into snarling beasts.

Gasping for breath, her stomach aching from laughing, Ellie took off her seatbelt and climbed into Jayce's lap. She grinned at the surprise on his face and pulled his lips down to hers.

When they finally came up for air, Jayce's eyes were like molten lava. "Wow, what brought that on?"

Ellie sighed and leaned her forehead against his. "I'm not sure, really. I guess I'm just worried about what we'll find at the end of this road. We don't know anything about these people, except Yvette says we can trust them. What if—"

Jayce put a finger to her lips. "Hey, come on. We have to trust someone; and take it from a guy who knows—worrying about all the 'whatifs' will drive you nuts. How about we just meet them and go from there? It's not like we'll be trapped here. We can always fly or teleport out."

"And where would we go? I don't remember hearing about any other options."

"Elle... let's just deal with one thing at a time. Hey. what about those 'feelings' of yours? Had any of those lately?"

"Hah! The 'bad' feelings have been almost non-stop since we left home, so I figured it best to ignore them. But now that I think about it, I haven't had one since we left Mr. Scumbag back in the forest."

"Well, there you go. Nothing to worry about, eh? Oh, we do have one problem, though. Much as I would love you to stay right where you are, driving like this would be a tad difficult." He kissed her forehead and raised an eyebrow.

Ellie chuckled, then sighed as she returned to her own seat. When she was settled, with her seatbelt back on, Jayce continued to crawl the car forward. Five bumpy minutes later, their tunnel-like surrounds fell away to be replaced by lush pastures with sheep, cows and horses grazing contentedly.

An old man stood in front of the first house, a two-story colonial-style farmhouse with wrap-around verandahs. The man watched them approach, the deep frown on his face making Ellie swallow nervously. His expression was far from welcoming.

The man sauntered around to the driver's side as they pulled up. Jayce wound his window down, and the old man leaned against the doorframe, his frown lessened only slightly by his dismal attempt at a half-smile.

"Howdy, folks. Looks like you took a wrong turn back there a'ways. This is private property."

Jayce kept his hands on the steering wheel and turned his face to the man. "Actually, I think this is exactly where we're meant to be. A mutual friend of ours, Yvette Fiora, said you might be able to put us up for the night if we happened to be passing by."

The old man's expressive face went from suspicion, to surprise, to understanding. "Well, I'll be damned. I do recall Yvette mentioning that some friends of hers might stop by. Forgotten all about it. How about you park around back, and I'll meet you at the kitchen door."

Ellie let out the breath she hadn't realised she'd been holding, grinning at Jayce as he moved the car to the back of the house. "So, I guess that's Jasper."

As soon as Jayce stopped the car, she threw her arms around his neck to pull him closer. "Jayce... I can't believe we're here..." she whispered, excitement and relief rushing through her. Over Jayce's shoulder, Ellie spied Jasper standing in the doorway watching them.

"You two coming inside, or ya gonna sit out here all day? Coffee's getting cold," Jasper yelled, chuckling and wheezing as he turned and headed back into the house.

Jayce and Ellie scrambled out of the car and followed the old man. They stepped into the kitchen to find an older woman with a cheery smile inviting them to sit at the table. Mugs of steaming hot coffee were placed in front of them, to which they eagerly added milk and sugar. They were soon relaxed and sipping the reviving brew.

Jasper pulled out a chair and sat down opposite them, shaking his head and smiling. "You'll have to excuse the less-than-friendly greeting earlier. I'm Jasper, and this is my wife, Isabel. Yvette told me to expect two eighteen-year-old runaways, not a doddering old couple of seniors. She did promise to put a glamour charm on you both, but I forgot how clever she was. So, I hope you had an uneventful trip?"

Ellie looked at Jayce and shrugged. Yvette said they should trust these people, so she took a deep breath and turned to the old man.

"I don't think 'uneventful' is how I'd describe it." She proceeded to tell Jasper and Isabel about their trials along the way. Isabel gasped and covered her mouth a few times, while the curiosity grew in Jasper's eyes.

The old man shared a look with his wife and sighed. "Well, sounds like you've lived through enough adventure to last a lifetime. Unfortunately, I think your troubles may be far from over."

"I'm afraid the bounty is now on both your heads," Isabel said, "and that kind of money can make people do terrible things. No one has any idea who to trust anymore." She sighed and moved over to her husband, draping her arm around his shoulders.

"This community was formed as a refuge for rogue dragons, every single one of whom was banished and lost everything. Now, rumours are starting to circulate that if a rogue happened to capture the runaways and take them to the Dragon Council, all past sins would be forgiven, and the one responsible would be welcomed back."

Jasper slammed his hand on the table, his eyes glowing like Jayce's when he was angry. "Fools! All of them! There is not one member of the Dragon Council with enough compassion to allow a rogue to return. They're using it as a ploy to track you two down."

Jayce stiffened, his eyes focused on his coffee mug. "I agree *some* of the Council members are corrupt, but are you sure they're *all* that bad?

Jasper rubbed his chin, frowning. "Well, I suppose anything's possible, son. Why? Do you know someone on the Council?"

"Thomas Raythawn. He's my father," Jayce said in a dull, toneless voice, his eyes still fixed on his coffee mug.

"You're Thomas Raythawn's son? The damned hypocrite personally responsible for declaring me a rogue? How dare—"

Shocked by the reaction of the old couple, the fear that had only just begun to settle leapt back into Ellie's throat.

Isabel rubbed her husband's back. "Now, now, Jasper, the sins of the father should never be avenged on the son. You're the one who taught me that."

Jasper appeared to be wrestling with his emotions. His expression went from anger, to acceptance, to shame. He relaxed and sighed. "I'm sorry, son, Isabel's right. I was way outta line speaking like that. As a matter of fact, knowing who you are sure explains a lot."

Jayce lifted his head. "What do you mean?"

"When we first heard the news, the bounty had been placed on an underage witch accused of putting a spell on an underage dragon and binding him to her as her familiar."

"I certainly did not! How many more lies—" Ellie spluttered, but Jasper raised his hand to let him finish.

"Now, I thought that was a bit strange. Witches and dragons are forbidden to meet before their eighteenth birthday. But I figured, in your case, someone stuffed up somewhere. Then we received a message this morning about the bounty also being on the young dragon's head. Strange indeed, I thought." He took a sip of his coffee and eyed the two of them.

"Yvette told us the real story of what happened, so knowing the Council as I do, I couldn't work out why they were now after the dragon as well. But now I understand. They've realised you left of your own free will. Which makes you not only a rogue, but also a hunted criminal for breaking one of the most important rules of the Dragon Realm."

Ellie had heard enough. She stood and slammed her hand on the table. "But we've done nothing wrong. How were we supposed to know about some stupid rule? We met by accident and bonded without even realising it. There has to be something we can do to clear our names? Seriously, I'm about ready to go kick some Dragon Council butt!"

Jasper and Isabel stared at Ellie in shock. Jayce chuckled and coaxed Ellie back down into her chair. "You're lucky she didn't point at you, or you'd probably be suspended from a wall somewhere about now."

Jasper raised his eyebrows. "Sorry, but I'm a bit confused. Your mother said you weren't trained, that you only discovered your powers three days ago. So, who taught you to use a power thrust?"

"No one taught me; it just sort of happened. I got super angry with Jayce the other day, and the next thing we knew, *BAM*, he was glued to the wall. And then Jayce thought of using it on the bounty hunter, and... well... it *worked*." Ellie shrugged, her face burning at the awe in Jasper and Isabel's eyes.

She was starting to get the feeling that what she could do was a *long* way from normal.

Jayce

JAYCE FINISHED his coffee and excused himself, stepping outside to retrieve the backpack from the car. He was unaware that Jasper had followed him until the other man spoke.

"I really am sorry for what I said earlier, Jayce. You're not to blame for what your father did. But I find it hard to believe the Raythawn heir would willingly walk away from the Dragon Realm. Are you sure the young witch didn't put a hex on you? I've known Yvette for a long time, and I'm sorry to say I wouldn't put it past *her.*"

Jayce smiled as he grabbed the backpack and flung it over his shoulder. Hearing Ellie discussing her wound with Isabel in his mind, he chose his words carefully, aware that Ellie could hear everything he said if she wanted to.

"As you said earlier, Jasper, the sins of the parent are not the sins of the child. Until a couple of days ago, Ellie had lived her entire life not even knowing her mother was alive. She was raised as a mortal, totally unaware of the political intrigue in both the dragon and witch realms. So why would she bother to put a hex on me?" Jayce shrugged.

"Besides, I was already questioning my desire to follow in my father's footsteps long before I met Ellie. So you see, we're both very much a product of our own experiences and life lessons. If we're banished from the realms of magic for wanting to be together, then so be it. But we don't deserve to be hunted like criminals for our choices."

Jasper's eyes were damp, and he patted Jayce on the back. "Well said, son. I think you and I are going to get along just fine. And I still have a few tricks left up my sleeve. They won't be finding you that easily here." He winked, and they headed back inside.

Ellie

ELLIE WAS STARTING to squirm under Isabel's intense gaze as the old woman studied her wound, so she was relieved when Jayce and Jasper entered the kitchen.

"Jasper, you need to see this, "Isabel said, as she waved Jasper over to where she sat. "When did you say this happened, Ellie?"

Ellie's eyes lifted to Jayce for the answer. She'd lost way too many hours in the last twenty-four to be sure of times.

"Around five o'clock this morning?" Jayce guessed.

Jasper whistled, his eyes wide and confused. "Holy cow! Did you do this healing yourself, Ellie?"

Jayce cleared his throat. "Well, we sort of did it together. Ellie was on the verge of delirium, so she repeated the spell after me."

Jasper shook his head. "Hot damn, this story gets more interesting every minute. Those scars look to be weeks old."

Ellie shook her head in confusion. "But isn't that normal after using a healing spell?"

Jasper chuckled. "Hmmm... maybe if two or three powerful witches chanted the spell together."

Ellie frowned. "So how come—?"

Isabel stood and flapped her hands as if she wanted to cut off any further questions. "I'm sorry Ellie, but you two must have been existing on pure adrenaline for days. You

both look practically dead on your feet. There's a spare room upstairs with a freshly made-up bed... unless you want two rooms?"

Ellie glanced at Jayce, blushed and shook her head. She didn't want to be too far from Jayce just yet. He'd become her rock in an insane world.

Jasper just nodded. "Thought you might want to stay close for a while. Anyway, go get some sleep, and we'll wake you in a couple of hours for a late dinner. *Then* I'll answer some more of your questions."

"But..." Ellie looked from Jasper to Jayce and back.

"Come on, Elle... I recognise that look in Jasper's eyes. We will *not* be learning any more until after we've slept. Thank you so much, Jasper and Isabel... for everything. We'll see you at dinner."

Jayce wrapped his arm around Ellie's waist as they headed up the stairs to get some sleep. *Will you please give the old man a break? He's not ready to talk yet, but he will be by tonight. Trust me, for once.*

ELLIE LEANED BACK in her chair and rubbed her aching stomach. The dinner had been amazing, and she was so full she thought she might burst. Jayce's eyes moved from her plate to where her hand sat, and he grinned.

Then don't eat so much next time.

I can't help it. Ever since we left home, I never know how long it might be 'til the next meal, so I'm stocking up. You know, like a camel does with water.

Jayce chuckled, reaching out and patting her bulging belly. Ellie scowled and slapped his hand away.

Jasper cleared his throat, and Ellie was hit by a pang of sadness at the memory of her mother having to do that around them so often. Even though Yvette had only been in her life for such a short time, Ellie missed her badly.

"Do you mind if I ask a personal question? Jasper said.

"Not at all. What would you like to know?"

"Can you and Ellie... ummm... communicate telepathically by any chance?" The interest in Jasper's eyes belied his casual tone.

"Yeah, we can," Jayce said, grinning at Ellie. "We realised that using dragon speak broadcasted our conversation to any and all interested parties, so we tried using our bond as witch and familiar to communicate privately... and it worked."

Jasper looked at Isabel with raised eyebrows. Apparently, this was another thing that was far from normal. "Which brings *me* to a question. Is there a way to use dragon speak without broadcasting?"

Jasper nodded thoughtfully. "Sure is. All dragons are taught how to do it after their Coming-of-Age Feast. When do you turn eighteen?"

"Saturday... we both do," Jayce replied.

"*Of course* your birthdays are on the same day. Somehow, I'm not surprised. Well then, after your birthday, there are a few things I can teach you, private dragon speak being one of them."

Isabel sat forward in her chair. "So Ellie, that means your Choosing Ceremony is on Saturday. Have you decided what you want to do yet?"

Ellie smiled. "Well, I figure as a mortal, I'll be a useless piece of baggage Jayce has to cart around while constantly risking his life to protect me. At least as a witch, I'll be more of an asset than a liability."

Jayce laughed. "That remains to be seen. So far, I think the scales are about even."

"Hey," Ellie said, punching his arm. "I helped heaps. Don't you dare even suggest I'm..." She bit her tongue when she saw the twinkle in his eyes. "Yeah, yeah, you were just baiting me, and I went off half-cocked again, didn't I?"

Jayce draped his arm around her shoulders and chuckled. "Yep, sure did. You'll work out when I'm teasing one day... maybe."

CHAPTER SEVENTEEN

Jayce

Jayce sighed with pleasure, as he leaned back against the soft cushions of the lounge. With his legs stretched out in front of him, and Ellie snuggled up close beside him, he couldn't remember the last time he'd felt so relaxed.

His eyes met Jasper's across the room, and the older man nodded. Reaching down beside him, Jasper pulled open a concealed drawer at the bottom of the recliner on which he sat. Lifting a large, heavy-looking book out, he placed it on the coffee table in front of him, flipping it open to a bookmarked page.

"This book is not supposed to exist. It's my family history, ordered destroyed back when the law regarding witches and dragons was first passed. Fortunately, one of my clever ancestors created an exact copy and submitted that instead. I think you may find some of the information in here very interesting."

"This bookmarked section chronicles the time leading up to the law about dragons and witches being imposed, and why it came to pass. It certainly explains why the Council want one or both of you dead."

Ellie sat forward, excitement radiating from every pore. Jayce chuckled, slipping his arm around her waist and pulling her back beside him. "Would you mind reading it aloud, Jasper? Before little-miss-impatient here bursts."

Ellie threw him a *just you wait* look, then sighed and sat back.

"Before I start reading, though, there are a few things I need to explain first. It's common knowledge that a witch's familiar can combine their own magic and strength with those of their witch, thus amplifying the witch's powers accordingly. So, if a powerful witch were to bond her powers with an equally powerful creature, such as a dragon, the results would be phenomenal. After seeing Ellie's scars from the healing you did together, I think I understand why the Council is nervous."

Jasper leaned over the book and began to read:

·　·　·

A number of disturbing incidents have come to the attention of the ruling Councils in the magical realms. A certain bad element of witches has been found guilty of hexing dragons in an attempt to bond them as their familiars and thereby enhance their own magical ability. This has prompted the need for a new law prohibiting a witch from taking a dragon as her familiar, regardless of the circumstances. The law is to be enforced in the realms of both dragons and witches, and any infringements will be punishable by death.

Jasper looked up at Jayce and raised his eyebrows. "There's another entry underneath this, which I fear tells a more accurate story:

Above is the official announcement regarding the introduction of the new law. It is rumoured, however, that the ruling Councils had ulterior motives for instigating the law. A young witch and dragon, drawn together and bonded by mutual consent, became a threat to the ruling Councils. The pair were separated, and both reported banished from their realms, but as no witnesses can attest to the banishments, it is feared the Councils disposed of the ill-fated couple.

Ellie looked ready to explode. "So this is all about us being a threat? Well, if anyone had bothered to ask, I'd have been happy to tell them we couldn't care less about power or their stupid Councils. All we want is to be left alone."

Jasper shook his head sadly. "I'm sorry, Ellie. I'm afraid you would be wasting your breath. Just the possibility that your bonding with Jayce could pose a threat is enough to throw them into a tailspin. I'm not sure they'll ever give up searching for you. But we can live in hope. Who knows what the future may hold?"

Ellie

ELLIE SAT in a numbed state of shock as the conversation continued to flow around her. Until Jasper had explained exactly how much trouble they were in, she hadn't quite grasped the enormity of their situation. She'd just assumed that if she and Jayce disappeared for a while, the Councils would realise they weren't a threat and let them be.

Jasper's words echoed around and around in her head. No way this would 'blow over' like they'd hoped.

So what was the point of running and hiding? It was hopeless.

When she realised Jayce stood in front of her holding out his hand, she forced her mind back to the people in the room.

"Sorry, I got lost in my own little world there for a while. Are we going to bed?"

Jayce smiled and nodded. "I thought you looked beat, so I suggested we call it a night." From the worry on his face, Jayce had heard the thoughts tumbling around inside her head. Giving him a grateful smile, she took his hand and got to her feet.

"Thank you so much for the lovely dinner. I'm sorry if I appeared rude... been a rough couple of days," she muttered.

Isabel stood and surprised her with a warm hug. "Don't be silly, love; you have nothing to apologise for. Get some rest, and tomorrow, we'll think about where to go and what to do from here."

Ellie's eyes filled with tears at Isabel's comforting words. With a watery smile, she followed Jayce from the room, up the stairs and into their room. She was moving on autopilot, going through the motions of appearing normal, while on the inside, she was falling apart.

But she couldn't fool Jayce. He was privy to everything going on in her head. Without a word, he picked her up and sat down on the window seat, cradling her in his arms.

"Hey, beautiful girl. I know what Jasper told us tonight was hard to hear, but you can't give up hope. We'll find a way out of this, I promise. We can't let them win, Elle, and we need to keep fighting. You and I are a force to be reckoned with, and they have no idea what they're up against."

The numbness slowly receded into the background. Jayce was right. If she allowed herself to sink into mindless despair, the Councils had already won. Ellie's battered emotions roused themselves, fighting their way back to the surface. The tears finally found release, and she turned her face into Jayce's chest and sobbed.

"That's my girl. You need to *feel* all the hurt and anger and then use it as a weapon against them. We can beat them, sweetheart, but only if we're strong... and we do it together."

Some of the fear, anger and frustration that had been building up for days eased. She needed to *feel* the knot in her stomach and the ache in her chest as a constant reminder of what they were up against. She refused to give up and make it easy for these people who wanted them dead. Whatever happened, she would *not* go down without a fight!

CHAPTER EIGHTEEN

Jayce

*J*ayce woke the following day filled with grim determination. Watching Ellie start to shut down the previous night had made him realise how innocent and fragile she was. The rugged exterior she presented to the world was all for show.

A week ago, she'd been an ordinary seventeen-year-old mortal girl whose toughest decisions involved what she wanted to do when she left school and whether to date a particular guy.

That last thought caused a sharp stab of jealousy in the pit of his stomach. *Stop it. This is about Ellie, not you.* Her whole world had been flipped upside down and inside out, and he needed to figure out a way to help her deal with the changes and new realities that had become a part of their everyday existence.

"Morning," Ellie's soft voice murmured from beside him. "Will you please stop stressing about me... I'll be fine. You reckon inside *my* head is a busy place."

Jayce chuckled, *of course* she could hear his every thought. Although he'd *thought* she was asleep. "How long have you been awake listening?"

"About as long as you've been awake thinking." She grinned and rolled toward him, placing her hands on his chest and propping her chin up on them. "I particularly liked the jealousy... and you're *so* cute when you're embarrassed."

Jayce rolled and flipped her onto her back, pinning her beneath him. "Listen here, you. We need to work out a way to keep *some* of our thoughts private. Otherwise, you may not think I'm quite so 'cute' the next time you 'overhear' what I'm thinking." He grinned as she blushed, her eyes widening. "And *you* look *absolutely gorgeous* when you're embarrassed."

A cheeky grin emerged. "Okay, you win. Next time, I'll let you know I'm awake. So can we please have breakfast now?"

He laughed and rolled onto his back. "Well, at least you're back to normal. Come on then, let's go eat. I think I'm gonna need a lot of coffee to keep up with that *yo-yo* you call a brain."

Ellie sat up and pointed towards the window seat. A pile of clothes began to grow where she indicated.

"Man, you sure you'll need all those today?"

Ellie shrugged and grinned. "It's a girl thing. I need lots of stuff to choose from. Deciding what to wear is not easy, you know."

"Pity I didn't take you to my place so you could fetch me some clean clothes. I've had these on since Monday morning... and today's what, Thursday?"

"Eewww, so that's what the smell's been."

"Hey, enough with the 'let's-pick-on-Jayce' stuff, okay?" He reached out to grab her, an instant too slow, as she jumped up and turned to face him, hands on hips and a triumphant look in her eyes.

"Okay, can you please be serious for a minute? I was thinking about something Jasper said last night about how our bond strengthens both of our abilities, like when we did the healing spell together. I wonder if we could fetch something as long as *one* of us can picture where it is."

"From what I can gather, nobody knows what we can and can't do, so I guess trying stuff is the only way to find out. You wanna see if we can fetch you some clean clothes from home?"

Jayce grinned. "Not just beautiful, but brilliant as well. I love the way your mind works. So, what do we do?"

Ellie shrugged. "No idea, really. Except I think we'll need to be touching."

Ellie laughed as Jayce dived out of bed and had her wrapped in his arms before she could blink. "Like this, you mean?"

Ellie's heart skipped a beat as his lips hovered just above hers. His hands rested on the small of her back, and she slipped her arms under his, tingling everywhere his body touched hers. She felt giddy, unfamiliar sensations making her head spin.

"Ummm... I *will* need to concentrate, though. And so will you. So, ummm... I'm struggling with that a bit right now. Maybe we—"

Jayce's lips caught hers, the tenderness in his kiss turning her legs to jelly. For a brief moment, all the fear and worries ceased to exist. Nothing else mattered. Her heart blossomed with love for this man who had given up everything to be with her, vowing to keep her safe and asking nothing in return. *This* was real... the rest was just random crap.

Jayce lifted his head and smiled. "Well, I think I may have found a solution to the 'eavesdropping' problem. I was way too busy with my own thoughts to listen to yours, and I'm assuming you were the same?"

Ellie tilted her head. "How on earth did you figure that out?"

"Because you are *definitely* not looking at me like someone who just read the thoughts that were going through my mind."

Ellie threw back her head and laughed. "I'll have to

remember that in future... maybe I'll just take a sneaky peek."

Jayce shrugged, but his grin gave her butterflies. "Don't say I didn't warn you. Enter at your own risk." His voice was deep and husky, and Ellie shivered at the sensations flooding her body.

He kissed the tip of her nose, cleared his throat and stepped back, holding her at arm's length. "Now... where were we? Oh yeah, clean clothes for me."

Ellie took a couple of deep breaths to slow her rapid heartbeat. "Okay... just give me a minute. I need to think."

"I'm in no hurry. Take as long as you need." His ability to go from passion to casual normality irritated her. How could he—?

She realised her mistake the minute she let his thoughts into her mind. Her entire body was on fire, a burning need making her blood sing. Her eyes flew to his, and he groaned.

Jayce crushed her against him, his passionate kiss inflaming the chaotic needs ignited by his thoughts. Ellie was lost, adrift in a sea of unfamiliar sensations. Her emotional response terrified and excited her at the same time. She moaned in protest when Jayce started to pull away.

He leaned his forehead against hers, breathing hard. "Elle... I'm sorry, babe. I had no idea you'd react like that. You caught me totally off guard. I thought you'd slap me, or laugh, or..." He tilted his head back and ran a hand through his hair. "Damnit all! You just weren't supposed to feel the same way."

Ellie reached up and placed her shaking hands on either side of Jayce's distraught face. "Hey... please don't apologise. I know you think you need to be big, and strong, and responsible for everything, but sometimes things get out of control... and this is just one of them. I know it should be too soon to feel this way, but... I love you, Jayce. And when you're hurting, I'm hurting too."

Jayce wrapped her in his arms. "How did I ever get this lucky? I feel like I've been waiting for you forever, and loved you the whole time. As for what *almost* just happened, I don't think this is either the right time or place."

Ellie nodded, slid her arms around his waist, and laid her head against his chest, the strong, steady beat of his heart soothing her jangled nerves.

"Ummm... so do you think we could try the clothes fetching thing anytime soon?" he murmured against her hair. "Now I really need a shower... a cold one."

AFTER SPENDING a few minutes sharing images of his room and closet, Jayce focused his thoughts on his black jeans, neatly folded on the second shelf, and was utterly blown away when they appeared on the bed.

Within minutes, a good collection of clothes and personal items sat in a pile. He kissed Ellie's neck, whispering "thank you" into her ear before grabbing what he needed and heading for the bathroom.

Yeah, don't worry about me. It's not like I'm hanging for a shower or anything, Ellie's voice floated into his mind as he closed the door.

Jayce chuckled as he turned on the taps, a steady stream of water bouncing off the tiled floor. *I thought I'd give you time to choose an outfit. I know how hard it can be.*

He stripped off his grimy clothes and stepped under the steaming jets of water, still chuckling as he listened to the plans for revenge flash through her mind.

And stop sitting out there listening to my every thought. Didn't you learn your lesson last time?

Her silence made him burst out laughing. *Damn, he loved that girl!*

SHOWERED, and happy to be in clean clothes, Jayce and Ellie arrived in the kitchen to the smell of freshly cooked bacon and eggs. Ellie was almost drooling by the time she piled her plate with food and pulled up a chair at the table. Jayce followed behind her, amazed that someone so small could eat so much.

"Good morning." Jasper looked up from reading the newspaper. "Sleep well?"

Ellie nodded, her mouth full, and Jayce smiled at the old man. "Yes, thanks Jasper. Slept like a log."

"Excellent," Jasper said, folding the paper and putting it aside as he reached for his coffee mug. "Isabel and I had a long talk after you went to bed, and I think we've come up with a few ideas that might make things a bit easier for you."

Isabel joined them at the table. "Well, we thought you might like to have your own space, seeing you could be here for a while. There's a cottage out behind the back gate. The place is old and needs work, but it's empty, and you're welcome to it if—"

"Yes, please," Ellie and Jayce both said at the same time, and they all laughed.

"That sounds fantastic. Thank you so much," Jayce said. "When can we start fixing it up?"

"Whenever you're ready, son. I have nothing else planned for the day. How about we go see what needs doing after you finish breakfast."

Jayce reached under the table and squeezed Ellie's leg. She grinned, her eyes sparkling with excitement.

As soon as they finished eating and clearing away breakfast, the four of them headed out the back door, past the rental car and through a small gate. They followed a path barely discernible under the overgrown weeds and shrubs... and there it was.

Jayce gazed at the small, dilapidated cottage, almost

invisible beneath the feral plant life, and a warm feeling settled around his heart. He slipped his arm around Ellie's waist, looking down at her smiling face. "Whadya think?"

"I think we're going to be extremely busy for the next few days finding our new *home* under all this mess. Can we go inside?"

"Of course." Isabel pulled a set of keys from her apron and stepped up on the verandah. Jasper moved up beside her, pulling a pair of gardening sheers from his back pocket and cutting away most of the vines covering the doorway. Isabel inserted the key, and with a bit of persuasive shoving, the door opened.

Jayce guessed from the shapes under the numerous dust-covers that the cottage was furnished, the decor old-world and charming. His fingers itched to rip off the covers and throw open the windows. He grinned at Ellie, hearing the same thoughts racing through her mind.

"So, can we start now? What should we do first?"

A loud buzz coming from the kitchen stopped them in their tracks. Jayce caught the look of fear between Jasper and Isabel and reached for Ellie.

"What's that, Jasper?"

"A car's coming through the pass. The buzzer is a form of early warning system. There's one in the house too. You two need to move to the back bedroom and stay there until we get back."

Jasper's stern face indicated he'd brook no argument, and Jayce nodded, moving Ellie toward the back of the cottage. Isabel and Jasper pulled the front door closed as they left.

Ellie

ELLIE'S STOMACH churned as she sat on the floor in the back bedroom with Jayce, dreading the sound of bounty hunters bursting in the door. She heard similar scenarios racing through Jayce's mind, his thoughts focused on protecting her, and his frustration at not having a weapon.

Remembering the gun in the backpack, she opened her hands, the gun appearing in one, the bullets in the other. Jayce's smile and sigh of relief warmed her shivering insides. He took the gun from her hand and kissed the top of her head—*just another reason why I love you, beautiful girl.*

They tensed at the sound of heavy boots on the verandah, followed by the key in the front door. Ellie held her breath as the door shuddered open, mentally preparing herself to face the inevitable.

"All clear." Jayce's shoulders sagged with relief when he recognised Jasper's voice. They scrambled to their feet and found Jasper and Isabel waiting in the lounge room.

"Damned arrogant sons of—" Isabel put her hand on Jasper's arm, and his mouth snapped shut. "Three Dragon Council guards looking for the morwitch and her rogue. Refused to leave until I let them search the house, raving about it being Council's orders. They even produced a letter giving them the right to do whatever was necessary to apprehend the criminals.

I had to do some quick thinking to explain your clothes in the spare room. Told them Isabel collects off-casts from the op-shops in town to give to the poor."

Jayce stepped forward, his face stiff with anger. "Jasper, we can't stay here and put you and Isabel in danger. If they find us—"

"Now you listen here, son. I don't care if a hundred Council Guards come here and search my house. Besides, even if they saw you, they'd have no idea you were the ones they're looking for. As long as you maintain your glamours, you should be safe. We'd like you to consider this your home for however long you need it to be."

Jasper looked at Isabel, and she nodded. "Up until a year ago, our son and his wife lived here in the cottage, which is why we installed the early warning system. Ren, our son, brought his wife Tammy here to protect her from an abusive stalker ex-boyfriend. They were here almost six months when the man tracked them down, although we still don't know how. He shot them both while they were asleep in bed."

Tears poured down Isabel's weathered old face. "Tammy was pregnant with their first child... our grandson." Ellie moved to envelop the old woman in a hug, unable to find the words to console Isabel for such a tragic loss.

Jayce's heart ached at the older man's haunted eyes. "Did they catch the guy?"

Jasper gave a hollow laugh. "The mongrel didn't even know Ren was a dragon. So, he never thought to look up when running toward the car he left at the other end of the pass. Dragons take care of their own, and he got what he deserved." The old man placed his hand on Jayce's shoulder. "So don't you worry about anything, son. I have no intention of letting lightning strike in the same place twice."

Jayce nodded, understanding why Yvette had sent them to these people. If anywhere was safe from those hunting them, it was here. Relieved that Ellie's initial fears were unwarranted, he knew they could trust Jasper and Isabel with their lives.

"Anyway, the guards have gone to search the rest of the community, which is about another kilometre down the road. So, how about we stop standing around gawking and get to work? The sooner this place is presentable, the sooner you can move in."

CHAPTER NINETEEN

Ellie

By lunchtime, Isabel and Ellie had made a huge dent in cleaning the inside of the cottage. Ellie's excitement every time she found something new under the dust soon had Isabel laughing and sharing in the fun. When Ellie's stomach started to growl in protest, she realised she was starving.

"Come on, Isabel, something tells me it *must* be time for lunch." Ellie linked arms with the older woman and headed for the front door. "I don't know about you, but I'm starv—"

Jayce and Jasper stood in the doorway, cracking up laughing as Ellie and Isabel emerged from the house.

"Okay, what's the big joke?" Ellie asked. She turned

to Isabel to see if she knew what they were laughing at and grinned. A thick layer of dust covered Isabel from head to toe. The older woman's dirt-streaked face broke into a smile, telling Ellie she was in a similar state.

"Lucky you fetched a few extra clothes this morning, sweetheart. Looks like you'll be needing them."

"Ha ha, very funny. We're heading up to the house to wash up and have some lunch." Ellie's jaw dropped at the massive mound of weeds. "Wow, from the look of that, I reckon we've all earned a break."

"No worries. We'll be right behind you." Jayce screwed up his nose as he kissed her grimy cheek.

The two women chuckled as they walked back to the house. They had just entered the kitchen when the rumble of tyres skidding on the loose gravel out front alerted them to the guards' return. Isabel's eyes scanned the room, pushing Ellie inside the walk-in pantry, her finger to her lips. Ellie nodded and moved backwards as Isabel closed the door. Ellie crouched down and waited, alone in the darkness.

Jayce, where are you?

It's all good, babe. We heard them too. Where are you?

In the pantry... you?

Hiding in the bush behind the cottage. Jasper's on his way to deal with them. Stop stressing; they can't know we're here... they're just fishing.

Jasper's boots stomped through the house towards the front door. "What's up boys, leave somethin' behind?" Jasper boomed. Ellie smiled, knowing he was practically yelling so she and Isabel could hear them.

"Seems you left out some relevant information, old man. Some of your neighbours seem to think you have had some visitors in the last few days. You wanna tell me about that?"

The guard's tone was rude and menacing. Ellie shuddered, wishing Jayce were here to hold her and stop her shaking.

I'm right here, Elle. I can hear them through you. Stay calm, babe; it'll be over soon.

Jayce's soothing voice in her mind helped to quell the feeling of isolation. She closed her eyes and wrapped her arms around herself, trying to convince her terrified mind they were Jayce's arms.

"Ah hell, some old friends from up north dropped by yesterday," Jasper growled. "Did my *neighbours* also happen to mention they were even older than me and the misses? I thought you were lookin' for a couple of runaway teenagers?"

The guard mumbled something unintelligible, and someone else replied. "Yeah, well, apparently, no one thought to question their age. But we also learned about the other house out back of here. I guess you forgot to tell us about that, too. We'll be needing to search that before we leave."

"Hey... I got nothin' to hide. You go right ahead and search wherever you want. No one's lived in the cottage for over a year. The wife and I are working on fixing the place up. She's thinking of taking up painting, so we plan to set it up as a studio. I'll show you the way."

The heavy boots moved away, and Ellie sucked in a slow, deep breath. Lucky she'd called a stop work when she did, or the guards would have found her and Isabel in the cottage. Okay, so she knew their glamours should prevent them from being recognised. But she had a feeling that *any* strangers, without a convincing explanation for why they were there, would be under suspicion.

Deep breaths, Elle. I can see them heading into the cottage now. They'll soon give up and move on.

Ten minutes later, Ellie heard a car's engine turn over, followed by the crunching of tyres on gravel as the guards pulled away from the house. She sat on the floor in the dark and waited for someone to give the 'all clear'.

Ellie breathed a huge sigh of relief when light flooded into the darkened space as the door opened and strong arms lifted her from where she was huddled. The heavy breathing in her ear told her Jayce had run from wherever he'd been hiding.

They found Jasper cursing and pacing back and forth in the lounge room. "I always suspected we had a snitch in the community. This isn't the first time we've taken in fugitives, and the authorities *just happened to stumble upon them.*"

"I think it might be time to call a community

meeting and introduce you two to the locals. I'll tell 'em Jayce is a rogue, and we're old mates, so when I heard you wanted a climate change, I offered you the use of the cottage."

"But I'm gonna make it my business to find out who the snitch is and call for a community vote on how we deal with them. Oh, and one of the guards wrote down the number plate of the hire car out back as well. It shouldn't take 'em long to verify my story that you're old anyway. I told 'em you flew home to organise the move, and we offered to return the hire car for you."

Jasper finally stopped pacing and dropped down on the lounge. "I reckon they'll be back, though. That one in charge is a nasty piece of work, suspicious of everyone and everything. He'll wanna do a thorough check on you, seeing you turned up right when the runaways went missing. We'll need to get word to Yvette so she can set up an unbreakable paper trail for Mr and Mrs Jones' existence."

He rubbed his hands over his head, making his salt and pepper hair stand on end. "Damned arrogant Council pups," he muttered as Isabel calmly announced that lunch was ready.

Jayce

THEY SPENT the rest of the day and most of Friday fixing up the cottage. On Friday afternoon, Jayce and Ellie stood hand in hand in front of their new home, amazed by the transformation before them. The richly vibrant and well-cared-for home bore no resemblance to the sad-looking, dilapidated little cottage they'd first seen.

"You ready?" Jayce squeezed Ellie's hand, smiling into her upturned face.

"I sure am." Before she could argue, he'd reached down and slid an arm behind her knees, sweeping her up and holding her against his chest.

"Hey," she laughed, her eyes wide. "You're supposed to be married to do the whole 'carry me over the threshold' thing."

"Is that a proposal?" Jayce asked, his eyes searching hers for a response. "Because if it is, I accept."

Jayce turned the handle on the front door and pushed it open with his shoulder. Ellie's silence was freaking him out.

Why couldn't he have kept his big fat mouth shut? She probably thought he was a complete idiot. They'd known each other for what... six days?

Ellie reached up and rubbed her hand against his

cheek, tilting his face toward her. The raw emotion in her eyes took his breath away.

"You know what? Maybe it was a proposal... and you are extremely lucky you accepted it."

"Seriously?" Jayce held his breath, sure he'd wake up any minute and discover the whole thing had been an incredible dream.

"Absolutely," Ellie said, sliding her hand through his hair and pulling his face towards her. "But we might need to convince my mother and the aunts first that we haven't lost our minds."

Jayce chuckled and brushed her lips with his. Two long strides brought them to the lounge, and he dropped down into its welcoming softness, his shaky legs relieved to find they no longer needed to function.

"So I'm thinking..." *kiss*, "you'll want to wait..." *kiss*, "until after our birthdays tomorrow... *kiss*, "to break the news?" Jayce said, feathering kisses all over her smiling face.

Ellie's tinkling laugh raised goosebumps all up and down his body. His pulse raced, and something was doing backflips in his stomach. *Damn, this girl drives me nuts.*

"I'm so glad you're as crazy as I am. Imagine feeling like this, and discovering that the feelings weren't mutual. It would be a living nightmare."

"Hmmm... I never considered myself crazy until I met you. Yep, I think I can live with crazy. Although,

I'm not sure I've achieved your level of craziness just yet. I might need to work on that."

Ellie

ELLIE WOKE the following day to find Jayce's side of the bed empty. Disappointed he hadn't woken her before getting up, she wandered into the kitchen, the smell of freshly brewed coffee tantalising her taste buds. She snatched up the piece of paper she spied on the kitchen table, scanning the message as she poured her first cup of coffee for the day.

Happy birthday, beautiful. Gone to town with Jasper to pick up supplies. Be back soon.

Love You xxx

She sighed and carried her coffee outside to the verandah, sitting down on the outdoor swing she'd fetched earlier from her old home. She hoped the aunts didn't mind. They rarely used it and knew it was her favourite place to 'sit and ponder the meaning of life', as they described it.

Thoughts of the aunts caused a pang of homesickness in the pit of her stomach. She'd been so busy running, hiding and surviving the last few days, she hadn't even considered how they must have felt when they returned from their trip to find her gone. This would be the first birthday she'd ever spent away from them, and her heart ached for the comforting warmth of their hugs.

She snapped out of her sombre mood at the sound of the squeaky hinges of the gate, accompanied by Isabel's cheery voice.

"Ellie honey, are you up yet? It's only me." The first time someone had come through the gate when Ellie was alone in the cottage, not long after the visit from the Council Guards, had sent her into a panic attack. They had all since agreed to call out from the gate to avoid unnecessary stress.

"Good morning, Isabel," Ellie called, smiling as the woman came into view. "Yep, I'm up, and there's coffee made in the kitchen. Jayce must have set the timer before he left. Grab a cup and come join me."

Isabel stepped up onto the verandah and bent to give her a hug. "First things first... Happy birthday, sweetie," she said, before releasing Ellie and stepping back. "*Now* I'll grab that cuppa and join you."

Ellie smiled as Isabel bustled her way inside. A blossoming friendship had developed between the two women as they worked together to turn the cottage into a home. The older woman's comforting presence eased some of the pain from missing her aunts.

"Well, the boys should be back any minute." Isabel reappeared and joined Ellie on the swing. "I'm so sorry Jasper dragged Jayce away so early on your birthdays, but we're running low on supplies. We've been so busy over the last few days that I didn't think to check."

"Please don't apologise, Isabel. It's the least we can do to help after all you've done for us. Besides, we've got the whole day to celebrate our birthdays. How long ago did they leave?"

"Goodness... they left before first light. Jayce drove the hire car back, and Jasper took the truck for the supplies. To be honest, I'm surprised they're not back already."

As if on cue, a horn blasted from the direction of the main house. The two women shared a smile and hurried to help unload the truck.

Jayce

JAYCE'S HEART skipped a beat as Ellie's smiling face appeared around the side of the house. He'd been worried she might be annoyed at waking up to find him gone, but her warm smile told him everything was fine.

"Hey, sleepyhead. Nice to see you're finally up and about."

"How do you know I haven't been up for hours?"

"Because I heard you reading my note and sighing over the coffee."

Ellie chuckled. "Damn... busted again."

Jayce reached for the coffee cup in her hands and passed it to Isabel, then picked her up and swung her around, singing Happy Birthday in a loud, slightly off-key voice. Ellie laughed, squirming in a feeble attempt to escape the deafening cacophony.

"Okay, okay, I get it. Happy birthday to you, too. Now, can you please stop singing? The milk will be curdled before it even comes out of the cows."

Jasper burst out laughing and slapped Jayce on the back. "She's got a point there, son... and happy birthday, Ellie," he spluttered through his laughter. Then he turned and slipped his arm around Isabel's shoulder. "And we'll be back in five minutes to start unloading the truck."

"So you didn't like my singing? You know you just ripped my heart out and stomped on it, right?"

Ellie giggled at his wounded martyr act. "Would you shut up and kiss me already? Jasper said five minutes."

Heaving a sigh, he cupped her face and gazed into her beautiful eyes. "Your wish is my command, fair maiden," he whispered as he captured her lips with his.

Ellie moaned against his mouth, her arms stealing up around his neck as she entwined her fingers in his hair. Her kiss was passionate and hungry, driving his senses wild and making his head spin.

Slowly, she pulled them both back from the brink, nipping softly at his lower lip as she ended the kiss. The whole experience had been totally mind-blowing.

"Happy birthday, babe," she said, her voice quivering and husky in his ear. "I never was much of a singer."

Ellie

ELLIE HELPED TO unload the truck in a hazy state of euphoria. She hadn't planned to kiss Jayce like that; it had just happened. She giggled like a six-year-old at the dazed look that still lingered in his eyes.

Ellie was startled out of her stupor when Isabel threw her hands in the air and placed them on her hips. "Oh, for goodness' sake, will you two please go home while I put these groceries away? I'm sick of trying to avoid running into you every time I turn around. Go on... scoot!"

Isabel shooed them out the back door towards the cottage, failing to suppress the smile that made the corners of her mouth twitch. "Lunch is at twelve," she called after them, laughter in her voice.

Jayce grabbed her hand as they stepped outside the back door. "Woohoo, birthday girl. We've got two hours to ourselves. What would you like to do?"

"Hmmm... I'm thinking a cuppa and a snuggle on the swing. How does that sound?"

"Perfect. Let's go."

They strolled towards the cottage hand in hand, Ellie trying desperately to keep all thoughts of his birthday present out of her mind. This 'never having a private thought' was starting to get annoying.

"I agree," he said, squeezing her hand. "Jasper is going to teach me how to use private dragon speak tomorrow. Maybe I'll pick up some tips that might help block our minds. Either that, or we need to work out our own 'early warning system'."

"You won't get an argument from me on that one."

They stepped up onto the verandah, and Ellie pushed Jayce down on the swing. "Okay, close your eyes; I have a surprise for you."

Jayce chuckled. "You're just full of surprises today."

"Behave, or I won't give you your present."

"Wait... I thought you already did. You mean there's more than the mind-blowing kiss?"

"Will you stop!" Ellie's body tingled as memories of the kiss flooded through her again. She giggled and dragged her mind back to the present. "Do you want your birthday present or not?"

Jayce grinned and closed his eyes. Ellie pointed to the empty space beside him and fetched the crossbow she and Jasper had been restoring in secret.

"Okay, you can open them now."

Jayce looked at her in confusion and then followed her eyes to where the bow sat. "Wow, Elle... where did you get this?"

"Do you like it?"

"I love it." He picked the bow up and laid it on his lap, rubbing his hands over the smooth timber. "How...? Where...?"

Ellie sat down next to him on the swing. "It was in the storeroom in Darwin. I remembered seeing it ages ago and asking the aunts about it. Apparently, it belonged to my dad. Jasper helped me restore it and said it was really well-made and still in excellent condition. Oh, and he offered to give you some lessons on how to use it."

Jayce looked up, his eyes shining with tears. "This is the best present ever. Thank you, sweetheart..."

He leaned over and kissed her gently, then laid the crossbow down beside him. He jumped up from the swing and stood in front of her. "Okay, my turn. There are two parts to your present. Are you ready?"

Ellie nodded, her eyes fixed on his.

Jayce reached for her hand and went down on one knee. "Ellie Fiora, I've loved you since the first time I set eyes on your beautiful face. I can't imagine my life without you. I know our lives are a crazy mess right now, but you and I together forever is the only part that makes complete sense. I love you, my gorgeous, funny morwitch. Will you marry me?"

Jayce pulled a small box from his jacket pocket and flipped it open. The most beautiful ring Ellie had ever seen was nestled in a bed of velvet inside it.

"Yes... yes... and *yes*! Stars, Jayce... as Yvette would say. How did you—?"

"After our talk last night, I couldn't sleep. You were fast asleep, so I went for a walk, thinking I needed some dragon time. I noticed the light was still on at Jasper and Isabel's, so I went in and told them every-thing. Jasper offered to lend me the money and take me into town so I could buy your ring as a birthday/en-gagement present. Is it okay? Do you like it?"

"Oh, Jayce, it's perfect. Should we see if it fits?"

Jayce removed the ring from its box and slid it onto the third finger of her left hand, his own hands shak-ing. The diamond-encrusted gold band slipped into place as if it were home.

Ellie pulled Jayce back down on the swing beside her and threw her arms around his neck. "This is the best birthday ever. There seriously are no words to tell you how much I love you, Jayce Raythawn. Thank you."

CHAPTER TWENTY

Jayce

Jayce sat in the kitchen with Jasper, his new crossbow on the table between them. Watching Jasper's hands intently as they loaded a bolt into the bow, Jayce's fingers itched to try it out. Jasper's running commentary made him smile. The old man was enjoying this almost as much as Jayce.

They'd had a fantastic day, Isabel and Ellie 'oohing and aahing' over Ellie's ring, while Jasper gave Jayce a quick demonstration of the power of his crossbow. Jasper promised to start their lessons the next day, and Jayce had tried to hide his impatience and disappointment.

Isabel cooked a mouth-watering feast of roast pork

with all the trimmings for their birthday dinner, and Jasper had managed to smuggle a cake into the truck without Jayce's knowledge. It had been, without a doubt, the best day of Jayce's life.

He jumped up from the table at Ellie's startled cry from the lounge room. "Elle... what's wrong?"

"My choosing ceremony! I forgot all about it. We only have until midnight tonight, and Yvette promised to send someone to help me. What if she's forgotten? I don't even know what I'm supposed to do."

Jayce and Jasper put the crossbow aside. They shared a long-suffering *'the women are going to work themselves into a frenzy without us'* look as they moved to the lounge room.

"Don't panic, Ellie," Jasper said as he settled into his armchair. "I'm sure your mother has it all under control. She's not likely to forget what day it is, and if she can't come herself, she'll send someone who can help you. It's only just after nine o'clock... plenty of time left."

A look passed between Jasper and Isabel, and at Isabel's slight nod, Jasper cleared his throat. "There's something Isabel and I wanted to talk to you about, and we thought maybe now, while we're waiting for Yvette or her stand-in to turn up, might be a good time."

Ellie snuggled into Jayce as he joined her on the lounge, her worried eyes constantly darting to the clock on the wall. Changing the subject was just what she needed to distract her from dwelling on her upcoming ceremony.

"Sure, Jasper, what's up? Is it something we've done?"

Jasper waved his hand and chuckled. "No, nothing like that. I need to tell you something about us. You see, as it turns out, the Councils *should* be worried about your powers and what you're capable of. From what we've seen and heard over the last few days, you two wield more power together than I ever thought possible."

"I hadn't planned to tell you this tonight, but you may as well know it all. Yvette, Isabel and I... well... we're part of a group of rebels who want to overthrow the corrupt ruling Councils in both realms. And having you two on our side could be just what we've been prayin' for."

Ellie

ELLIE STARED at Jasper with her mouth open. She must be hallucinating again, because it sounded like the old couple sitting in front of them, in collusion with her own mother, wanted her and Jayce to join them in a revolution.

Jayce looked as stunned as she felt. "Excuse me? You want what?" His eyes had started to glow.

Jasper lifted his hand as if to ward off an attack. "Now, hold on there a minute, son. Before you get all hot and bothered, how about you listen to what I have to say first? You've seen an example of what the Council Guards are like. Do you really think the Council who sent them should be allowed to continue to run the realm unchallenged?"

Jayce folded his arms and gave the man a curt nod. "I'm listening," was all he said. Ellie slipped a hand into his folded arms, and he grabbed it and squeezed. They were in this together.

"Over the last couple of years, more and more dragons have been declared rogue and banished on trumped-up charges. Coincidentally, many of these dragons are from well-respected and affluent families who've been forced to forfeit their lands and their gold. When a dragon is banished, their property becomes that of the Council, to do with as they see fit."

"Added to this is the fact that all dragons are drafted into the army for five years when they turn eighteen, making them responsible for protecting the Council and doing their bidding. Those three who turned up here the other day are a result of the army's training techniques. Any dragon who refuses to take up this duty is also declared rogue and banished."

Jayce sighed and squeezed Ellie's hand. "That part is true enough. It's one of the reasons I was already considering going rogue before I met you."

Jasper's eyes widened. "So you had seriously considered it? Even with your father being who he is?"

Jayce half-smiled. "Even more so because of him. I enjoyed the freedom of living in the mortal world and was dreading a future filled with political battles and strictly enforced rules and regulations. And then, of course, I met Ellie, and even when I thought she was only a mortal..."

Jayce sighed and shrugged. "Ah hell, I guess it's time I came clean about a few things as well. Apparently, my past has no intention of staying where I thought I'd left it."

Jayce proceeded to tell them a shortened version of growing up as the son of Thomas Raythawn. When he got to the part about his trip home the night before he met Ellie, he directed every word to the girl he loved more than life itself.

A heavy silence hung in the air when he finished. Jayce was kicking himself for not telling them about the situation between him and his father before now, but he'd hoped never to have to deal with the man again.

Finally, Jasper nodded. "Thanks for sharing with us, son. Suddenly, everything makes so much more sense.

Ever since I learned that Thomas Raythawn raised you, I wondered how someone with your ethical values and honourable practices had survived living with that man. Now I understand."

"You bested him, Jayce, something a man like your father will never let go unpunished. If you hadn't met Ellie, Thomas would have found another way to make you pay. The night you walked out of his house, you became the enemy."

Jayce felt like a huge weight had fallen from his shoulders. He hadn't realised the burden his secrets had become. He'd spent his whole life afraid of being judged, or having his words dismissed as lies, if he tried to expose his father's true nature. And then there was the shame of allowing his father to beat his mother because of him.

"Jayce, the man is a monster. I've suspected it for years. Don't *ever* blame yourself for his deeds; that's what he wants you to do. Blame the criminal, not the victim."

"So, you are at least partly aware of what's going on in the realm, and I fear Thomas' power over the other Council members is growing. The Council must be aware of the rumblings of unrest and are probably already expecting trouble from some disgruntled rogues. But I doubt even *they* realise the magnitude of the problem. I believe the situation is almost as bad in the Witch Realm, but I'm not qualified to comment on that. Yvette would be the best person—"

"Speak of the devil, and she appears." A stunned silence filled the room as they all stared at Yvette, standing in the centre of the lounge room, grinning like a Cheshire cat.

Jasper recovered first, jumping to his feet, a worried frown on his face. "Yvette, you're not supposed to come here. This is way too dangerous for everyone."

"Oh pooh." Yvette waved her hand at Jasper. "I was extremely careful. I put a glamour on a friend, and she is currently impersonating me. So why would anyone be looking for me?" She turned towards Ellie and Jayce, and her grin faded at her daughter's 'less-than-happy-to-see-you' face.

She sighed. "I'm going to assume from that face that Jasper told you everything. I'm sorry I didn't explain, sweetheart, but if you remember, we were on a rather tight schedule. My biggest priority was getting you two to safety."

Ellie took a deep breath and smiled at her mother. "I know, you're right. It was better that you all waited until we understood what the Dragon Council were capable of. I think Jayce and I have seen enough to understand our only hope of survival is to deal with the Council once and for all."

Ellie laughed at the stunned faces. "What?"

"Who are you, and what have you done with the volatile daughter I met a week ago?" Yvette asked with a smile.

Ellie looked down at the hand Jayce squeezed, the

sight of her new engagement ring giving her butterflies. "I think you'll notice quite a few changes. It's been an... interesting week."

Yvette's eyes dropped to Ellie's hand, and she gasped in shock. "You can't be serious? What's it been... a week?" She turned on Isabel and Jasper. "Surely you didn't condone this? Have you all lost your minds?"

Jasper bristled at her tone. "Exactly how much time have you spent around these two people, Yvette? It's as plain as the nose on your face that they're meant to be together. So get down off your high horse and stop letting your stupid pride stand in the way of your daughter's happiness."

"Jayce came to us for advice because he didn't know how long it would be until we saw you again. And yes, we gave him our blessing. I took him to town this morning to buy the ring he wanted to give Ellie for her birthday."

Yvette's shoulders drooped, and she turned back to Ellie and Jayce. "Fine. What's done is done. I just wish—"

Isabel cleared her throat, and all eyes turned to her. "Well, this squabbling isn't getting anyone anywhere. Yvette, I assume you're here to assist and witness Ellie's choosing ceremony before midnight? I suggest you get that done first, and then we all need to sit and have a civilised conversation."

Ellie was surprised by the commanding tone of Isabel's voice, but even more by the glow in her eyes.

Ellie had assumed the older woman was a dragon from her aura, but it was the first time she'd seen the old woman's eyes glow like Jasper and Jayce's.

Isabel winked at Ellie's stunned expression. "Always expect the unexpected child. The quiet ones are usually the ones to watch." Isabel's face softened into a smile. "And I'm glad you understand your mother's reasons for not telling you about the rebellion. She was loathe to involve you in any of this. We suggested asking for your and Jayce's help. And I do mean *ask*. It is entirely your decision whether you *choose* to join us or not."

Isabel sighed and sat back in her chair. "Now, I believe you and your mother need to attend to some important business. We'll be right here waiting when you're done."

Ellie kissed Jayce, stood, and followed her mother from the room, flipping the switch on the outside floodlight Jasper had resurrected between the house and their cottage.

She was proud of herself for not doing her usual 'totally over-react-and-run-off-at-the-mouth-without-all-the-facts' thing. Maybe she was finally getting better at dealing with the crappy situations life threw at her. *Well, it was definitely a start.*

CHAPTER TWENTY-ONE

Ellie

Ellie turned to Yvette with an apologetic smile as they stepped out the back door. "I'm sorry we didn't wait to speak to you about the engagement thing. I get that you think this all happened too quickly, but seriously... it's not like we can or *would* choose someone else. We're already bonded for life."

"And as for the whole rebel business, well... I did think about snapping at you. But I'm trying to break the habit of shooting my mouth off before thinking things through. Apparently, I do that a lot!"

Yvette draped an arm around her shoulders and smiled. "I'm afraid you inherited that from me. I don't do it as often anymore, but I used to be exactly like you." She chuckled. "The only reason I'm better now, is because I got sick of needing to apologise.

And I'm sorry I overreacted to your engagement with Jayce. I guess I was feeling a bit miffed about being left out of the 'happy family' scene I interrupted."

Ellie pulled her mother in for a hug. "You don't ever need to feel like that. I'm just so glad you're here. Thank you for coming. I *so* didn't want to do this choosing thing with a complete stranger."

"I thought you might be nervous... which is why I set up the glamour double. So, have you made your decision yet?"

Ellie nodded, smiling. "I choose to be a witch. It's become blatantly obvious that I'm a lot more useful with magic than I ever was without it."

Yvette grinned. "Oh, Ellie, I'm so happy. I can stay until tomorrow night; I thought it might give us the chance to start your training."

Ellie chuckled. "Ummm... about that... There've been a few... developments... since I last saw you..."

Ellie proceeded to tell Yvette about the events of the past week, and when she got to the part about the healing, she lifted her shirt to show her mother the scars.

Yvette gasped in shock. "And you say this only happened three days ago?" Ellie nodded, and Yvette began to chuckle. "No wonder the Council is in a panic. I knew the bond between you and Jayce would increase your powers, but this is... unbelievable."

Snippets of the conversation Jayce was having with

Jasper and Isabel floated into her mind, and Ellie knew the moment he agreed to help with the rebellion. She smiled at her mother.

"Jasper and Isabel are doing a much better job of explaining the situation in the Dragon Realm since we left. I think Jayce will be convinced by the time we go back in there."

Yvette stared at Ellie. "How are you...? Don't tell me you and Jayce...? You can hear everything the other person is thinking?"

Ellie chuckled and shrugged. "Yep. Makes keeping a secret a pain in the butt."

Yvette shook her head, a glow of pride in her widened eyes. "You never cease to amaze me. I am so proud of you."

Ellie gave Yvette another quick hug and stepped away. "It's almost eleven-thirty. Don't you think we should get this Choosing Ceremony thing started?"

Yvette sobered instantly. "Of course. Sorry, I got a bit side-tracked. Okay, we need you to be inside a candle circle like you were for the awakening ceremony. Somewhere that's open... over there looks good." Yvette waved her hand, and a circle of candles appeared in the clearing in front of them.

"Right, now for the correct attire". She waved her hand again, and Ellie found herself wearing a silky, soft, floating white gown. Yvette chuckled. "Well... that answers a question a mother would never ask. The gown is white, so at least you're still—"

Ellie's face burned. "We are *so* not having this conversation." She moved into the circle and glared at Yvette with her hands on her hips. "Now, can we *please* just get on with it?"

Yvette grinned and waved her hand toward the sky. Ellie tilted her head back, her jaw dropping open as the Stars moved into alignment, forming a circle above her head.

"My daughter, the morwitch Ellie Fiora, comes before the Stars to declare her intentions regarding her future. The choosing is made of her own free will, and I am here only to witness the event."

The Stars above Ellie's head began to flicker, and she looked at her mother in confusion. "The Stars are eager to hear your choice. You need to tell them what you want and convince them you are aware of what your decision entails."

Ellie smiled, focusing her gaze on the flickering Stars. Feeling both comforted and safe in their presence, she formulated the words she wanted to say.

"I, Ellie Fiora, choose to forego my life as a mortal and take up my birthright as a witch. I understand the responsibilities I undertake and swear to use my powers only for good. I will always defend those less fortunate and deserving of my help."

The Stars swirled, dropping down and dancing around her as sparks of brilliant light shot into the air. Ellie spun around with them, laughing as she reached out to touch their tantalising presence.

And then, one by one, they abandoned their dance and rose slowly upward, shooting across the sky and leaving a blazing trail of light behind them. The last Star hovered in front of her for a moment, and Ellie thought she could discern a smiling face in its depths.

You will do well, daughter of the Stars. A soft, lilting voice spoke in her mind, and the Star touched Ellie's cheek before shooting up into the sky as the others had.

Completely mesmerized, Ellie stood in the middle of the circle, her cheek tingling, her entire body buzzing with energy. When the world came back into focus, she realised her mother was staring up at the sky with tears streaming down her face.

Ellie stepped out of the candle circle and ran to her, throwing her arms around Yvette's stiff body. "Hey... what's wrong? Why are you crying? Everything's fine."

Yvette turned her gaze to Ellie, her eyes filled with wonder and awe. "Oh, Ellie, that was *so* beautiful. I've witnessed quite a few Choosing Ceremonies over the years, but I have *never* seen a young witch touched by one of the Stars. This is a huge honour, one that I think declares you a favourite."

"Wait... you mean this doesn't happen at every ceremony? So why would they pick me?"

Yvette shrugged and put her arm around her daughter's shoulders. "Who knows why the universe chooses to do anything? Besides, who cares why? Being marked as a favourite is... amazing."

Ellie's smile evaporated as Jayce's thoughts barged into her mind, her blood turning to ice at his shock and fear. What the hell was going on?

"Something's wrong with Jayce. We need to get back to the house." She grabbed her mother's hand, and they ran for the back door.

Jayce

JAYCE STARED at the burning coffee table in horror. He heard Ellie and Yvette's feet approaching and sighed with relief as the fire spluttered and died, leaving a badly scorched table sitting in the middle of the room.

"What the hell was *that*? All I did was cough, and the damn table caught fire. How is that even possible?"

Jasper and Isabel burst into fits of laughter. Jayce scowled at them in confusion. *Great. So now* everyone's *gone insane?*

Ellie joined him on the lounge and wrapped her arms around him. He buried his head against her shoulder, her energy restoring his equilibrium as he tried to make sense of what had happened.

"Well, *that's* a first. I've heard stories about things like this happening, but I always thought they were myths invented by dragons after a few too many brews," Jasper spluttered.

"Can someone please tell me what the hell's going on? How in Hades did that fire just come out of me?" Jayce demanded.

Jasper, no longer laughing, rubbed his chin as he studied the scorched coffee table. "I'm not sure I *can* explain this, son. Like I said, I've only ever heard *stories* of dragons who could breathe fire when in human form. But seriously, it's supposed to be impossible."

Yvette stepped forward and cleared her throat. "I think I understand what's going on. At the end of Ellie's choosing ceremony, the last Star touched her face."

Jasper and Isabel stared at the young couple sitting on the lounge, their mouths gaping.

"Ellie is a *favourite?*" Isabel's voice held a touch of reverence.

Yvette nodded. "And if Ellie is, there's a very strong chance that Jayce is as well. He missed his Feast, but I think the Stars have been able to favour him through Ellie and their bond."

Jayce felt Ellie's frustration building to match his own, and he sat forward on the lounge. "Excuse me, but do you think someone could explain to the people involved in all this *exactly* what the hell you're talking about? Otherwise, I may let Ellie loose on you, and that won't be pretty!" Jayce's eyes moved from one face to the next as he spoke. Ellie's body shook as she chuckled beside him.

Yvette sat down and sighed. "I'm sorry. But you need to understand that what we've seen tonight has only ever been mentioned in stories handed down for generations. Nobody really believed any of them were true. I always thought they were like fairy-tales, invented to encourage children to strive toward becoming a favourite. I even remember being disappointed that nothing special happened at my own choosing ceremony."

Jasper nodded and smiled. "Yep, sounds familiar. I was raised with the constant fear of being named a 'fallen', which my parents told me was the opposite of a favourite. Now *that* part I'm sure they made up just to make us behave. I was so relieved at my Feast not to be deemed a 'fallen', I didn't care about not being chosen as a favourite."

Isabel smiled at her husband. "Did you honestly believe there was such a thing as being 'fallen'? Why didn't you ask your friends about it?"

Jasper shrugged. "I just assumed everyone already knew about it."

Isabel chuckled. "You poor thing. Still, if thinking that way kept you out of trouble, your parents probably did us both a favour.

Jayce sighed. "Okay, so this whole 'favourite' thing has always been shrouded in mystery. But you must know *something* you can tell us. What did the stories say about this 'being favoured'?"

The three looked at each other as if deciding which one would tell the story, and then Isabel nodded. "I suppose it *is* my turn to do some explaining. Okay, so all children in the magical realms are raised to believe they may earn the right to be chosen as a favourite at their Coming-of-Age Feast or Choosing Ceremony. Nobody ever seemed to know exactly what you had to *do* to be chosen, but the thought of being so honoured was always a great incentive to be the best you could be."

"Unfortunately, though, there are no records of what benefits come from being favoured or how the knowledge of this honour was imparted in the first place. I guess we'll just have to wait and see. Although the fact that you two can do things I never believed possible tells me, it will definitely be interesting."

CHAPTER TWENTY-TWO

Ellie

By the time they were headed toward their cottage, Ellie's head was spinning. She was glad Yvette had decided to stay over; it meant they'd have the whole next day to spend together. By the sound of things, Jayce would be busy working with Jasper, what with learning how to control his fire breathing—*so the furniture would remain intact*—on top of his crossbow lessons and private dragon speak instruction.

As soon as the front door closed behind them, Jayce reached out and pulled her against him. "Man, I was starting to think we'd never be alone again." His eyes twinkled with mischief.

"I've been dying to tell you something ever since you came back in from your choosing ceremony. Seeing you in that dress played havoc with my concentration all night. Damn, you look gorgeous." Ellie shivered at the intensity in his eyes.

"Do you have any idea how hard it is to..." he sighed. "Yeah, you do, don't you?"

Ellie reached up and kissed him, as she'd wanted to do all night. Today had been the most incredible day of her life, thanks to this amazing man. How could she continue to question whether they were meant to be together? This wasn't about the number of *days* since they'd met. Their bond was for life. Suddenly, it all became clear... *this* was the right time and place.

Jayce groaned as she poured all the emotions she'd been holding back into that kiss. Scooping her up into his arms, he walked to their room, never breaking the kiss as he lowered her tenderly onto the bed beneath him.

"Are you sure about this? Because if not, now's the time to—"

"Absolutely... I love you, Jayce..." Ellie tingled at the burning passion in his eyes. No further words were necessary.

Jayce

JAYCE WOKE UP the morning after his eighteenth birthday ready to take on the world. Nothing and nobody would stop him from spending the rest of his life with the incredible woman who lay beside him.

Ellie's face broke into a cheeky grin, her eyes still closed. "Mmm, I happen to think you're incredible too... just sayin'."

Jayce grinned and pulled her into his arms. "Listen here, witch. We've got a lot to do today. Damn it. I wonder if there's a spell to speed up time so we can get everything done and end up right back here in about... let's say an hour?"

Ellie giggled. "Goodonya, I now have an image of us whizzing through the day as if someone hit the fast-forward button on the TV. Although, the part where you're flexing your muscles as you reload the crossbow double-time is pretty hot."

"Good morning. Anyone up yet?" Yvette's voice floated in the bedroom window. Ellie squealed and dived out of bed, grabbing her clothes and heading for the shower.

You don't mind entertaining my mother while I take a quick shower, do you, babe? I did warn you the last time you beat me that I'd get you back.

Jayce laughed as he watched her rapid retreat. He really was marrying a witch! Ellie's tinkling laughter floated through his head as he went to greet his future mother-in-law.

Ellie

"EXCUSE ME SLEEPYHEAD, you need to pay attention. You're never going to learn how to use your powers if you're forever floating off into la-la land somewhere. Oh, and the goofy grin has *got* to go," Yvette said, with the hint of a smile lifting the corners of her mouth.

Ellie jumped as her mother's words penetrated her thoughts, too busy reliving every moment of the most perfect night of her life to follow what her mother had said.

"Sorry," she said, shaking her head to clear the images floating through her mind. "I promise to give you my undivided attention from now on."

"Fine. So, as I was saying, have you noticed that

using spells takes more energy than something like fetching?"

Ellie remembered her exhaustion after using the memory-erasing spell so soon after a power thrust on the bounty hunter. "Yeah, now that you mention it. I spent almost an entire day fetching stuff from Jayce's and my rooms, and I was tired, but nothing like after I cast two spells back-to-back."

Yvette frowned. "How did you fetch from Jayce's room? I didn't think you'd ever been there?"

"Oh, I didn't. But we found if we linked my powers with Jayce's mind, we could fetch things he could picture as well."

"Are you serious? I've never heard of anyone being able to do that before."

Ellie chuckled. "We figure since there aren't any records of what we can and can't do, we'll just keep trying things and see how we go." The frown was still on Yvette's face. "That's okay, isn't it?"

"Okay? It's fantastic. Maybe we should ask Jayce to work with us for a while. I'd love to see the two of you casting spells together."

"Well, he's busy with his crossbow training this morning. Maybe after lunch Jasper might 'lend' him to us."

"Sounds like a plan. In the meantime, I thought we might practice some spells to build up your energy levels. I'm thinking, under the circumstances, a few more defensive ones might be best."

Jayce

"OKAY, now slow your breathing and concentrate. Don't take your eyes off the target. You need to anticipate where it will be when the bolt releases, not where it is now." Jasper's voice was soft and calm beside him.

Jayce lowered the bow and turned to Jasper in frustration. "Easier said than done. Every time I'm almost centred, a random thought from Ellie's mind blows it all to pieces. Maybe we should work on learning private dragon speak first. I'm hoping whatever you do to make it private will help shut Ellie's thoughts out when I need to concentrate."

Jasper chuckled. "I can't say I envy you sharing a mind with Ellie. Must be like being caught in a whirlwind inside there sometimes."

Jayce groaned. "You have no idea. I love the woman, but there are *some* thoughts that just shouldn't be shared."

Jasper threw back his head and roared with laughter. When he recovered enough to speak, he put his hand on Jayce's shoulder, his eyes full of sympathy.

"Damn, I never even thought of that problem. Well, it's almost lunchtime. How about we take a break and work on the dragon speak after lunch?"

"Sounds great. I just hope it works; 'cause if I don't find an on/off switch soon, I may go stark-raving mad."

Jasper slapped his back, still chortling as they headed for the house. No doubt, he was sifting through the thoughts *he* wouldn't want anyone else to hear.

Ellie

ELLIE WAS STARVING, and so tired she was struggling to stay awake. She tried to focus on the conversation at the table, but decided her brain must already be asleep.

The mention of her name penetrated the fog. "So Jayce. Ellie and I thought it might be good if you two practiced casting some spells together while I'm here."

Jayce chuckled, draping his arm around the back of Ellie's chair. "Ummm, Yvette. You may not have noticed, but Ellie is almost asleep with her eyes open."

Yvette's eyes flew to Ellie. "Why didn't you tell me you were exhausted? You need to sleep."

Ellie shrugged. "I knew you could only stay until tonight, and I didn't want to waste any of the time we had left together."

"Oh honey, you probably only need an hour's rest. How about you take a nap, and I'll come and wake you? I don't want you collapsing."

Ellie nodded her head and pushed her chair back from the table. Jayce moved to go with her, but she put her hand on his shoulder. "I'll be fine. You finish your lunch."

Jayce raised an eyebrow. "And find you curled up asleep on the ground halfway between here and home? I don't think so. Come on... you'll be asleep before your head hits the pillow, and I'll be back to finish my lunch in five minutes."

Ellie nodded, too tired to argue. Jayce stood and slipped his arm around her waist, and she fought the urge to sag against him.

"Oh, for goodness sake. Stop being so stubborn and admit you're ready to collapse for once, will you?" Jayce reached down and picked her up, grinning at the three people watching the show. "I'll be back in a couple of minutes," he said to the silent onlookers and strode out the door.

Ellie smiled at his determined face. "Thank you...I didn't realise how tired I was."

"You looked like you did after wiping that bounty hunter's memory. I knew you wouldn't make it home alone."

Ellie rested her head against his chest and sighed. "Love you, babe," she mumbled as she nodded off to sleep.

Jayce

JAYCE TUCKED ELLIE into bed and smiled. She was so exhausted that she hadn't even stirred when he laid her down on the bed. He kissed her forehead and headed back to the house to finish his lunch, feeling guilty about enjoying the silence of his own thoughts for a while.

Everyone stopped talking when he re-entered the kitchen, a sure sign the topic of conversation had been him, Ellie, or both. He sat down at the table and turned his eyes to Yvette.

"So, how about you share what you were discussing? Ellie's asleep, so this is a rare moment when we can talk freely."

Yvette looked ready to plead ignorance, but the look in his eyes must have convinced her otherwise. She breathed a huge sigh and shrugged. "Something terrible is happening in the mortal world. People are getting sick and dying from some kind of wasting disease... and Ellie's aunts have been affected."

Jayce frowned. "You realise we can't keep this a secret from Ellie, right? And the first thing she'll want to do is go and help the aunts?"

Yvette nodded. "Which is why I waited to talk to Jasper and Isabel when you two weren't around."

"Yvette, much as I appreciate you trying to protect us, Ellie needs to know what's going on as well. We *live* in the mortal world, and Ellie has friends and family in Darwin. How long has this been going on? Does anyone know what's causing it?"

Yvette shrugged. "No one seems to know. The disease, or whatever it is, manifests in different symptoms, which appear to be dictated by age. The middle-aged and elderly become hyper-passive, losing the desire to live and wasting away from malnutrition and dehydration. While the young get hyperactive and aggressive. It's getting harder to control the spread of the disease."

"You suspect magic is involved, don't you? What do the Councils have to say about it?"

Yvette shrugged, looking down at her hands wrapped tightly around her coffee mug. "That's just it. They're refusing to do anything, saying what happens in the mortal world is not their business. But... something weird is going on there, too. I've been trying to work out exactly what's wrong, but no one else seems to think there's a problem, almost as if nobody cares anymore."

Jayce put his elbows on the table and dropped his head into his hands. Ellie would want to go straight back home to Darwin. *How the hell was I supposed to convince her she needed to put her own safety before that of her aunts?* He growled and lifted his head.

"So what are you suggesting we do, then? Hide here like scared rabbits and let people die?"

Jasper leaned forward in his chair. "I know you're angry and frustrated, son. But nothing'll be decided until we receive more information about what the Councils are up to. I'm expecting news tonight. So how about you and I go do some target practice and work on the private dragon speak while we wait? "

Jayce nodded and got to his feet. "I'm sorry I snapped. Of course, I'll do whatever's necessary to keep Ellie safe. And we do appreciate everything you've done for us. I just hate feeling helpless. This constant need to run and hide is gnawing away at my insides."

Jasper patted his shoulder. "I understand. But exposing yourselves at this stage won't help anyone. Save your energy and anger for when they're needed."

Jayce walked outside with the old dragon in silence. Jasper was right, but hiding made him feel like a coward. It had taken every shred of his self-control to stay hidden when the Council Guards had spoken to Jasper like he was garbage. But Jayce had to consider Ellie's safety, too. *Life really sucked sometimes!*

CHAPTER TWENTY-THREE

Jayce

As Jayce had predicted, Ellie flatly refused to accept the fact that she couldn't go and help her aunts. Jayce tried every argument he could think of, knowing it was hopeless before he even started. Stubborn, and determined not to abandon the aunts, she was way past listening to reason.

Jayce rubbed his chin thoughtfully. "What if we teleport to the aunts' house, find out what we can about what's going on, and come straight back? We could be in and out in less than an hour."

Yvette shook her head. "No way. You know magic leaves a trail for anyone who's looking. There's bound to be at least one bounty hunter watching the house."

Ellie frowned. "What if I went alone? They're expecting two of us, and I'd just look like an old friend visiting them."

Jayce almost choked. "There is no way you're going without me. We go together or not at all."

"But..." Ellie started, but at the look in Jayce's eyes, she threw her hands in the air. "Well, we can't just sit here and do nothing!"

Yvette sighed. "There might be another way. We can try scrying for the aunts. I wanted to teach Ellie anyway, and we may learn something about what's causing the outbreak to spread. Sometimes, the presence of dark magic is more noticeable when looking through a magical filter, so to speak."

Everyone looked at Ellie, Jayce holding his breath in anticipation of her reply. She sighed and nodded. "But if we don't learn anything, I *will* be going to see them, whether you like it or not!"

Ellie

ELLIE CLEARED her mind of all thoughts except those related to her aunts. Holding her hands above the bowl of water, she jumped when it bubbled and began to swirl. She clung to the comforting feel of Jayce in her mind, his presence helping to calm her frayed nerves. Suddenly, the water calmed, and an image of Serena and Emelda took shape on the reflective surface.

Ellie smiled at the sight of her two aunts sitting in their favourite armchairs. But the smile froze at the lack of animation on their usually bright and cheerful faces. At first glance, they appeared simply lost in their own thoughts, but Ellie shuddered at the vacant expression in their eyes as they stared unseeingly at each other.

She concentrated on expanding the image, scanning the aunts' surroundings for anything unusual. The room was abnormally neglected, a dusty haze suspended in the still air. A slight movement caught Ellie's attention; Emelda was wringing her hands in her lap. Ellie zoomed back in and gasped. Emelda's hands looked withered and blackened, as if burned. Serena's were in the same state.

Whatever had infected them must have come from something they touched. She scrolled through her memories of the years they spent as a family, searching for clues that might explain what happened. Then she spotted the small gardening spade on the floor beside Serena's chair.

Why would a gardening tool be sitting discarded on the lounge room floor? The aunts were always meticulous about putting things where they belonged.

Ellie waved her hands over the bowl again, forming a mental image of the aunts' prized rose bushes. Once again, the water swirled, settling to reveal the area of the garden she sought. The gardening tool carry-all sat abandoned next to the two kneeling frames the women used when working in the garden. And the rose bushes were reduced to wilted, blackened sticks.

What the hell is going on? She felt the same confusion in Jayce's mind as she stirred the water one more time and concentrated on the park across from her house. When the image appeared, she reeled in shock.

The lower half of the tree trunks were charcoal, the branches and leaves withered and dying; the previously lush green grass dried and blackened.

About to end the scrying, she caught sight of two young boys moving into view. One boy wielded a base-ball bat, beating the other boy mercilessly. When the victim finally dropped to the ground, still and lifeless, the boy with the bat reached into his victim's pocket, pulled out some coins, shrugged and moved on, his bare feet black and withered.

Ellie closed the image and stumbled backwards, nauseated by the senseless violence. Jayce's arms caught her before she fell, as the tears slid down her face.

"The disease is coming from the earth," she whispered, still unable to process the reality of what was happening. "How could someone poison the earth?"

Yvette finally recovered her voice. "I don't know,

honey. But damage on this scale shouldn't be possible... unless the Tree of Life herself is sick. This is much bigger than I feared, and I have no idea how to fix it."

"SO WHAT IS this Tree of Life anyway? And how do we find it?" Ellie asked when Yvette finished telling Jasper and Isabel about the vision.

Yvette snapped. "You can forget the *we* right now! Ellie, the Councils of two magical realms are hunting you because they want you dead. Which part of that don't you understand?"

Ellie's eyes flared. Taking a deep breath, she exhaled slowly. "Mother, I get that you are only trying to protect me, but I don't want to live like this. Do you really expect us to spend our whole lives hiding? 'Cos no way that is *ever* going to happen."

"Jayce and I are favoured, and between us, we must be powerful enough to fight off a bevvy of bounty hunters. No one else is prepared to lift a finger to help the people of the mortal world, and you expect us to do the same?" She shrugged and reached for Jayce's hand. "At least we'll die doing something useful instead of hiding in a cupboard!" She turned to Jasper. "Now, can someone *please* answer my questions?"

Jasper shook his head. "The Tree of Life, sometimes

called Mother Nature or Mother Earth, is the guardian of the mortal realm. Her roots sustain all life in this world. If She were somehow poisoned, it would leach into the earth, killing everything it touches.

As for finding Her home, I'm afraid that's an impossible task. No one knows where the Tree is located. It's been kept a secret for this very reason, to avoid any harm coming to the Tree Herself."

Ellie frowned. "But someone or something *did* find Her. What about rumours or stories hinting at Her location? People can't help but leak information when it comes to something secret."

Isabel sat forward, leaning her arms on the table. "Of course, there've been rumours, but how do we eliminate the false ones and find the true ones? If any of them *are* even true."

"But that's my whole point, Isabel; someone else found Her, so they managed to work it out somehow. Either that or the information is written down *somewhere*. There must be someone we can talk to. Who would have access to this kind of knowledge?"

Jayce snapped his fingers. "What if someone leaked the location? It would have to be someone who's been around for thousands of years and is privy to all kinds of secrets..." he smiled, "... and I think I have an idea who it might be. When we were kids, there was an old dragon everyone called 'Grandfather', who used to tell fantastical stories to keep us entertained. Maybe, just maybe, some of them were true."

A rush of excitement tingled along Ellie's nerve endings. "Awesome. Do you know where he lives?"

Ellie reeled as Jayce's mind slammed shut. "Yes, I do, and there's no way you're going to the Dragon Realm, so stop trying to pull the image of where he is out of my mind."

Ellie's face burned. "Seriously? As if I'd—"

"Don't bother denying it. I can read *your* thoughts too, remember?" He chuckled and hugged her, but his eyes held a distinct warning. "I can just see you trying to sneak off without me. Not. Gonna. Happen."

Ellie sighed, but she was still annoyed and confused by the sensation of Jayce's mind blocking her. "Fine, but I still wanna know how you shut your mind like that.

Jayce glanced at Jasper, and the old man winked. "Dragon secret... and seeing you're not a dragon..." Jayce shrugged, giving her a smug grin.

Ellie stood and punched his arm. "What a load of crap! We're bonded, and we both agreed to the mind-sharing thing. No way you should be able to shut me out like that."

"Hey, I distinctly remember telling you some of the stuff mentioned in the book didn't consider dragons as familiars. So, for once, I can do something you can't, and you need to get over it." His fiery eyes sparked dangerously, but Ellie was way too wound up to heed the warning.

"Get over it, huh? Fine, keep your stupid dragon

secrets. But don't expect me to hang around while you gloat!"

Jayce

JAYCE REACHED for Ellie an instant too late, groaning as she vanished before his eyes. What the hell had he been thinking, goading her like that? He'd spent an hour working with Jasper while she was asleep, learning the art of closing off his thoughts. He'd planned to teach her how to do it as soon as they got the chance.

Damnit! He'd been so angry with her for refusing to listen to reason that he'd reacted without thinking it through. But he had to admit it felt good to be able to do something Ellie couldn't for once. Sometimes, his male ego rebelled at the fact that she had such incredible power and he brought so little to the partnership. Sure, he could fly and breathe fire, but she could do so much more!

Yvette moved over to sit beside him, draping her arm around his shoulders. "Don't beat yourself up about it, Jayce. I love Ellie too, but sometimes she can be a frustrating pain in the butt."

Aware of the sympathy in his friends' eyes, Jayce shrugged. "Yeah, but knowing how stressful this last week has been, I should have seen the signs and backed off."

Yvette smiled. "I know I haven't spent much time with Ellie, but she is so like me when I was her age. I always reacted first and regretted it later, a scary trait in a witch. But I was nowhere near as strong as Ellie is becoming, which makes it even more dangerous in her case."

Jayce sighed. "So what do I do now? I don't even know where she's gone."

Yvette nudged him. "I doubt she would go far. I think you'll find the whole thing was more about the exit than the destination. I'd try the cottage first."

CHAPTER TWENTY-FOUR

Ellie

Pacing back and forth in the bush behind the cottage, Ellie's heart felt like it would jump out of her chest. Damnit, she was sick to death of being treated like a child. She picked up a stone and hurled it at the nearest tree.

What was the point of being 'safe' if you had to spend your whole life scared and in hiding to achieve it? *Enough was enough.* She would not sit around and do nothing while her friends and family could be dying.

She hurled another rock at the hapless tree. And what was with Jayce anyway? She was stunned when he slammed his mind closed on her. So what if she *did* briefly consider using the image of the Grandfather's house to find him? He still didn't need to...

Ellie sunk to the ground and covered her face with her hands. She hated to admit it, but Jayce had done the right thing by blocking her out. Frustrated by everyone telling her what she could and couldn't do, she probably would've teleported there just to spite them. What an idiot. Jayce had been trying to keep her safe, as always, and she was too stubborn and pigheaded to listen.

The sound of crunching leaves under heavy boots alerted her to Jayce's arrival. She lifted her face and gazed into his warm golden eyes.

"I'm so sorry—" they both said at once.

Jayce dropped down beside her and pulled her into his arms. Which, of course, just made her feel worse. She'd done nothing but argue with him and act like a spoiled brat... and as usual, he was prepared to apologise when the whole thing was mainly her fault.

"Please let me talk first," Ellie said, comforted by his heartbeat beneath her cheek. "I'm a stubborn, self-centred idiot. I spent all day arguing with you when you were only trying to keep me safe. I over-reacted to the blocked thoughts thing because I was angry, and worried, and scared—"

Jayce's kiss was tender, healing the anger, and worry, and fear—just as he always did. Ellie pushed all other thoughts aside and allowed her bruised emotions to recover in a place where nothing existed outside their love for each other.

Jayce lifted his head, his eyes filled with adoration. "Okay, so my turn now. Jasper taught me the private dragon speak thing while you were asleep, and I *do* plan to teach you how to use it, too. I guess I just lashed out, angry at you for dismissing my concerns. Ya' know, sometimes loving you, and trying to keep you safe at the same time, can be a damned frustrating job."

Ellie snuggled against him and gave him a sheepish look. "Yeah, sorry about that. I'm a total pain in the butt. But I'm *your* pain in the butt, and you just have to put up with me. But please remember I'm trying really hard to change, okay?"

Jayce kissed the tip of her nose and smiled. "I love you, warts and all witchy girl. But we really do need to discuss this whole 'going to the Dragon Realm' thing."

Ellie sighed and nodded. No way she would win *this* particular battle.

Jayce

AN UNCOMFORTABLE SILENCE hung in the air when Jayce and Ellie returned to the kitchen.

"I'm so sorry I went off like that. I'm such an idiot..." Ellie burst out, fresh tears welling in her eyes. Jayce guided her over to the seat she recently vacated and sat down next to her.

"Okay, so Ellie and I discussed the situation, and we agreed that Yvette should teleport me to the Grandfather's house."

Jayce grinned as three sets of eyes looked up, surprise on all their faces.

"And you're okay with that, Ellie?" Yvette asked hesitantly.

"Yep. I understand it's way too dangerous for me to go to the Dragon Realm. I'm worried about Jayce going too, but this is our best chance of getting the information we need." She shrugged and smiled at her mother. "How long before you need to go home?"

"I'm staying until we have a better idea of what's going on. I'll send a message to my glamoured friend asking her to stay holed up a bit longer. So when would you like to go, Jayce?"

"How about now? I don't think we can afford to waste any more time. I'm ready whenever you are. Hopefully, we won't be gone long and can slip in and out without raising any alarms. The Grandfather's house is in a secluded valley not far from the Dragon Council's castle. Do you think you can get us there?"

"No problem. I've been to the castle a few times with messages for the Council. We'll be fine."

Jayce turned to Ellie and grinned, kissing her on the forehead. "Won't be long, sweetheart."

Ellie raised a quivering smile. "Please be careful..." she whispered.

He moved over next to Yvette, offering her his arm, as the floor fell away beneath him.

JAYCE AND YVETTE landed in the Dragon Realm, which is a short walk from the Grandfather's house. Fortunately, the place appeared deserted, and they moved silently between the trees toward their destination.

"The Grandfather's house is just up ahead. I think it might be best if I go alone. Would you mind waiting here among the trees? This shouldn't take long." Jayce spoke softly as the house came into view. Yvette nodded and squeezed his arm.

Jayce crept toward the dimly lit hovel where he hoped the Grandfather still resided. As he tried to peer through the windows yellowed with grime from years of neglect, a voice entered his head.

Come in, Jayce Raythawn. I have been expecting you. Jayce froze, wondering how the old man knew he was there. *Don't worry, no one else knows you are here, and the door is not locked.*

Jayce opened the door cautiously, praying to the Stars that this wasn't a trap. When the silence continued, he signaled to Yvette to stay put and stepped inside.

"Good to see you again, young Jayce. I was deeply saddened to hear of your troubles. Please sit and make yourself at home. I feared you wouldn't come before—" The old man's emaciated frame shook as he wheezed and coughed for a moment. The painful truth hit Jayce immediately. The Grandfather was dying.

"How did you know it was me outside the house? And how did you use dragon speak while in your human form?"

"I never forget the scent of a dragon who is bound for greatness. I knew it the first time you came to visit me. As for the use of telepathy, let's just call it an old family secret." Wracked by another coughing fit, the old dragon waved his hand weakly in front of him.

"But enough of the pleasantries, we have important business to discuss. I have been poisoned, and I am not sure how much longer I can fight the effects." He spoke in a matter-of-fact voice, utterly devoid of emotion.

"Who did this to you, Grandfather?"

"I wish I knew, son. But I'm sure all will be revealed in *time*. That's the one thing I don't have much left of, unfortunately. So... I'm afraid I may have inadvertently shared some information that has the potential to cause a great deal of grief. What do you know of the Tree of Life?"

Jayce's jaw dropped open at the old man's words. "That's what I came here to talk to you about. My friends and I believe the people of the mortal world are being poisoned by something leaching into the earth."

"Then my worst fears are coming true. You think the Tree of Life is sick, don't you?" When Jayce nodded, the Grandfather's wizened old face crumpled.

"Then I will die a failure. I was the only one left in the three realms who knew the location of the Tree and swore to keep the secret to my grave. But I grew old and careless, letting some of my secrets slip in the delirium caused by the poison. I failed to recognise the presence of dark magic until too late."

"What makes you think dark magic was involved?"

The Grandfather leaned over and spat into a bowl beside his chair. "Its presence leaves a distinct smell and taste in the air. I emerged from my delirium suspecting someone evil had witnessed the ramblings. I prayed to the Stars that the location of the Tree was not among the secrets spilled."

The old man coughed again, and this time, Jayce saw the blood on the cloth he pulled away from his face. "When I picked up your scent tonight, I dreaded learning why you were here."

"But I fear you may be too late. These events occurred weeks ago, and if the poison is spreading that fast, the Tree's defenses are breaking down. It's only a matter of time before—"

"No... please don't say it. Surely, there is something we can do. I'm bonded to a witch as her familiar, and she's not only powerful but was favoured by the Stars at her choosing ceremony. If we can just talk to the Tree, She might know something we can do to save Her."

The Grandfather sat up a little straighter at Jayce's words, a tiny glimmer of hope appearing in his old pain-filled eyes. "She's a favourite, you say? Well, well... it's been a very long time since I heard of anyone receiving that blessing. I was beginning to think the Stars had abandoned us. Maybe there is hope after all..."

Jayce sat forward in his chair, resting one of his hands on the old man's knee. The Grandfather's eyes went wide with awe at the contact. He chuckled and wheezed, his eyes filling with tears. "You didn't mention that *you* are also a favourite. Why is that?"

Jayce was astonished by the old man's words. "Ummm... what makes you think I am? I was banished before my Feast and couldn't attend my own ceremony."

"Then the Stars must have used the bond between you and your witch. Trust me, son. I have only ever had contact with one other favourite in the last thousand years, and you possess the same energy."

Jayce shook his head in wonder. Yvette had said something about that being possible after Ellie's ceremony, but he'd disregarded it at the time. His chest swelled with pride at the honour the Stars had bestowed upon him.

"So *now,* do you think we may be able to save the Tree? I need you to tell me where She is so we can ask Her if there's a cure. Will you trust me with the secret? I swear we will keep Her location a secret as long as we live."

The old man sighed and nodded his head. "Yes, Jayce Raythawn, I believe you and your witch are the only hope for the Tree of Life, and I will tell you everything I know. You might like to invite your friend in first, though. The one waiting out in the trees. The air is quite chilly tonight." The Grandfather chuckled at the look of surprise on Jayce's face as he stood to call Yvette inside.

CHAPTER TWENTY-FIVE

Ellie

Ellie paced the floor, chewing her nails and watching the clock. Jayce and Yvette had left over an hour ago, and the waiting was killing her.

Isabel emerged from the kitchen carrying a teapot and five cups. "Come sit down and have some herbal tea. I'm sure they'll be back any minute, and you'll be no help to them if you're a blithering idiot."

Ellie smiled at the old woman and shook her head. "You don't believe in mincing your words, do you, Isabel? I love your honesty."

Jasper came up behind his wife, chuckling as he slipped his arms around her waist. "You got that right,

Ellie. I can always rely on Isabel to tell me when I'm being a complete idiot. Although I don't always agree with her view of the situation." He kissed his wife on the cheek. "Now, herbal tea sounds like just what the doctor ordered... shall we?"

Jayce and Yvette appeared in the room just as they settled around the table. Ellie jumped up and threw herself at Jayce, giggling as he nearly toppled backwards from the impact. Oblivious to the room full of people, she kissed him desperately, pouring all the fear and worry of the last hour into his mind.

When she finally allowed him to come up for air, his dazed expression made her smile. "Hmmm... I may need to go away more often. The welcome home is spectacular."

Ellie blushed and giggled. "Don't even think about it!"

Yvette cleared her throat, reminding Ellie they weren't alone. She buried her face against Jayce's chest, wondering if there'd ever be a time when they could live their own lives without the constant scrutiny of others.

Jayce kissed the top of her head. *There will be, babe, when this is all over.*

Yvette managed to look almost as uncomfortable with the situation as Ellie. "Sorry, but we have so much to tell you, and time is rapidly running out."

By the time Yvette and Jayce finished relating what

the Grandfather had told them, Ellie couldn't decide whether to laugh or cry.

Yes, they'd learned the location of the Tree of Life, but what if it was too late to save Her? And even if the Tree knew of a possible cure, would they have time to find and administer it before She was too far gone? The questions were endless; the answers always just leading to more questions.

Jayce reached for her hand under the table, his troubled eyes telling her he had all the same questions, doubts and fears. But when he smiled at her, she found his determination contagious.

Ellie sat up straighter in her chair and turned to Yvette. "So, we need to leave as soon as possible. Every second we spend sitting here is time wasted. Jayce, did the Grandfather communicate an image of the area you can send to me?"

For once, Jayce didn't explode and told her she couldn't go. "For once, Ellie's right, we need to do this together. Until I told the Grandfather about Ellie being favoured by the Stars, he believed there was no hope. Oh, and he also confirmed I was favoured as well. Said he felt it when I touched him."

Everyone in the room erupted into cries of congratulations, sharing hugs and some backslapping. Ellie smiled when Yvette whispered, 'I told you so' into Jayce's ear as she hugged him.

Jayce finally threw his hands in the air, his enjoyment at the fuss relegated to second place behind the importance of finding the Tree.

"Okay, so we know the Tree is located in a hidden valley somewhere deep in the Amazon. The Grandfather admitted it had been hundreds of years since he last visited Her, but he sent me an image of the entrance to the sanctuary itself. He said magical wards were in place when he first sought entry, which the Tree removed when he declared his presence. So if this wielder of dark magic managed to find a way in, I'm sure we'll be able to as well."

Yvette put her hands on her hips and glared at the two of them. "I'm coming with you. Don't bother arguing. My mind is made up."

Jayce and Ellie smiled at each other and nodded. "We'd love you to come with us," Ellie said. "It's not like either of *us* knows what we're doing."

Yvette nodded, the worry in her eyes tempered by relief. "Right, so we leave at dawn." She raised her hand as Ellie and Jayce opened their mouths to argue.

"We don't know how long this will take or what we'll be dealing with. There's no point going off exhausted and starving before we start. We'll meet back here for breakfast at first light, rested and ready to leave. Now, goodnight, and make sure you get plenty of *sleep*." Her mouth definitely twitched, belying the stern look in her motherly eyes.

Jayce

JAYCE SIGHED as Ellie's breathing deepened, relieved she'd finally succumbed to the exhaustion they both felt. It had been a long, stressful day, and he got the feeling that the journey ahead of them would be worse.

Unable to sleep, he pondered the meaning of the message the Grandfather sent him as he left the old man's cottage.

I fear your journey will be long and arduous, fraught with many trials. But I believe the Stars favoured not only each of you individually, but your union as well. Your task can only be accomplished together. Do not allow anything to destroy what the Stars have blessed. Love has the power to conquer all, but remember—it requires trust to survive.

Jayce brushed a stray curl back from the face of the woman he loved more than he'd ever thought possible. She stirred at his touch, and he smiled as she snuggled closer. They would do what needed to be done together, and he would die protecting her if necessary.

JAYCE SMILED and squeezed Ellie's hand under the table at breakfast the next morning. His mind was reeling as he tried to follow the thoughts racing through Ellie's head.

Man, it's busy in there. I can't even begin to keep up with your thoughts. Jayce chuckled

Tell me about it! You should try it from this side. Ellie answered with a sigh.

Breakfast had been a quiet affair, the group sitting around the table seemingly lost in their own private thoughts.

Jasper finally broke the silence. "I'll send word to a few reliable rogue dragons while you're gone and see if we can get some idea of the situation in the Dragon Realm. Please be careful. Just keep in mind that whoever or whatever poisoned the Tree of Life obviously possesses powerful dark magic, and is not going to be happy about you interfering with their plans."

Ellie jumped as a voice boomed through the house. "Jayce Raythawn, I know you're here. It's me, Rhett. I need to talk to you."

Jayce didn't even think before jumping up to run outside and greet his old friend, but Jasper grabbed his arm.

"Jayce, you can't just go barreling out there with no idea of why he's here. How did he even find you, huh? We don't know what's been going on in the Dragon Realm, son... he may not be the friend you once knew any longer."

"Just let me go out first and see what happens. You'll soon be able to tell if he's not himself by observing his behaviour and listening to our conversation."

Jayce wanted to tell the old man he didn't know what he was talking about. That he and Rhett had been friends since they were babies, and Rhett would never try to hurt him.

But Jasper might be right. His old friend could be tainted, or infected, or whatever the hell was wrong with the worlds, and Jayce had responsibilities he couldn't ignore. He nodded to Jasper and backed off.

Ellie's arms slid around him as he slumped back into his chair. They watched Jasper open the front door and walk outside as Rhett stepped out from behind a tree. So far, he appeared to be the same person Jayce had known all his life.

"Howdy, Rhett. My name's Jasper, and this here's my house. What makes you think this Jayce Raythawn fellow is here?"

Rhett almost snarled. "Don't mess with me, old man. He went to the Grandfather's house. I recognised his scent, so I followed the magic back here." Rhett looked past the old man and glared toward the house.

"I know you can hear me, Jayce. Just answer me this.

How could you abandon your family and friends for a damn girl... 'specially a witch girl who's ruined your damned life?" Rhett spat on the ground next to him as if the word gave him a sour taste.

Jayce's eyes filled with horror. "Jasper's right, the Rhett I know would never speak to *anyone* like that. This is crap... what the hell is going on?"

Ellie's heart ached at the pain in his eyes. "We have to assume that no one outside this house is who they used to be any more.

We need to find the Tree of Life and work out how to fix things in the mortal world, and *then* we can concentrate on whatever is going on in the magical realms. Confronting Rhett now would be disastrous for both of you."

Jayce nodded and looked back outside. Jasper stood in front of Rhett, scratching his head as if confused. "Well, son, a man and a woman arrived here last night seeking refuge for the night, but when we got up this morning, they were long gone. I'm afraid I've no idea where they were headed."

Rhett kicked the ground, his eyes full of suspicion. "So, you're telling me they *were* here, and now they're gone? How come the magic trail ends here then, huh?"

"Maybe they left using other means. Is this Jayce fellow by any chance a dragon?" Rhett nodded. "Guess they must've flown outta here then. Sorry, young fella, looks like they gave you the slip."

Rhett morphed into his dragon form, roaring in frustration as he took off without another word.

Jasper turned and re-entered the house, shaking his head as he walked over to Jayce. "I'm gonna go ahead and assume that's not how you remember your old friend Rhett?"

When Jayce shook his head, Jasper patted his shoulder. "Guess we won't be needing to send anyone into the Dragon Realm to see what's going on after all. I think we just saw a perfect example of it."

CHAPTER TWENTY-SIX

Ellie

$\mathcal{A}$s soon as they were finished breakfast, Ellie insisted they start their search for the Tree of Life. They teleported to where the Grandfather had said they would find the Tree, landing in a dense jungle that stretched out endlessly in every direction.

After a quick search of the surrounding area, they were convinced that the layout of the trees and the terrain where they currently stood, was the only place that bore any similarities to the Grandfather's image.

Well, everything except the entrance itself. Instead of two ancient trees, whose branches intersected overhead to form an archway, a thick wall of tangled brush and vegetation stood before them. Ellie was starting to think the Grandfather's memory wasn't as good as they'd hoped.

Jayce moved closer to the thick wall. "I don't get it. This should be the exact spot. I know it's been over a hundred years since his last visit, but you'd think—"

"Jayce... stop!" Jayce's hand was mere centimetres from the wall when Yvette shouted. "Sorry, I didn't mean to yell. Maybe just let me check this out first. Something feels... *wrong* about this area."

Jayce shrugged and nodded, moving back to stand beside Ellie. Yvette examined the tangled vines, taking care to avoid touching the area, and began to chant softly. As her voice penetrated the silence, black tendrils of smoke appeared, snaking their way through the tangled mess. Yvette gasped and stepped back.

"Damn... just as I thought. This *is* where the entrance was the last time the Grandfather visited, but we failed to consider that someone or something evil has been here since then. The entrance is sealed with a curse to prevent others from entering. Ellie, time to learn some spells for dealing with curses."

Yvette held out her hand, and a tattered book appeared. She sat on the ground, beckoning Ellie and Jayce to sit beside her as she flipped through the pages. "I get the feeling we may be needing these particular spells a lot in the near future. I *studied* all the spells used to combat dark magic but never needed to *use* them before now. Ahhh, here it is..."

"So what were you chanting before, when the smoke started?" Ellie asked.

"Ahhh, yes... I'll add that spell, and this one, to your little book. In fact, you should probably try to memorise them. In situations where you need to use this type of spell, more often than not, time is of the essence. Having to look it up could mean the difference between life and death. I'm sorry if I sound overly dramatic, but I'd hoped never to encounter this kind of powerful dark magic in my lifetime."

Yvette took a deep breath and continued. "Okay, moving on. So, the spell I chanted earlier needs to be repeated three times: *Contineo et Aperio Pestis*, which loosely translated means 'contain and reveal any curses present'.

Please make sure you always start with *Contineo*, which is the containment part, or you might accidentally activate the curse, allowing it to cause whatever harm it was created to do. Right, so this spell should nullify and remove the curse: *Concido et Abjugo Pestis*. It might be more effective if we all say it together. Ready?"

Ellie chuckled as Jayce practiced the pronunciation over and over in his head before getting to his feet and reaching down to pull her up.

Holding hands, with Jayce in the middle, the three recited the words of the spell, Ellie and Yvette each pointing their free hand toward the cursed obstacle. Ellie's eyes widened as the tangled mess began to sizzle, disintegrating in front of them. In its place was a gaping hole... the entrance to the hidden valley.

Large, blackened patches of earth, the same as they'd seen in the park near Ellie's home, dominated their view of the valley. The smell of death and decay hung in the still air. Yvette dropped Jayce's hand and cautiously moved forward.

"Well, at least whoever did this appears to be gone. I suppose they thought the cursed wall would keep the entrance hidden. Come on, we need to find the Tree and pray She's still alive," Yvette said, her face distraught as she viewed the desolate scene before them.

"It might be quicker if I do a scout from the air rather than waste time walking in the wrong direction." Jayce morphed into his dragon form and lifted into the air before anyone could argue.

Ellie frowned and chewed her lip. "Should he be doing this? What if someone sees him?"

Yvette squeezed her hand. "I'm sure the valley is secluded enough to hide his presence. Besides, Jayce is right, this will save us a lot of time."

Within minutes, Jayce swooped down towards a spot barely visible from where they stood, lifting back up and making a bee-line straight toward them.

I found Her, and there might still be time. Get Yvette ready to climb aboard, Jayce's voice said in Ellie's mind.

Ellie chuckled and turned to Yvette. "So, are you ready for your first-ever dragon ride?"

Before Yvette could respond, Jayce landed and swung his tail around for them to climb on.

"Ummm... I don't really..." Yvette paled, looking at Jayce's scaly tail as if she expected it to bite her.

"Oh, come on, it'll be fun. I'll hold onto you... don't look so worried." Yvette finally nodded and climbed aboard Jayce's tail.

They scrambled across Jayce's broad back and settled against his neck, Ellie sending a message when they were ready to go. Within seconds, they were in the air, Yvette's arms wrapped tight around Ellie's waist.

A few minutes later, the Tree of Life came into view, and Ellie's heart raced. A small ring of green grass still surrounded the base of the Tree, a bare scattering of leaves remaining on Her branches.

As they approached, a leaf detached itself and floated to the ground. Where it landed, the earth was soon withered and blackened, encroaching on the small area valiantly fighting the effects of the poison.

Jayce landed as close to the Tree as he dared, worried the wind from his wings would do more damage to the sickly Tree. Ellie and Yvette scrambled down off his back, and together, they walked toward the desiccated remains of what had once been the heartbeat of the mortal world.

Without thinking, Ellie stepped forward and placed her hand on the withered trunk, sending messages of love and sadness in the hope that the Tree still held onto some remnant of life. She jumped as the Tree shuddered beneath her hand.

Ahhh... morwitch, daughter of the Stars... I had begun to despair that you would arrive in time. Thank the Stars you found the Grandfather before he died. I fear I will share his fate before long.

The soft, lilting voice of the Tree was in her mind, full of pain and sadness. Tears ran down Ellie's face as she felt Jayce's arm slide around her waist.

Unfortunately, my overriding purpose of self-preservation worked against us. Since the Dark One tricked me into admitting him into my sanctuary, I was able to purge the poison by pushing it into my leaves and shedding them. But the leaves are spreading the poison through the earth, and I am unable to stop the process. Once the last leaf falls, I will no longer be able to fight the poison; my magic will be overpowered, and I will die.

But there must be something we can do. Is there no cure? Ellie implored through her tears.

Jayce, too, had tears streaming down his face. *Please tell us what we need to do to save You, and we will move Heaven and Earth to get it done.*

It is good that you are here also, dragon-born son of the Stars and witch's familiar. The task I must set for you will not be an easy one, but together, you may have a chance to succeed.

The waters of the Living Lake contain powerful healing qualities. But I cannot guarantee the waters will be able to combat the dark magic. I would be sending you on a dangerous journey that may be pointless, and procuring the water may take more time than I have left.

Ellie closed her eyes, praying to the Stars for a solution. They needed to somehow buy more time. If the Tree could just hang on until they found this Lake and brought back the water...

"Wait... the spell book. I'm sure I saw a spell to slow time. It might buy us the time we need?"

"I'm not sure whether the spell would be able to penetrate the dark magic, Ellie. From what I know, dark magic is much stronger..."

"But we need to at least try! I mean, what've we got to lose?"

"Maybe if the three of us tried casting the spell together?" Jayce suggested.

Yvette nodded and sighed. "Okay, fetch the book. But I don't recall...?"

"I don't need the book. I remember all the spells already."

"How did you...? Never mind."

"The spell is *demoror tempore*. I think it might be best if we are all touching the Tree when we try it." Ellie held out her hand to Yvette, and she joined them.

"Okay, are we ready? Pray to the Stars that this works. After three. One... two... three."

Demoror tempore, the three chanted as one.

Ellie held her breath as she waited for the spell to take effect. She smiled as a faint mist began to rise from the ground, wrapping around the Tree and cocooning it in its centre.

"Woah, looks like the spell is working," Jayce said in awe.

I believe you are right, dragon son. The flow of my sap is indeed slowing. This may allow us the time to find the cure. But are you sure you are willing to take the necessary risks, even with no certainty of success?

Ellie met Jayce's eyes, knowing there was never any question of what they would do.

Of course we'll go. Can you tell us where we can find this Living Lake?

I'm afraid I do not possess that knowledge. Only that your journey will be treacherous, and you may not survive. But if you plan to try, you must leave now. Even with time slowed, I fear the end is not far off.

We'll be back before you know it, Jayce said, the false bravado in his voice not fooling anyone.

May the Stars guide and protect you. Remember, your greatest strength lies in your union. Take care of each other. Now you must go. I am tired and need to rest to maintain my energy. Farewell and Starspeed.

CHAPTER TWENTY-SEVEN

Jayce

Jayce was every bit as emotionally strung out as Ellie when Yvette gently pulled him and Ellie away from the Tree and teleported them all back to the secluded farmhouse. The group sat around the table; Jasper and Isabel stunned as they absorbed what had transpired. A heavy silence fell over the room as they contemplated the enormity of the task the two had been set.

Jasper frowned. "I've heard of this Living Lake you need to find, and I don't think you're going to be too happy about the location."

Ellie sighed and leaned against Jayce. "Of course, the

damn Lake is somewhere no one in their right mind would ever go. So just tell us, Jasper."

Jasper stood up and pulled a piece of paper and a pencil from the drawer. He laid the paper on the table and began to draw what appeared to be a map.

"Okay, so here is the Dragon Realm, and over here is the Witch Realm," he said, drawing two large circles on the far left and far right of the page. "There's never been any love lost between the inhabitants of the two realms, so whenever a meeting of the ruling Councils is necessary, it needs to be held in neutral territory."

"This," he drew another circle below and between the two realms, "is where those meetings take place. On a world called Brevis, which can only be accessed when there is a need for it. According to the rumours, the Living Lake is on Brevis too."

Jayce frowned at the old man. "So how does this Brevis know when and why something is needed?"

Jasper drew a long tube linking the Dragon Realm to Brevis, and an identical one from Brevis to the Witch Realm. "You need to travel using the Aqueous Flow, the entrance to which is inside each of the Council's meeting halls." He looked up at Ellie and Jayce.

"Here's the part you're not going to like... only a dragon can use the dragon's entrance, and a witch the witch's entrance. Which means you'll be travelling separately."

Jayce felt as though he'd been kicked in the guts. Separation from Ellie had *never* been part of the plan.

"No way I'm exposing Ellie to that kind of danger alone. We need to find another way."

Jasper shook his head. "I'm sorry, son, but this is the only way to travel to and from Brevis."

"If it helps," Yvette said from the other end of the table. "I'll go with Ellie and make sure she gets to the entrance safely. I'm more concerned about how you're going to reach the Dragon Council's meeting hall, Jayce. Any ideas about how you'll manage that?"

Jayce stared at the faces of his friends, convinced they'd all lost their minds. Surely they didn't expect him to agree to this plan? It was unthinkable.

Isabel cleared her throat and rose from the table, collecting the empty coffee cups and giving Jayce a sympathetic look. "Well, I know time is short, but it's been a huge day, and we're all struggling to process this new information. I'm going to prepare a quick meal, and then we'll discuss the plan. Jayce, why don't you and Ellie go shower and freshen up."

Jayce gave Isabel a grateful smile and stood as well. "Awesome idea, Isabel, thanks. You're right, processing *this* is definitely going to take a while."

Ellie

. . .

ELLIE FLOPPED DOWN on the lounge and looked up into Jayce's smouldering eyes. "You know we have to do this, right? There's no other way. The Tree of Life did say it wouldn't be easy."

Jayce ran his hands through his hair and dropped down next to her. "But she *also* said we needed to do it *together*," he growled.

Ellie leaned against him and sighed. "We *will* be doing it together. It's only the 'getting there' part we have to do alone. I'm sure it'll be fine, and we'll only be apart for a couple of hours, max."

Jayce groaned, pulling her into his lap and wrapping his arms around her. "*Only* a couple of hours? Which will feel like a lifetime!"

"I know, babe, but we don't have a choice. The Tree of Life *needs* this water. So, let's start dealing with the reality of what we need to do. Like how you're going to reach the entrance to this Aqueous Flow. It's not like you can just fly into the Dragon Realm and walk into the Dragon Council's meeting hall."

Jayce tightened his arms, kissing the top of her head. "Will you stop worrying about *me* and start thinking about yourself for a change? I'm sick to the stomach at the thought of you doing this without me. I don't even want to *think* about all the things that could go wrong with this plan."

Ellie tilted her head back and sighed. He was right

about one thing: the thought of separating, even if only for a short time, had her stomach in knots, too. She took a deep breath and pushed the thought aside. She needed to focus on getting to this Brevis place.

"I'm thinking Yvette can take you to the Dragon Realm like she did last time, then come back for me. Your glamour will disguise you well enough while you're in human form, you just need to avoid getting too close to anyone who might recognise your scent. What do you think?"

Jayce blew out a long, slow breath and nodded. "I don't like it, but you're right... it has to be done. If Yvette can teleport me in, I'm sure I'll find a way inside the Council chambers."

Ellie grinned and slid her hands through his hair. "Great, then it's all settled. So... we still have about an hour to kill before we need to be back at the house. Any suggestions about what we can do to fill the time?"

Jayce chuckled. "Do you really need to ask?"

"Well, I have some board games back home in my room I can fetch. Unless you—"

She squealed as Jayce stood and threw her over his shoulder, cutting her off mid-sentence.

"If I'm going to survive for hours away from you, I'll need to create some new memories to keep me going. And we *won't* be needing boards for the games I have in mind."

CHAPTER TWENTY-EIGHT

Jayce

$\mathcal{A}$ couple of hours later, Yvette teleported Jayce into the Dragon Realm. They landed among the familiar trees near the Grandfather's house, relieved to find the place once again deserted.

"Please be careful, Jayce. I can't believe I'm letting you two do this alone," Yvette said, squeezing his arm, her eyes filled with fear.

"Hey, we'll be fine. You just focus on getting Ellie into the Aqueous, and I'll be waiting when she gets to Brevis. Nothing to worry about, right?"

"Please promise me you'll take care of her. I only just found her, and... well..." He pulled Yvette into a hug as the tears leaked from the corners of her eyes.

"It's okay, Yvette, I understand. I promise to protect her with my life."

Yvette stepped back and smiled up at him. "Thank you, Jayce. I'm glad you two found each other. Now I need to get back before Ellie comes looking for us." She squeezed his arm one more time and vanished.

Taking a deep breath, Jayce turned and walked toward the castle. Before leaving the farmhouse, Yvette had altered his glamour in an attempt to disguise his scent. Knowing that Rhett had recognised it when Jayce visited the Grandfather, they'd agreed not to take the risk again.

The spell made him feel weird, as if he was inside someone else's skin. But it would be worth the discomfort if he ran into anyone he knew. His only problem now was that he had no idea how to get inside the castle gates, let alone into the meeting hall.

Jayce reached the winding dirt road leading up to the castle and spent some time leaning against a tree. Studying those using the road to come and go, he was concerned by the general air of apathy of the people.

He remembered standing in this exact spot when he was nine or ten years old, watching the hustle and bustle of workers entering and leaving the castle. Someone had always been laughing, or shouting a greeting to a friend, and he had longed to be a part of the excitement.

He turned his attention to an old man struggling up the hill with a cartload of fresh produce, obviously bound for the castle kitchen. Suddenly, the cart hit a large hole in the dirt road, and a wheel came loose, causing it to lurch sideways and spill some of its contents into the dirt.

Jayce was astonished when the old man scratched his head, threw his hands in the air and turned to walk back down the hill. The cart lay abandoned, and no one seemed to care.

Jayce waited until the man moved out of sight, and then another few minutes in case he decided to come back, before stepping out from behind the tree and strolling toward the cart. He bent down and managed to manoeuvre the wheel back into place, securing it as best he could. Then he picked up the least damaged produce, lifted the handles of the cart and headed toward the castle gates.

The guards ignored him as he pushed the cart through the entry gates. To them, he was merely another old man bringing in supplies, a common and boring sight as far as they were concerned.

Jayce had only ever been inside the castle grounds once before, and it was a long time ago. In a rare moment of generosity, Thomas had allowed his son to accompany him on business. Jayce's eyes had absorbed every detail, as young boys given such a treat were want to do.

Keeping his head down, he pushed the cart toward the back entrance to the kitchen, dreading that someone he knew would appear, recognise and arrest him. When he reached the door to the kitchen without encountering anyone, he sucked in a huge calming breath. So far, so good.

The sound of boots scuffing on the cobblestone alerted him to the man emerging from the other end of the massive structure. He glanced over his shoulder and almost threw up when he recognised the man as his father.

Jayce stood frozen outside the kitchen door, holding his breath and dreading what would happen next. The boots paused. Thomas Raythawn stood halfway between the castle and the gates, lifting his head and sniffing the air as he looked around.

Stars... please let the glamour have worked! His thoughts flew to Ellie, and how she would react if he didn't make it to Brevis. He didn't care what happened to him, but the thought of leaving Ellie alone and unprotected wrenched at his heart.

His father's eyes brushed over the old man hunched beside his cart. Shaking his head, Thomas shrugged and took another few steps. A heartbeat later, he morphed into his dragon and leapt into the sky. Relief washed over Jayce as his father's dragon form faded into the distance.

Buoyed by the fact that his own father hadn't recognised him, Jayce started to believe he might have a chance of pulling this plan off. Leaving the cart, he slipped inside the castle and went in search of the meeting hall.

Excitement burned through him a few minutes later when he recognised the massive double doors heralding the entrance to the Dragon Council meeting hall. Stepping inside, he almost cheered when he found the room deserted. Luck seemed to be on his side for once. Now, all he had to do was find the pool Jasper had told him about.

Apparently, this pool provided access to the Aqueous Flow. He was supposed to dive in, and allow the Flow to transport him to Brevis. Jasper had been unable to give him any more details, never having used this particular mode of travel himself. Jayce shrugged. He just hoped there was nothing else he needed to know to survive the journey.

Then he saw it. Light streaming in through the windows reflected off the surface of the water, announcing its presence like a beacon. He moved silently around the edge of the room until he stood in front of a pool of soup-like liquid.

The murkiness of the water was a little off-putting. He hadn't imagined it looking quite so... ominous. Well, too late to turn back now. Taking a deep breath, he stepped up to the edge.

Right, here goes nothing. See you on the other side, gorgeous girl, he thought as he plunged headfirst into the pool's murky depths.

Ellie

ELLIE WAS nervous about what to expect from her first visit to the Witch Realm. So when they landed in a house filled with furnishings very similar to the one she grew up in, she was pleasantly surprised.

Yvette smiled and waved her hands around. "Well, this is my home... What do you think?"

"Wow, it's almost an exact replica of the aunts' house. But I don't understand. How is that possible if you had no memories of your time in the mortal world?"

Yvette shrugged, looking down at her hands. "To be honest, I have no idea. I can only assume my subconscious tried to make it at least *look* like the only place I was ever really happy. It's amazing what the mind can do."

Ellie's heart twisted at the sight of the forlorn woman standing in front of her. She couldn't even begin to imagine what her mother had gone through, losing both her husband and her child under such tragic circumstances. Nausea churned in Ellie's stomach at the very thought of losing Jayce, knowing that if she lost him, she would never be whole again.

She smiled and draped an arm around her mother's shoulders. "Well, I'm glad to finally be here. Better late than never, right?"

Yvette gave a huge sigh and seemed to pull herself back together. "You're absolutely right...I never thought I'd live to see the day you forgave me, let alone be standing here in this house. I'm so proud of you, Ellie, and I feel like the luckiest mother ever."

A hint of sadness returned to her eyes. "I only wish the circumstances were a little different. I hate the thought of you going into this unknown world without me. I only just got you back in my life, and I couldn't bear the thought of—"

Ellie enveloped her mother in a warm hug. "Don't stress. I'll be fine. You'll be there with me right up until I enter the pool, and Jayce will be waiting at the other end. What could possibly go wrong?"

Yvette returned the hug and then held Ellie in front of her at arm's length. "Promise me you'll be careful. Don't do anything to put you or Jayce at risk. If there's any sign of danger, you need to come straight back. Okay?"

Ellie patted her mother's shoulder and nodded. "I promise. Now, can we please get going? I want this whole thing over with."

Her mother grinned. "Not to mention you're missing Jayce already, hmmm?"

Ellie's face burned at her mother's light-hearted jibe. "Maybe..." Ellie mumbled as they headed out the door.

No one paid them any attention as they strolled down the street arm in arm. If anything, the few people they encountered went out of their way to avoid making eye contact. Was it always such an inhospitable place? Because so far, Ellie felt no regret for turning her back on the Witch Realm.

Yvette stopped in front of an old manor house. "We're here," she whispered to Ellie. "If anyone asks, we're visiting the Elder Minerva. She's a friend of mine, and no one will question my visiting her."

Ellie swallowed nervously and nodded. "Okay, lead the way." Hunching her shoulders, she tried to make her old hag persona appear as unobtrusive as possible.

They stepped through the front door and walked down a long hallway, totally ignored, just as they'd been on the street. Ellie was just starting to think no one here ever spoke, when a voice behind them interrupted her thoughts.

"Yvette, what brings you here? I thought you would be out searching for that brat morwitch daughter you had the misfortune to produce. Any news on her whereabouts?"

Ellie stiffened at the woman's insulting words, wanting nothing more than to slam the old witch into a wall.

Yvette squeezed Ellie's arm and turned to the

woman. "As you well know, Davina, it was suggested I not take part in the search. I have no desire to set eyes on the ungrateful wretch ever again. She deserves everything she gets!"

Yvette turned back and almost dragged Ellie down the hallway, Davina's cackling laughter following them until Yvette stopped outside an intricately carved door, and they hurried inside.

Yvette sagged against the door, looking at Ellie with tears in her eyes. "You know I didn't mean one single word, don't you?"

Ellie smiled and rubbed her arm. "Of course I do. But that doesn't mean I won't be coming back for the nasty hag as soon as this is all over. I have an over-whelming desire to see her writhing in agony."

Yvette chuckled, the relief evident in her eyes. "That's my girl," she said, giving Ellie a quick hug. "So... this is the meeting hall. Now, all we need to do is find the pool before anyone else appears."

Ellie took in the circular room, her eyes widening at the symbols scrawled on the walls, floor and ceiling. "Wow, how do you even remember which symbol means what? They're everywhere!"

Yvette sighed. "Well, a witch is usually exposed to all these symbols from the time they're born. You have quite a bit of catching up to do—"

"Oh, I think I see the pool," Ellie interrupted, pointing to an open doorway on the other side of the room. "The light is reflecting off something in there."

Ellie raced across the room, pausing at the sight of the pool filled with murky water. "Doesn't exactly look inviting, does it?"

Yvette moved ahead of her to the pool, a frown on her face. "It certainly doesn't. In fact, I don't like this at all. Something feels... wrong. Maybe I should..."

They both froze at the sound of a door opening on the other side of the meeting room.

Ellie turned to her mother in horror. "What do we do now?"

"*We* won't do anything. *You* will be diving into this pool and finding Jayce, and *I* will deal with whoever's here. Now go... and I love you."

Yvette's face told her it was pointless to argue. Her mother would think of something to tell whoever entered the room, and Ellie had an important 'date' waiting at the other end of her journey. She blew her mother a kiss, sent a silent message of love to Jayce, and dived into the uninviting depths.

CHAPTER TWENTY-NINE

Jayce

Jayce's lungs burned from lack of oxygen. He was beginning to doubt he would survive long enough to reach Brevis. No one had mentioned how *long* the trip took, and he couldn't believe he hadn't thought to ask.

Breathe, a voice whispered in his head.

I can't... I'll drown, he replied desperately.

I will breathe for you. Just breathe... trust me.

Okay, so the options were to die of asphyxiation or drown from inhaling the water? What the hell kind of place was this?

Sorry Elle'... he thought as he exhaled and sucked in the water surrounding him, astounded when air entered his lungs. The water was gone. Instead, he existed in some kind of void, as if suspended within a cloud.

Relief washed over him as he sucked the air into his aching lungs. He was alive, and he might still make it to Brevis yet. And then the voice returned.

You are not a member of the Council. Yet you feel special. Why are you here?

I need to go to Brevis to save the life of a friend, Jayce improvised.

The voice stayed silent for a minute as if weighing up this unusual situation.

So be it. Your survival depends on what is meant to be.

What the hell did that mean? He waited for the voice to speak again, but the silence prevailed.

Ellie

PANIC CREPT into Ellie's mind. Why hadn't she thought to ask someone how *long* the trip took? She'd assumed it would be quick.

Dumbarse! What if she couldn't hold her breath long

enough? Had Jayce survived, and was he waiting for her on Brevis? Stars, what was she supposed to do now?

Breathe, a voice whispered inside her head.

What? Who said that? What kind of ridiculous joke is this? I can't breathe! I'll swallow the water and drown, Ellie replied, exasperated by the voice's idiotic suggestion.

Trust me... The voice sounded amused.

Why should I trust you? Ellie challenged.

Because if you do not, you will die...

Fine... but this better work or... or...

Damn, she must be hysterical. Did she really just try to threaten a disembodied voice with the power to decide whether she lived or died? *Unbelievable.*

Ellie exhaled and opened her mouth, dreading the sensation of the murky water entering her lungs. And then, by some miracle, she breathed air. The water disappeared, and she floated in some kind of void. Silently thanking the Stars for her survival, she sucked the air into her deprived lungs. But the annoying voice hadn't finished.

Only Council members are permitted to use the Flow. Why do you wish to travel?

Ellie wracked her brain for an answer. *Because the Tree of Life sent me here on a quest.*

How can that be? Her location is a secret.

A wielder of dark magic has poisoned Her. The Tree is dying, and I need to find the Living Lake.

The voice went quiet for a minute.

You may yet regret accepting this quest. But your fate is out of my control.

Great, so who does control it? Ellie waited for a response from the disembodied voice, but there was nothing.

Jayce

JAYCE FLOATED IN THE SILENCE, unaware of how much time had passed since he entered the Aqueous. He focused his thoughts on memories of Ellie, smiling as a kaleidoscope of images ran through his mind.

Wait, what was that? I don't remember that happening.

Jayce examined the unfamiliar memory. Maybe it was one of Ellie's? He frowned as he concentrated on the scene unfolding in his mind.

Ellie and Yvette stood outside Jasper's house, talking and laughing.

"So he really believes coming to you was his own idea? He doesn't suspect being hexed?" Yvette asked softly.

Ellie laughed. "He hasn't got a clue! He seriously thinks

I'm in love with him, and the bonding was by mutual agreement. You were right; my powers are incredible. And the fact he hates his father means he'll be more than willing to fight for the rebellion."

Jayce's mind reeled as the memory faded. Everything inside him screamed that the memory had to be a lie. He knew her every thought. How could this be possible?

Insidious doubts began to creep in, eating away at what he believed to be true. What if she'd known how to shut him out of her mind all along?

Ellie had shown him the book about telepathy, which specifically said *he* needed to agree for the link to work. Damnit, he'd fallen for every lie they'd fed him like some stupid, lovesick fool.

Jayce felt as if his heart were being ripped out of his body. How could she do this to him? What kind of a monster was she?

Hot, unbridled anger surged through him, replacing the pain of betrayal. It burned inside his chest as the full impact of what he'd seen hit him like a sledgehammer.

They were *all* in on it! Jasper and Isabel, too. The whole thing had been a ploy to make her more powerful. Jayce's mind screamed in anger and frustration as he plummeted through the air before hitting the ground with a resounding thump.

Ellie

ELLIE WAS SO over floating around in the middle of nowhere. She wanted to see Jayce. Was he already on Brevis waiting for her? It felt like forever since they parted that morning.

Sighing, she let her mind wander through the memories they'd built together in such a short time. She lingered over a few of the most recent ones, shivering at the intensity of the emotions they evoked.

An image of Jayce sitting with Jasper and Isabel at the kitchen table, talking quietly, floated into her mind. She couldn't remember being there, so the memory must be one of Jayce's.

"You've done well so far, son," Jasper smiled at Jayce. "Are you sure she'll agree to help us?"

"Of course, she will. She thinks I'm madly in love with her, would do anything I asked. She has no idea the whole bounty hunter thing was a hoax created to get her here."

Isabel put her hand on his shoulder. "Well, make sure you keep up the facade. We need her power boosted by yours to succeed. I think the engagement thing is a nice touch. It will seal her commitment to you, and therefore, the rebellion."

Ellie's heart shattered into a million pieces as the image faded. She ignored the tears sliding down her face as the pain of Jayce's betrayal ate away at her insides. Everything had been a lie? Just so she would use her power to help them win their little war?

She burned with shame at the way she'd given herself to him. She should have known someone like him would never be attracted to her. He'd even told her that once himself. What an idiot.

Well, no more! As soon as she got to Brevis, she would find the damn Lake, and then she was out of there!

Dreading finding Jayce waiting for her when she arrived, yet wanting to escape the state of suspended animation more than life itself, she started to fall, landing on her butt on solid ground.

CHAPTER THIRTY

Jayce

Slowly getting to his feet, Jayce scanned the area, thanking the Stars when he found no sign of Ellie. The way he felt, he couldn't trust himself not to strangle her on sight. His stomach churned as the images of her duplicity played over and over in his mind. How could he be so stupid?

Well, if she thought he would be sitting here waiting for her, like some personal lapdog, she was in for a rude shock. As soon as he found the damn Lake, and got the damn water, he would walk away and not look back. Ellie and her stupid rebellion could go to hell.

Snapping his befuddled mind back into focus, he

took in his surroundings. He stood in a forest, the trees so tall he couldn't see where they ended. Obviously, the waters of the Living Lake were every bit as nurturing as the Tree of Life said. Lush green grass blanketed the ground, stretching in every direction.

Jayce heaved a huge sigh and spotted an area where the trees looked to be a little more sparse. He shrugged, not caring what direction he took as long as it was away from Ellie. His heart ached at the thought of never seeing her again. But she had betrayed his love and trust, and there was no going back. Remembering the link between their minds, he slammed the door to his thoughts shut. No way she would *ever* get inside his head again!

Ellie

ELLIE SAT FOR A MINUTE, stunned by the sudden landing and trying to gather her scattered thoughts. Jayce was nowhere to be seen—which was the *only* good thing to happen all day.

She jumped to her feet, determined to be as far

away as possible before he *did* arrive. If she could just find the Lake and leave here without having to see him, it would make things so much easier. Frankly, she hoped to never set eyes on him again... *ever!*

In all honesty, she wanted to curl up in a ball somewhere and lick her wounds. But she promised the Tree of Life she would try and save Her, and that's exactly what she would do. And she did *not* need some dragon who considered himself 'the Stars gift to women' to help her.

She stifled a sob and almost lost it. *Damnit all to hell!* Everything between them seemed so perfect. But it had all been an elaborate lie to gain access to her power. So much for the Stars favouring their union. The whole thing was a complete farce.

Well, no more... enough was enough!

She squared her shoulders and looked around at the towering trees and lush vegetation. The damn Lake could be anywhere, and she had no idea where to start looking. She shrugged and started walking, determined to put as much distance between her and Jayce as possible. How big could a transitory planet be? She was bound to come across the Lake eventually, so one direction was as good as any other.

Jayce

JAYCE'S THOUGHTS tumbled around in his head as he walked. He desperately wanted to dismiss the image of Ellie's duplicity as false, but the evidence was undeniable. The conversation with Yvette had taken place where they'd been working on Ellie's powers, at Jasper and Isabel's farmhouse. And if not a memory of Ellie's, where had it come from?

He thought back to when they'd first met. He should have listened to his first instinct—that she'd put a hex on him. Rhett had obviously worked things out, following him to the farm to try and warn him; and Jayce had ignored him. *What a stupid, blind fool!*

What he couldn't understand was how Ellie had faked the emotions he saw on her face, and in her eyes, every time he looked at her. *Wait.* What if the original plan to use him had backfired, and she'd developed real feelings for him? He groaned at his mind's wretched attempt to convince himself she loved him. *Get a grip, man! Someone who can do this to another person is incapable of 'real feelings'.*

Jayce staggered forward, trying to shut out the thoughts and questions his mind kept repeating. He almost cheered when he spied the sparkling waters of the Living Lake through the trees up ahead, thanking the Stars for sending him in the right direction. Hopefully, the whole nightmare would soon be behind him, and he could move on with his life. A life without Ellie, filled with shattered hopes and dreams.

He pulled the silver flask from his belt as he moved toward the pristine waters of the Lake. He'd expected to be trudging around all day looking for the healing waters the Tree of Life needed. But then, a world that popped in and out of existence according to the needs of others couldn't be that big. Could it?

Squatting by the Lake's edge, he dipped the flask into the water. It was almost full when a disturbance out in the centre of the Lake drew his attention. The hair bristled on the back of his neck as he stood to get a better look. The water had begun to bubble as if boiling or infused with air like a giant spa.

A sharp pain shot through his left ankle as his leg was ripped out from under him. *What the hell?* A pale, withered hand reached out of the water, its long, sharp claws wrapped firmly around his ankle, digging into his flesh through his boots.

Jayce kicked out at the hand with his other boot, but it only latched on tighter, pulling him closer to the water. A surge of anger ripped through him. He would *not* be a victim again!

His dragon would deal with this! Hysterical laughter bubbled to the surface at the slimy creature's ignorance. Wait until it discovered it held the foot of a dragon! But when he attempted to release his dragon, a dull thud reverberated in his chest. Something was seriously wrong... he couldn't morph!

Jayce broke into a cold sweat, the anger giving way to a growing sense of panic. He rolled onto his stomach, fear clutching at his aching chest. Searching for something to grab hold of, he scrabbled in the grass, digging his fingers into the dirt beneath it, anything to stop the creature from succeeding in pulling him into the water.

Pain shot through his right ankle as another hand latched onto him, rendering both legs useless. That's when he realised it was hopeless. The water was up to his knees, and unable to hold onto anything substantial, he slipped further in with every second.

He formed an image of Ellie in his mind, smiling that cheeky grin, her eyes sparkling with love and longing. Thoughts of the future he'd envisaged with her made him cry out with pain. If only she'd loved him even *half* as much as he loved her. The thought jolted him back to his predicament. The water had reached his thighs, his hands still scrabbling at the grass in a last desperate attempt to slow his journey toward certain death.

And suddenly, everything was clear. He opened the door to his mind and allowed his thoughts to connect with Ellie's. He had no idea whether she would hear him, or if she was even on Brevis yet, but he couldn't die without telling her how he felt.

Ellie... I know what you did, and I don't care. I know now that we *were just a lie, but I forgive you. I love you... more than you can possibly imagine. Take the water and save the Tree of Life. I just wish you had loved me... the way I love you. Goodbye, my love...*

With that, Jayce stopped fighting the creature's pull, tears streaming down his face as he slipped into the cool waters of the Lake.

Ellie

ELLIE WANDERED AIMLESSLY, her heart heavy in the face of Jayce's devastating betrayal. Even the marriage proposal had been nothing but a ploy to secure her allegiance. *How could anyone be so cruel? Maybe it was a dragon thing that allowed them to exhibit emotions they didn't feel.* Ellie had really believed Isabel and Jasper had cared about her, too.

Even Jayce's over-protective attitude took on a whole new meaning. The rebellion needed her alive. Keeping her safe had been his duty, not something he did out of love or caring.

Bitterness flooded her entire being. She needed to

accept the vision as the truth, no matter how much she wanted to deny it. Everything about their short-lived relationship, and their plans for a future together, had been based on lies. And now it was all over.

Ellie had just spotted the light reflecting off the waters of the Lake through the trees when Jayce's thoughts slammed through the barriers she'd erected in her mind.

Ellie... I know what you did, and I don't care. I know now that we were a lie, but I forgive you. I love you...more than you can possibly imagine. Take the water and save the Tree of Life. Tell Her I'm sorry I failed Her. I just wish you had loved me... the way I loved you. Goodbye, my love...

What the hell was he talking about? His words didn't make sense. Why would he think *she* had never loved *him*, when it was the other way around? Was this some new attempt to make her feel sorry for him? But that meant he knew she'd discovered the truth. How? Unless...

Realisation hit her like a bolt of lightning. The Aqueous had tricked them both! Jayce had been shown images similar to hers. The memories were all lies, cleverly planted to resemble the truth! She started running towards the Lake, sending out thoughts to Jayce as she ran.

Jayce, where are you? I'm coming... I love you too! She waited for his answer, but there was nothing.

Please talk to me... are you at the Lake? Still nothing.

Ellie took in the torn clumps of grass littering the

bank at the water's edge, drag marks ending at the water confirming what she feared. Something had pulled him into the Lake.

Without hesitation, she dived headlong into the water, begging the Stars to help her find him in time.

She pulled herself down toward the bottom of the Lake, her eyes picking up shadowy movement just ahead. It was Jayce, and he appeared to be standing up, suspended in the water surrounding him. As she got closer, she saw something attached to his ankles, holding him in place.

Ellie reached out and wrapped her arms around the man whose last thought was that she didn't love him. She couldn't bear the thought of him dying believing the lies. Her lungs burned, but she didn't have time to go up for air. Not without Jayce, anyway. She focused her eyes on the 'thing' holding Jayce in its grasp.

LET. GO. NOW. Ellie screamed the words in her mind, the power thrust impacting with two clawed and withered hands, which recoiled as if burned as she dragged Jayce upwards. Her limbs weak from lack of oxygen, her chest ready to explode, she drew on the last of her energy to propel them to the surface.

Ellie sucked the precious air into her deprived lungs as her face broke the surface of the water. Relief flooded her at the feel of Jayce's faint heartbeat under her hands—frighteningly weak but there, nevertheless. But wait, he wasn't breathing!

How long had he been down there? It couldn't have

been more than a few minutes since she'd heard his message. She wasn't going to have time to get him to shore. She needed to do something *now*. Rifling through her memory, she searched for the healing spell Jayce had helped her use on her injuries.

She smiled as the words of the spell surfaced in her mind, and she kissed Jayce's forehead.

Lenimentum Vulnus, she whispered, pointing at his chest. Jayce shuddered and then gasped as the fresh air hit his lungs. When he started to cough, Ellie turned his head to the side, allowing him to purge the water from his stomach. Finally, the coughing eased, and Jayce opened his golden eyes.

"I love you, Jayce Raythawn. How dare you almost die believing I didn't. You and I need to have a serious conversation about trust, my love. Seems we were both the victims of some extremely cruel and nasty lies."

"I've no idea what you're talking about, although you had my attention with your first three words. But can we please save the rest until we're out of the water?" Jayce croaked, a smile lifting the corner of his mouth. "I'm a tad waterlogged here."

CHAPTER THIRTY-ONE

Jayce

Jayce continued to splutter and cough as Ellie dragged them to the edge of the Lake, his head spinning as he tried to process Ellie's words. *Did she say they were* both *the victims of lies? What the hell did that mean?* He clambered up the grassy banks and rolled onto his back as Ellie collapsed beside him, groaning from exhaustion. Her hand reached for his, and he grabbed hold, sighing as her energy flowed into him.

"Jayce? Inside the Aqueous, did you happen to see a memory you thought was mine?" Ellie asked softly.

Jayce closed his eyes, the anger and hurt rising up

inside him. He tried to release Ellie's hand, but she held on tight.

"Yes, I did," he ground out. "So don't bother trying—"

"The same thing happened to me. So, can you please just listen before you say anything else?"

"Fine. But it won't—"

"Jayce. I was shown a memory I assumed belonged to you, talking to Jasper and Isabel, laughing at how you managed to trick me into believing you loved me. Did you see something like that too?"

Jayce's eyes widened as she spoke, an overwhelming sense of relief filling him with hope. It was all a lie? Ellie hadn't betrayed him. The Aqueous had warped and twisted their memories, planting the seeds of doubt with evidence based on tenuous but believable facts.

He rolled his head to find her watching him, tears streaming down her face. He groaned at the thought of how close they'd come to losing each other forever. Reaching over, he brushed the tears away from her beautiful face. She'd saved his life... even when she believed he'd betrayed her.

"I'm sorry, Elle'. I tried to dismiss the whole thing as a lie, but everything about the vision felt so *real*. I believed you didn't—"

Ellie leaned over and kissed him, her eyes burning with the intensity of her love. She lifted her head and smiled. "Hey, you don't need to be sorry. I guess you saw something similar, huh?" He nodded, and she smiled through her tears. "I believed it too, so we're both as bad as each other."

Jayce shuddered at the memory as he sat up and pulled her into his lap, cherishing the sensation of holding her close again. "Okay, how about we try to focus on something else? None of it was real, and I'm ready to make some new memories that will be *very* real. But first... how do we get out of this place?"

Ellie started to giggle and then froze, looking at him with horror in her eyes. "No way I'm going back inside the Aqueous. We need to find another way home."

Jayce tightened his arms and tried to muster up a reassuring smile. Inside, his stomach churned at the thought of the Aqueous being their only option. Unless...

"Wait... I just thought of something. Jasper and Yvette said no one can teleport on or off Brevis, but what if that's only because they're not powerful enough? According to what everyone's been telling us, we're not exactly your average witch and dragon. What if teleporting is only possible for a witch and dragon who are bonded? It would explain why the Aqueous was so determined to keep us apart."

Hope blossomed in Ellie's eyes. "Jayce, you're a genius! Why didn't we think of that *before* we used the Aqueous Flow? We could have avoided all the heartache."

"Hey, slow down a minute. It might not even work yet."

"Of course, it'll work. Although it probably wouldn't hurt to ask the Stars for a bit of help," she grinned.

"Good thinking. Okay, so what do we need to do?"

"I guess we both just need to focus on the same image, and think about being there."

"Mmmm... I can think of somewhere I'd like to be right now. How about—"

"The lounge in our cottage? Perfect! I assume you were about to suggest the same place?" Ellie batted her eyelashes, her eyes sparkling with mischief.

Jayce chuckled and nodded. "Of course. Where else could I *possibly* have been thinking of?"

Ellie rolled her eyes and snuggled in against his chest, before snapping to attention and jumping out of his lap.

"What *are* you doing?" Jayce asked, missing the feel of her in his arms.

Ellie bent down and picked up the silver flask he'd filled earlier. He'd forgotten all about it. Thank the Stars *one* of them was thinking straight.

"Well, I certainly have no intention of coming back here for this. *Now* I think we're ready to go home." She crawled back into his lap, holding tight to the flask.

Jayce held Ellie in his arms and closed his eyes, focusing his mind on an image of the big, soft, comfy lounge in their cottage. Sending a silent plea for help to the Stars, he held his breath and waited for the jolt telling him they were home. But instead, a familiar voice was in his head... the Aqueous Flow!

Teleporting on or off Brevis is forbidden. The rules are perfectly clear. Why did you try to do this?

Jayce opened his eyes and slowly released his breath. From the look of terror in Ellie's eyes, she'd heard the voice as well.

Do the rules also allow you to twist the thoughts of your passengers and plant lies inside their memories? Jayce growled.

The voice was silent for a moment as if pondering the question.

The Aqueous would never do such a thing. We are but a conduit between worlds. Why do you make this accusation?

"Because it's what happened, that's why!" Jayce realised he was no longer thinking his answers; instead he'd yelled, all the hurt and anger pouring out of him.

How can this be true? A new voice joined the conversation, and the Lake had started to bubble again. *Fear not, young daughter and son of the Stars. You have proven yourselves worthy of removing the water from the Living Lake, and are free to leave and take the flask with you. But your accusation of having your minds tainted while inside the Aqueous concerns me. How is this possible?*

We know nothing of this matter, Lord of the Lake. If what these two claim is true, the Flow must have been tainted without our knowledge. We must investigate these claims and purge ourselves of this corruption. Until then, we are unable to offer safe passage. I am sorry we failed in our duties, my Lord.

I will ensure our visitors are returned home safely. But you must be more vigilant in the future. This must never be allowed to happen again, the Lord of the Lake's voice boomed inside Jayce's head.

Yes, my Lord... as you wish, the Aqueous voice replied.

Jayce and Ellie sat through the entire conversation in stunned silence. Beginning to think himself inside another nightmare, Jayce seriously hoped he'd wake up soon. The creature in the Lake, who'd tried to kill him, was now offering them safe passage home? This was all *way* too weird!

Now, favoured of the Stars, the voice still boomed, but a little softer. *Close your eyes and focus as you did before. I will use the magic of the Lake to send you there. Farewell, and I wish you luck with your task. I was saddened by the news of the Tree of Life being poisoned, and I hope to hear that She is thriving again soon.*

Jayce closed his eyes as Ellie snuggled in closer against his chest. Once again, he held his breath and focused on their destination. Within seconds, the grass beneath them dropped away, and the soft fabric of their lounge at home was a welcome replacement. He opened his eyes to find Ellie's face grinning up at him.

"Man, it's good to be home," he whispered as his lips sought hers for a welcome home kiss.

CHAPTER THIRTY-TWO

Ellie

Ellie opened her eyes and sat up in a panic, the lingering traces of her nightmare fading when she found herself on the lounge beside Jayce. She sighed with relief and snuggled back down.

"What was *that* all about?" Jayce asked, his eyes still closed. Ellie chuckled. "Sorry, babe, just a nightmare."

Jayce propped his head up on his elbow and looked at her. "Something tells me those memories won't be easy to shake. Hell, the entire Aqueous trip is going to be hard to forget. I still can't get over how real those fake memories felt."

Ellie reached out and ran her finger along his stubble-covered jaw. "That's because the false memories were planted in with our real ones, using our bond to convince us the memories must be real too."

Ellie shuddered, and Jayce gathered her into his arms. "Thank the Stars you worked out it was all a lie. How many others have travelled in the Flow and still believe the lies? The Aqueous didn't even know how long it had been tainted."

Jayce's body stiffened. "Damn, Elle', I just had a thought. All the Council members from both realms must have used the Flow to travel to Brevis. What if the taint affects people in different ways, depending on their thoughts when they're in the Flow?"

"Well, it would explain what Jasper said about the Council members all being corrupt. Who knows how long the Flow has been tainted?" Ellie breathed a huge sigh. "So, I guess this means we have to tell Mum, Jasper and Isabel we're back?"

"Hmmm... I'd hoped to keep it a secret a bit longer, but we need to take this water to the Tree of Life. Come on, time to get cleaned up and put the old folks out of their misery."

ELLIE COULDN'T HELP LAUGHING at the stunned faces of the three people sitting around the kitchen table.

Yvette recovered first, jumping up to hug Ellie first, then Jayce. And then everyone started talking at once.

"How did you get here?"

"Did you find Brevis?"

"Did you find the Lake?"

"Are you both okay?"

Ellie held her hand up and smiled. "Hey, one question at a time. But first... Isabel, I would kill for a coffee. Would you mind...?"

Isabel jumped up, giving Ellie a quick hug on her way past. "Good to see you safe, honey. The kettle's not long boiled."

Ellie and Jayce pulled up chairs and sat down at the table. Jasper leaned across the table towards Jayce, and they clasped each other's wrists, the old man nodding in approval. "Welcome back, son. Can I assume you found what we need?"

Jayce reached down and unclipped the silver flask from his belt, a huge grin spreading across his face. "We sure did, although I must admit, we got a little more than we bargained for."

Isabel placed a steaming hot coffee in front of each of them, adding delicious-looking slices of banana cake on a plate.

Ellie sighed with pleasure. "Oh, Isabel... I love you. I didn't even realise I was starving until I saw that cake. Can we please eat before we talk?" She grinned at Jayce. "Or would you like to start while I eat?"

Jayce chuckled. "Yeah, don't worry about me... not

like *I'm* hungry or anything. Go on, you eat, and I'll talk."

Jayce launched into the story of his journey since Yvette left him in the Dragon Realm. When he reached the part about the lies in the Aqueous, he slipped his arm around Ellie's waist.

"I won't go into the details of the memories. Suffice it to say they were bad enough to convince me that Ellie betrayed me."

He shuddered, leaning over to kiss the top of Ellie's head. Sucking in a deep breath, he continued with his story, finishing with the hands dragging him into the Lake. Then he nudged Ellie and grinned. "Okay, do you think you could stop eating long enough to tell your story now?"

Having made short work of two pieces of cake while Jayce talked, Ellie nodded and took up where he left off. By the time she finished telling the rest of their tale, Yvette, Jasper and Isabel looked horrified.

Yvette was the first to speak. "So basically, it's a miracle you survived, both emotionally and physically."

Jasper rubbed his chin, deep in thought. "And you say the Aqueous had no idea the Flow was tainted? Who or what could have the power and opportunity to do such a thing?"

Jayce finished the last of his coffee and leaned back in his chair. "I'm willing to bet the same 'who or what' responsible for poisoning the Tree of Life. And if the Council members travelled after the taint was planted, it might explain their weird behaviour. Who knows what they saw while they were inside the Flow?"

No one spoke for a moment, considering the possible ramifications of this news.

Yvette cleared her throat. "Hey, I understand how hard it is to put this aside, but we all agreed the fate of the mortal realm is our first priority. The Tree of Life needs this water as soon as possible."

Ellie grinned and got to her feet. "Yep, I agree. So let's go." Her smile faded when she realised three pairs of eyes stared at her. "What...?"

Yvette chuckled. "I realise you think you're some kind of superwoman, honey, but from what you told us, I think you should take some time to recover first."

"Oh, we already..." Ellie covered her mouth, her face burning as she slid back into her chair. *Yeah, way to go, Ellie.*

Jayce chuckled. "Ummm... we got back a while ago, Yvette, and had a quick nap and cleaned up before we came over here."

Yvette appeared to be working hard not to laugh. "Of course you did," was all she said.

"So, when do we leave for the Tree then?" Ellie asked as if the conversation about resting had never happened. Before Ellie and Jayce could even begin to argue, Jasper and Yvette informed them they were going with them to the Tree of Life.

"Bottom line is, son, you and Ellie are too important to risk anything happening to either of you. We'll need your help to deal with the problems in the witch and dragon realms together. Who or whatever is wielding this dark magic is a powerful force. Yvette and I will be there in case they show up and try to stop you." Jasper shrugged. "Safety in numbers and all that."

Isabel draped her arm around Jasper's shoulder. "Much as I don't want him to go either, I'm afraid Jasper's right. I'd come too, but we're waiting on important messages from the Dragon Realm. Besides, with you all teleporting out of here, someone needs to stay behind and make sure you're not followed." She glanced at the shotgun near the front door and smiled.

Ellie had spent the last week ignoring her 'feelings', knowing the bad ones were inevitable, considering what was going on in their lives. But the bad 'feeling' she got about this trip made her double over in pain.

"Elle... what's wrong?" Jayce jumped out of his chair and knelt beside her.

Ellie groaned, her stomach churning and her head pounding. "A really... bad... feeling. The worst... ever." She ground out the words through gritted teeth.

Yvette's face turned deathly pale. "We need to change something about the plan." She turned to the others. "What were we talking about when the pain came on?"

Jasper frowned. "Ummm... teleporting, messages from the Dragon Realm, Isabel guarding our trail?"

Yvette gasped. "Isabel! I think you should come with us. I'm not sure you staying behind alone is such a good idea."

Ellie lifted her head and looked at Yvette in wonder, the pain subsiding as fast as it had come on. The feeling had been about Isabel! She shuddered at the thought of what might have happened if they left her behind.

"Well, at least it appears that problem's solved," Yvette said. "Isabel, you might like to prepare for a trip to the Amazon."

No one said another word as Isabel turned and left the room. Ellie's eyes met Yvette's, and they shared a smile. Hopefully, they had averted one potential catastrophe.

Jayce

ALTHOUGH ELLIE APPEARED to have recovered from her premonition, Jayce was worried by her continuing silence. Something else was wrong. He could feel her stress, but her thoughts were so chaotic that he couldn't make sense of them.

Hey beautiful... what's going on?

Ellie's eyes stayed glued to the table. *I'm scared, Jayce. The bad feeling has lessened, but no matter how hard I try to ignore it, the damn thing won't go away.*

Jayce squeezed her shoulder and tilted her head up so she could look into his eyes. *Hey... what happened to the fearless morwitch I met not long ago? Since when did you become such a worry wort?*

Since I almost lost you twice in one day, Ellie replied, tears filling her eyes.

Ahh, but that only happened because we were apart. I have no intention of letting you out of my sight ever again... so it won't be a problem.

Ellie sighed and nodded her head. *I just wish this was all over. I'm so sick of being scared. Promise me that once we help the Tree of Life, we can spend some time doing nothing.*

Jayce reached up and put his arms around her neck, leaning his head against hers. *Absolutely. I'm thinking that when this is over, we'll take a supply of food to the cottage and lock all the doors for a week. How does that sound?*

Jayce was relieved to see some of the fear leave her eyes. *It sounds perfect.*

Ellie

BY THE TIME Isabel returned to the kitchen, Ellie was itching to leave. Yvette and Jasper had been whispering at the other end of the table, and it appeared they could finally get going.

"Right, so change of plans," Yvette said. "Since Isabel won't be here to guard our trail, Jasper and I agree it might be best to fly out, land somewhere deserted not too far from here, and teleport from there."

"But we can't fly in daylight! What if someone recognises Jayce and—?"

Yvette held up her hand and smiled. "Which is why Jayce will be leaving here as a passenger, the same as you and I. Jasper and Isabel will be flying us out."

A strangled curse came from Jayce as he jumped to his feet. "You don't seriously expect me to sit on another dragon's back as a *passenger*? Sorry, but that's just plain *weird*."

Jasper chuckled and slapped him on the back. "Come on, son... where's your sense of adventure? I gotta say I never expected to carry another dragon on my back either, but desperate times call for desperate measures."

Ellie grinned. "Yeah, Jayce, it'll be fun. And I get to ride on a dragon's back with you!"

"Fine. But no one outside this room is ever to find out about this, or I'll never live it down!"

CHAPTER THIRTY-THREE

Ellie

fter much huffing and puffing, Ellie finally convinced Jayce to climb aboard Jasper's dragon, watching Yvette hook herself into the harness on Isabel's back. Ellie had insisted that Yvette needed it more than she did, since Jayce would be holding her tight on Jasper's back. She smiled at the thrill racing through Jayce's mind as Jasper spread his wings and lifted into the sky.

They had been flying for less than twenty minutes when Ellie spied a cluster of black wings lifting out of the trees below them. She turned to look back, thinking they were too large to be birds, and realised they were heading toward them... fast.

Ummm... Jayce, I think we've got company.

Jayce turned his head and groaned. *Damn... Wyverns.*

O-kay. What's a wyvern?

They're the black sheep of the dragon family. And their 'services' are usually available to anyone who can afford them. It's unlikely a bounty hunter would pay to hire six of them, though, which means our 'dark magic' friend probably sent them.

Jayce slipped his mind into dragon speak. *Jasper... problem. Check out what's behind us.*

Jasper's neck flexed beneath them as he turned his head. *Damned Wyverns. Nothing to worry about as long as you don't let them get too close. We need to make sure we burn 'em up before they're within striking distance. I'm surprised they'd even attempt to take us on... guess they don't call 'em the dumb cousins for nothing.* He and Isabel both chuckled.

Isabel, please don't laugh. I already feel like I'm on the rollercoaster from hell just being on your back. Ellie was surprised to hear Yvette's voice join the conversation. She must be hearing her through one of the dragons.

Best you hold on real tight, Yvette, Isabel warned. *Things are about to get a whole lot worse, not to mention warmer.*

Isabel banked left and turned to face the oncoming wyverns. Opening her mouth, she released a long stream of fire at the two creatures out front.

Ellie held her breath, waiting for the creatures to

catch fire and fall from the sky. But something was wrong. The fire didn't have any effect on them.

Isabel, the fire's bouncing straight off them. You need to get outta there... now! Ellie cried, sending a power blast at the two wyverns closest to Isabel. The creatures spun backwards through the air, shook themselves, and fell in behind the other four.

Ellie, don't waste your energy. Yvette sounded stressed. *A power thrust is no good unless there's something for the victim to impact with. We need to find a way to remove the spell making them impervious to fire.*

Ellie paled at the memory of how weak she was after using two spells back-to-back. Her powers had increased since then, but Yvette was right, she still needed to conserve her energy.

Okay, so what do you suggest? Give me a minute, I'm thinking...

Well, don't take too long thinking, Yvette. Isabel was headed back toward Jasper, the wyverns still close behind her. *I don't know how long we'll be able to outfly them. We're carrying passengers, and they are smaller and quicker to start with.*

Ellie wracked her brain, trying to recall anything in her spell book that might work. She concentrated, and the images of the pages were in her mind.

Now that's impressive, Jayce said, obviously seeing the images too.

Anything useful?

Hang on, I'm looking...

Wait, Elle... stop there. Is that a sleeping spell? 'Cos, I'm thinking it would be hard to fly if you're asleep? Yvette, what about a sleeping spell? Worth a try?

What on earth made you think of...? Never mind, I'll give it a go.

Yvette pointed at the closest wyvern, her lips moving as she cast the spell. The wyvern faltered for a second, then shook its head and kept flying.

Damn, looks like they're impervious to that too, Yvette growled.

Ellie turned to Jayce and looked into his eyes. *Okay, babe, how about we try it? Sort of like a double whammy.*

Jayce's voice chuckled in her mind. *I thought you'd never ask. Let's try saying it at the same time. After three... one, two... three.*

Ellie pointed at the nearest wyvern as they chanted together. As soon as the spell hit its target, the creature reacted as if turned to stone, its wings folding in as it plummeted toward the ground.

Woohoo... one down, five to go. Jayce chuckled as Ellie's cheer entered his mind.

Be careful, Ellie; we don't know how much you can do without exhausting yourself. Yvette's voice was laced with pride and worry as she grinned at her daughter.

It's all good. Jayce and I are doing it together, so I shouldn't need to use as much energy. Besides, we don't have much choice.

I'm afraid Elle's right, Yvette. We don't want to let one of those things get too close. Their barbed tails are poisonous.

So, can we please stop wasting time and finish this? Jayce... one, two... three.

Jayce

THE SECOND WYVERN reacted the same as the first, as did the third and fourth. Jayce felt his energy levels drain a little more after each casting, and knew Ellie would be feeling it even worse. The last two wyverns dropped back, staying out of range of the spells.

I think it might be time to land and regenerate the batteries for a while. I'm not sure how much longer we can keep casting spells. How you doing, Elle?

Panic surged through him when she didn't answer. He attempted to tighten his arms around her waist, shocked to discover how little strength he had left. If they didn't land soon, they would both be in trouble.

Elle! Are you still with us, babe? We need to stay awake until we can land...

Elle... please answer me.

Hmmm?... Sorry, I'm fine. Just struggling to keep my eyes open. Jayce sagged with relief at Ellie's soft reply.

Jasper, you need to get them on the ground... now! Yvette's high-pitched, shaky voice sounded desperate. Jasper banked in a wide circle and headed for the ground.

Ellie, stay awake just a bit longer, okay honey? Keep talking to me so I know you're okay. Yvette's voice had calmed, but was still laced with fear.

Hey mum... did we get 'em all?

Sure did, honey. You were amazing... I'm so proud of you.

Jayce was amazing, too...we've got the whole 'double whammy' thing down pat...

Yep, you make quite a team. Okay, honey, you're almost back on the ground. Just hang on for one more minute...

Jayce sighed with relief as Jasper landed. He'd never felt so drained in his entire life. This spell-casting thing was hard work. Jasper swung his tail up and around for them to climb on.

Hey, gorgeous girl, can you manage to climb onto Jasper's tail so we can get back on solid ground? Come on... you can do it.

Ellie nodded, and he helped her to her feet. He staggered, his legs threatening to give out beneath him, but he managed to drag the two of them over to Jasper's tail. *Okay, ready when you are Jasper.*

Jayce slid off Jasper's tail, forcing his legs to support him as he helped Ellie. They collapsed to the ground in a tangled heap, and he reached out with shaky arms to gather her up and pull her into his lap. Her arms stole up around his neck, and he rested his head on hers.

"Man, what a day!" he groaned. He smiled as Ellie's deep breathing told him she was asleep.

Isabel landed close to where they sat, Yvette scrambling down off her back as soon as they were on the ground. Her eyes widened when she saw Jayce. "Stars, Jayce, you look terrible."

"You have no idea. Every single muscle in my body seems to have shut down. I didn't realise how exhausted I was until I tried to stand. I'm surprised Ellie stayed conscious as long as she did."

"Well, there are some benefits to being stubborn. I think it served her well today," she grinned as she looked down at Ellie. "Did you hear her call me mum? It's the first time she's ever..." her eyes filled with tears, and she shook her head, unable to finish the sentence.

"I understand Yvette. It was only ever going to be a matter of time. She's had a lot to deal with over the last few weeks, poor baby."

"So, I go to sleep for a minute, and we're back to 'her' and 'she' again. Damn, I wish you people would stop talking about me as if I'm not here!" Ellie giggled as she lifted her head from Jayce's chest.

"Well, good to hear you back in your usual fine form, honey. I'll leave you two alone for a minute while Jasper, Isabel and I discuss what to do from here. By the way, Jayce, I have no idea why, but the other two wyverns turned tail and left. Guess they decided they weren't getting paid enough to die."

Yvette turned and walked over to Jasper and Isabel, and Jayce felt the confusion in Ellie's mind.

"I thought she said we got them all?"

Jayce grinned. "D'ya'think maybe she figured out you wouldn't give in if she told you the truth?"

Ellie sighed and gave a sheepish smile. "Damn it, I hate people knowing me so well. Hey, I just realised something. This is the first time I can ever remember being in your arms without your energy seeping into me. Did the spell-casting affect you too?"

Jayce chuckled and kissed the tip of her nose. "You could say that. But don't you worry about me. I'll be fine after some rest."

The sound of a throat being cleared made them both look up. "Sorry, I should have thought of this before." Yvette was back. "I'm going to cast a healing spell on you. This won't completely restore your energy, but should speed up the process a little."

Ellie smiled up at her mother. "Sounds awesome. I'm ready when you are."

Yvette cast the spell on Ellie first, and Jayce was relieved to see the colour return to her face. It wasn't until Yvette did the same for him that he understood how effective the spell was. His arms and legs no longer felt like jelly, and the lethargy was almost gone.

"Wow, that was amazing. I think I could get used to this whole magic thing after all. Thanks, Yvette," Jayce said, a huge grin on his face.

"No, thank *you*... both of you. I shudder to think

what would have happened without you and Ellie. I'm thinking our nemesis has underestimated your combined ability. Oh, and Ellie, what made you think of using the sleeping spell?"

Ellie smiled. "I tried to think of something in the spell book we might be able to use, and an image of the entire book appeared in my head. I was flicking through the pages when Jayce spotted the sleeping spell."

Yvette stood in front of them with her mouth open. "I don't know why I keep being surprised by what you two can do. Needless to say, I've never heard of anyone else being able to do that." She shook her head and chuckled.

"By the way, Jasper, Isabel, and I discussed the situation, and we all agreed we should stop here and rest for at least a few hours. I'll organise some tents and bedding for us all."

Ellie frowned. "But we need—"

"Please don't argue with me, Ellie. Your energy levels are dangerously low. A healing spell doesn't replace food and rest. If we were to leave now, your energy wouldn't be restored enough to use your magic if the need should arise." Yvette smiled and looked at Jayce. "It'll only be for a few hours. It's almost dark, and you two have been going since dawn."

Ellie

ELLE, wake up, sweetheart... time to go.

Ellie was sure she'd just gone to sleep when she heard Jayce's voice in her head. Forcing her eyes open, she found him hovering above her face.

"Damn, I love watching you sleep. One day, when this is all over, I'm gonna spend an entire day doing it."

Ellie chuckled. "What makes you think I'd want to sleep all day so you could watch me?"

Jayce's smouldering eyes glowed. "Guess I'll have to make sure you're too exhausted to argue with me for once. I can think of a few ways I could guarantee that."

His lips found hers, the kiss hungry and filled with promise. Ellie sighed and revelled in the sensations racing through her body. She'd never admit it to him, but he wouldn't get an argument from her about doing this for hours on end, either. No point in giving the man a swelled head, though.

Jayce lifted his head and rolled onto his back with a groan. "Man, I'm so over the whole *'no, you can't do that —you need to save the worlds'* thing. Whatever happened to turning eighteen and being able to party every night?"

Ellie rolled towards him and put her chin on his chest. "I'm sorry, babe. I guess all that went out the window when 'we' happened."

He grabbed her around the waist and dragged her on top of him. "Don't you ever apologise for 'us' happening. Having you in my life makes everything else pale to insignificance. I'm not interested in partying every night unless it's with you."

Ellie framed his handsome face in her hands. "Well, it's nice to know we agree on something." She placed her lips on his in a soft, tender kiss.

Jayce groaned and rolled them over again until he was on top of her, pinning her hands above her head with his.

"So you wanna play huh?" Shivers ran up and down Ellie's spine as his whispering breath tickled her ear. "Well, two can play—"

They froze at the sound of footsteps approaching the tent. "Are you two ready to go or what? It's after midnight already."

Ellie giggled as Jayce released her hands and slumped onto his back with a soft moan. "You were saying?"

"Go talk to your mother and give me a minute, you seductive little witch. This isn't over..." She shivered at his whispered words, grinning as she scrambled to open the tent and step out into the cold night air.

CHAPTER THIRTY-FOUR

Ellie

Ellie smiled and accepted the thermos of coffee and plate of sandwiches Yvette handed her. "Thanks, Mum. I'm starving, as usual."

"I thought you might be, so I prepared this back at the house before we left, just in case. Anyway, enjoy. I just need to finish sending the tents and bedding back and we can get going. Is Jayce up?"

As if on cue, he emerged from the tent, his eyes lighting up at the sight of the thermos. "Yeah, I'm up. Looks like I got here just in time. Knowing Ellie, another few seconds and I'd have missed out on the refreshments."

"Careful, or you might still miss out," Ellie said, raising her eyebrows.

Yvette chuckled. "Okay, I'll leave you to sort this out. Please be ready to go in five minutes."

Ellie laughed as Yvette turned and walked away. She handed the thermos and sandwiches to Jayce, who burst out laughing as she fetched the swing-seat from their front verandah. "What? Where else are we gonna sit?"

"I didn't say a word," he said, shaking his head.

"Just as well." Without another word, she fetched two coffee mugs, holding them out for him to fill.

Jayce frowned as they sat down, and each took a sandwich. "Elle, stressing about whether the water will cure Her isn't going to change the outcome. We'll find out soon enough."

Ellie groaned, both annoyed and relieved. Jayce could hear the thoughts racing around in her head. When he lifted his arm, she slid closer, soaking up his energy. "Yeah, I know... easier said than done. I keep thinking about all the time we've wasted. Why didn't we—"

"How about you just drink your coffee and eat? I don't think the Tree would expect us to go without food and sleep, and that's about all the time we've 'wasted'."

Ellie sighed and nodded. "Fine, but if we're too late, or... or..."

"Then stop talking and eat!" Jayce smiled and squeezed her shoulder. "Unless you're not hungry anymore? 'Cos I'm happy to have your share if—"

"Not in this lifetime, buddy." She grabbed the other half of the remaining sandwich and was soon washing it down with her coffee.

EXACTLY FIVE MINUTES LATER, Yvette teleported them to the sanctuary. Ellie's head spun as she tried to adjust to the searing sun and sticky heat of the Amazon, which was not an easy task after the recent cool darkness of the Tasmanian night.

Horrified by how much She'd deteriorated, Ellie cried out and ran towards the Tree. The last leaf had fallen, Her limbs drooped in despair, and the ring of grass previously surrounding Her had withered and died. A sickly, oily black substance coated Her base, with long, thin tendrils snaking their way upwards, spreading the poison She was no longer able to purge from Herself.

"Jayce, hurry up," Ellie called, tears streaming down her face, her arms wrapped around the failing Tree. "She needs the water... now!"

Aahh... Daughter of the Stars. It is good you are here. But I fear you may be too late. The poison taints my sap, my magic all but gone.

No... it can't be too late. We brought the water from the Living Lake.

Jayce laid one hand against the Tree and slipped the other around Ellie's waist. "What do we do?" he asked Ellie.

"She says we're too late; the poison has progressed too far. Oh, Jayce... what are we gonna do? We have to save her."

Yvette stepped up beside them. "She did warn you that the water may not be enough, even before she was this sick. All we can do is use the water and pray to the Stars that it works."

Jayce frowned, running his hand through his hair. "What if we cast a healing spell, all three of us, while we pour the water on Her? That might add the boost She needs?"

Yvette bit her lip and shook her head. "I doubt it will—"

"Wait, Jayce is right. Remember my wounds, and how fast they healed from Jayce and I doing the spell together? And the 'double whammy' we used on the wyverns? This is not about what would 'usually' work anymore. You said it yourself—nobody *knows* what we're capable of."

Jayce pulled the flask from his belt and removed the lid. "Okay, so how do you wanna do this? I'm thinking we need to be touching the Tree as well as each other. We can ask Jasper or Isabel to pour the water while we cast the spell."

Ellie nodded and called Jasper and Isabel over,

explaining what they needed to do. Then she, Yvette and Jayce leaned against the Tree and joined hands.

The Tree's pain made Ellie's heart ache, and she sent a silent message to the Stars, begging for their help.

"Okay, are we all ready? NOW!"

Lenimentum Vulnus, the three chanted together while Isabel emptied the flask over the base of the Tree's blackened trunk.

They stepped back, watching as the black, oily substance began to bubble where the water touched, sliding away from the Tree's surface. Hope flared in Ellie's chest, only to die when the water evaporated. It hadn't worked; the dark magic was too strong.

Throwing her arms around the Tree, Ellie sobbed. Their failure had not only killed the Tree of Life but also meant the end of the mortal world. Millions of people would die because they took too long to bring back the cure.

"Elle, stop it. None of this is our fault. She told us the water might not work. The only one to blame for all this is the damned 'Dark One', whoever the hell he is. What we need to focus on right now is whether there's another way to heal the earth. This whole nightmare was caused by magic, and it's time the magical realms stepped in and tried to fix it!"

"But how many people will die in the meantime? The aunts..." Her sadness turned to anger. This couldn't be over. She gripped the Tree harder and concentrated all the love and energy she could muster through the rough exterior and into the Tree's heart. *Please don't give up. You have to keep fighting.*

Suddenly, the Tree shuddered, a faint glow emanating from her roots and spreading upwards. Tiny buds sprouted and unfurled into shiny green leaves along the no longer drooping limbs. Ellie waved the others over to come touch the Tree and share in Her joy.

A tinkling laugh sent shivers of delight up Ellie's spine. *Thank you... I felt your energy clearing a path for the water to reach me. You have defeated the dark magic and given me new life.*

In a matter of minutes, the Tree's rapid regrowth followed the path of what should have taken weeks, like watching a movie where someone hit the fast-forward button. Ellie looked around in awe as the entire valley transformed from a blackened wilderness into a beautiful meadow, sprouting lush green grass interspersed with an abundance of sweet-smelling flowers in a cacophony of colours.

Ellie rubbed the rough surface of the Tree's trunk reverently, feeling Her sigh with pleasure. Jayce's arm slipped around Ellie's waist, and he gasped as the sensations flooded into him.

Thank you, daughter and son of the Stars. I knew you would come, and prayed that you would succeed. This was your destiny, foreseen thousands of years ago and communicated to me by the Stars.

Ellie's heart was so full of love she thought it might burst. *But what if whoever poisoned you comes back?*

Do not fear. It will not happen again. The Dark One gained access to our hidden valley disguised by a glamour as the Grandfather. I was old and lonely, and welcomed a visit from an old friend. It was not until I had lowered the magic shield that I realised my mistake. I will not be so easily duped again.

The Dark One? Who is this monster?

He is a powerful wielder of dark magic. The blood of both dragon and witch runs through his veins, and hate has eaten away at his heart. An insatiable appetite for power and revenge drives his every waking moment. He laughed when I asked him why he wanted to destroy the mortal world.

The Tree shuddered as if just the memory of this Dark One's presence sent fear racing through Her.

He answered my question with a shrug and a sneer, spitting the words in distaste. 'Why not? They are a useless race who will no longer be able to provide a haven to lawbreakers from the magical realms.' He condemned an entire race to death because of indifference. He will stop at nothing to achieve his goals.

She sighed, creating a gentle breeze that shook her outstretched limbs. *I am sorry to be the bearer of sad tidings, but your destiny is yet unfulfilled. Although you succeeded in foiling the Dark One's plans for the mortal world, the dragon and witch realms are still under threat. You are tasked with destroying the Dark One and bringing peace back to the magical realms.*

Ellie sucked in a breath as Jayce's arm tightened around her. She wasn't exactly *surprised* by the task the Stars had set them, but the reality of what lay before them made her blood run cold.

Jayce's eyes were filled with grim determination. *Okay. So what can you tell us about this 'Dark One'? How are we supposed to find him without even knowing what he looks like?*

The Tree sighed again, her sadness washing over them. *I am sorry, Jayce Raythawn, for being the one who must tell you. But you already know where to find him. The Dark One is the man you know as your father, Thomas Raythawn.*

*END OF BOOK ONE *

FROM JENNIFER

Thank you so much for reading Book 1 in the Morwitch Series. I hope you enjoyed reading it as much as I did writing it. Originally, this series was written as a duology, but Jayce and Ellie really wanted me to continue their story. So… the story continues

You can visit my website for further updates and release dates, as well as subscribe to my newsletter at:

jenniferredmile.com

I WOULD BE FOREVER GRATEFUL IF YOU WOULD CONSIDER LEAVING A REVIEW ON AMAZON .